Praise for
THE ANGELAEON CIRCLE

"Karyn Henley spins a lyrical young-adult tale of mythical and legendary beings, of reimagined angels and terrifying malevolents, in a small kingdom where the world's fate rests on a young priestess's shoulders."
> - KATHY TYERS, author of *Shivering World* and the Firebird series

"Karyn Henley's novel starts with a jolt, grabs the reader by the collar, and doesn't slow down one minute. This author infuses her text with imagery, suspense, and a cast that will appeal to all ages. In addition, it has a feeling that I can only describe as "folklorish," with all the best elements that come with that – music, magic, and mystery. I think it's destined to become a classic."
> - KATHI APPELT, author of *The Underneath*, National Book award finalist, Newbery Honor Book, PEN USA Award

"This lusciously written fantasy has it all: epic battles, earthbound angels, immortal humans, and a bright, engaging heroine. Henley's young priestess-turned-warrior is forced to put her past together like a jigsaw puzzle with pieces so sharp they cut. Her story is nearly impossible to forget, so readers will be eager for more!"
> - LOUISE HAWES, author of *Black Pearls: A Faerie Strand*, AAUW Juvenile Literature Award nominee; Gold Award, Hall of Fame, teensreadtoo.com

"Followers of fantasy novels will want to put *Eye of the Sword* at the top of their reading list. It is not to be missed." - ALICE D., Readers Favorite

"Written in solid prose, with excellent physical descriptions and believable dialogue, the story zips along … the love between Melaia and Trevin is compelling, as is Trevin's quest and all he discovers about himself."
> - PUBLISHER'S WEEKLY ONLINE

Five stars: "This is a wonderfully imaginative and thrilling fantasy tale."
	- NIGHT OWL REVIEWS

"It has everything a good fantasy should have - quests and mystery and fighting and romance and traveling through distant lands."
	- HOBBITSIES

"*Eye of the Sword* is so heroic, romantic and full of action that I couldn't stop reading." - KRISTEN, thebookmonsters.com

"A great tale, filled with action, treachery, and great characters."
	- PAMELA, thesongsontheway.com

"The writing style has a very Anne McCaffrey flavor . . . I loved this book . . . I award *Eye of the Sword* my highest rating."
	- scribblesonthebackofjanuary

". . . a delightful read . . . actionpacked plot . . . everything I was hoping for in a sequel." - thebookcellarx.com

THE ANGELAEON CIRCLE

BREATH OF ANGEL

EYE OF THE SWORD

THROAT OF THE NIGHT

ANGELAEON CIRCLE
BOOK THREE

THROAT OF THE NIGHT

A NOVEL

KARYN HENLEY

ANDON PRESS
NASHVILLE

THROAT OF THE NIGHT
PUBLISHED BY ANDON PRESS
an imprint of Child Sensitive Communication, LLC

www.ThroatoftheNight.com

ISBN 978-1-933803-36-4

❖❖❖

*To all the readers
who want to know what happened next.*

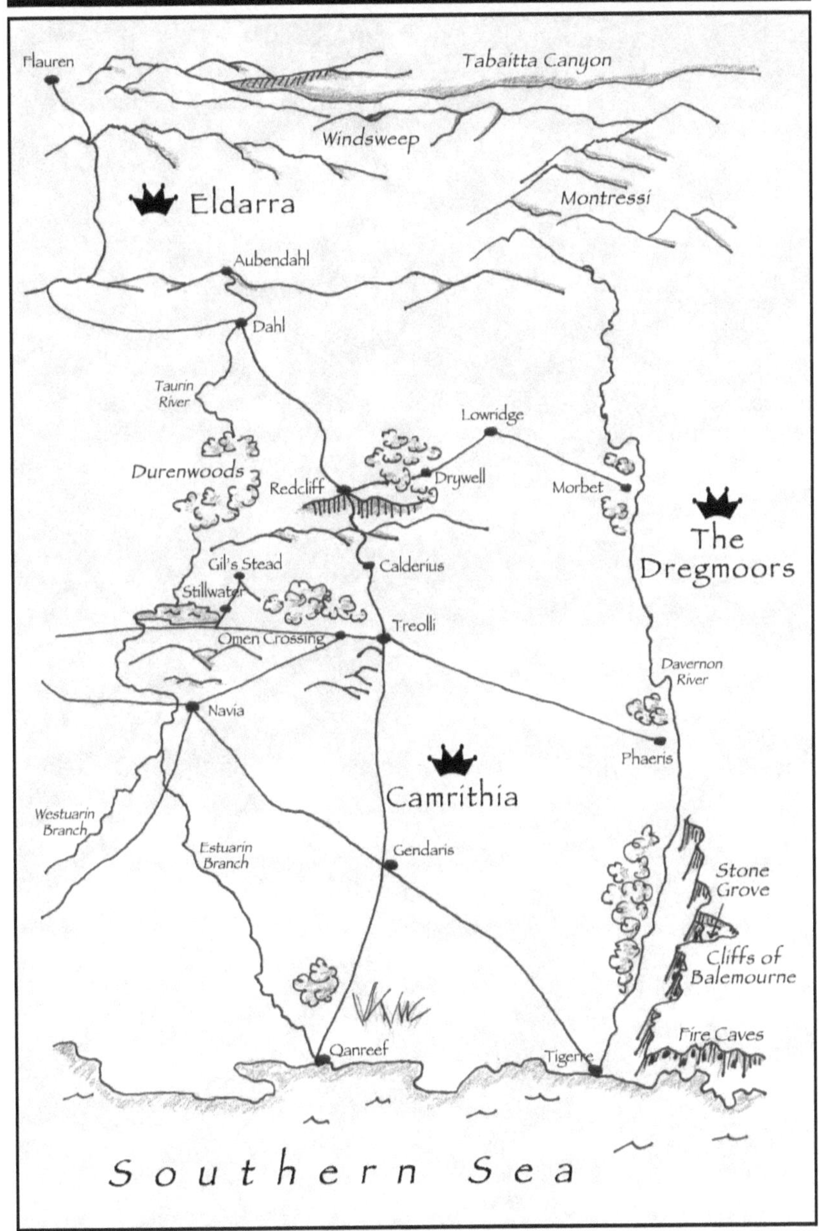

THE THREE KINGDOMS
Flauren
Tabaitta Canyon
Windsweep
Eldarra
Montressi
Aubendahl
Dahl
Taurin River
Lowridge
Durenwoods
Redcliff
Drywell
Morbet
The Dregmoors
Gil's Stead
Calderius
Stillwater
Treolli
Omen Crossing
Davernon River
Navia
Phaeris
Westuarin Branch
Camrithia
Estuarin Branch
Gendaris
Stone Grove
Cliffs of Balemourne
Fire Caves
Qanreef
Tigerre
Southern Sea

Cast of Characters

Ambria: Queen of Eldarra.

Arelin: Trevin's father; Angelaeon; a warrior angel also known as the Asp.

Lord Beker: King Laetham's advisor.

Baize: Camrithian gash runner.

Benasin: Second-born immortal, father of Jarrod.

Catellus: A comain of Camrithia, commander of men-at-arms.

Cyprian: Eldarran caravan-master.

Dio: Bard for the court of Eldarra.

Dreia: One of the Archae. Guardian of plant life and the Wisdom Tree.

Dwin: Sixteen-year-old brother of Trevin.

Earthbearer: One of the Archae. Guardian of ground and underground; also known as Lord of the Under-Realm.

Esper: A sylvan earth-angel, wife of Noll.

Flametender: One of the Archae. Guardian of fire.

Haden: Brother of King Kedemeth and a horseman of Eldarra.

Hanni (Hanamel): High priestess of the city of Redcliff.

Hesel: A Dregmoorian gash runner.

Iona: Fifteen-year-old priestess of Navia.

Jarrod: Nephili; half-brother of Melaia; admitted to the ranks of Angelaeon as Exousia.

Kedemeth: King of Eldarra, brother of Haden.

Laetham: King of Camrithia, Melaia's father.

Livia: A servant-messenger of the lower order of angels.

Melaia: Seventeen-year-old princess of Camrithia, Nephili.

Nuri: Fourteen-year-old priestess of Treolli.

Noll: A sylvan earth-angel, steward of the Durenwoods.

Peron: Novice priestess at Navia; turned into a drak at the age of six.

Lord Rejius: Firstborn immortal; ruler of the Dregmoors.

Seaspinner: One of the Archae. Guardian of water.

Serai: Angelaeon; Melaia's handmaid.

Silas: Overlord of the city of Navia.

Stalia: Immortal daughter of the Firstborn; queen of the Dregmoors.

Trevin: Twenty-one-year-old comain of Camrithia; brother of Dwin.

Windweaver: One of the Archae. Guardian of wind.

Windwings: Winged horses under the protection of the Angelaeon.

Yareth: Son of the overlord of Navia.

THE ANGELAEON

FIRST SPHERE

The three highest ranks are not strictly angels but winged heavenly beings who serve in the presence of the Most High.

CHERUBIM
Guard light and sound (music)

SERAPHIM
Personal servants of the Most High

OPHANIM
Guard celestial travel

SECOND SPHERE

KURIOTES
Regulate duties of lower angels and govern worlds

ARCHAE
Guardians of the world's elements: wind, fire, water, plant life, and earth

THRONOS
Negotiators and justice-bearers

THIRD SPHERE

EXOUSIA
Warriors and keepers of history

ARCHANGELS
Guardians of people groups; influential in politics and commerce

ANGELS
Messengers

WORLD SPHERE

NEPHILI
The "clouded ones"; half-angel, half-human

SYLVANS
Elflike earth-angels; inhabit forests and woodlands

WINDWINGS
Winged horses

THROAT
OF THE
NIGHT

Chapter 1

Without waiting for bodyguards Melaia dashed out of the palace and ran to the main gate of Redcliff, hoping to see Trevin among the returning warriors. Instead she found wagons of wounded rolling into the city, accompanied by clumps of refugees on foot. Melaia elbowed through the gawking townsfolk who blocked the first wagon. As the rig creaked to a standstill, the gate guards yelled, "Let the wagons pass."

The crowd ebbed back, but before the wagon pulled forward, Melaia hoisted herself in. A half dozen wide-eyed children scooted aside to make room for her as she moved through the wagon, looking for anyone she could help. Other than dirt and scratches, the children appeared fine. Beyond them a pale, disheveled old woman cradled the head of groaning man. As a death-prophet, Melaia could see the flicker of his spirit bordering his body, but it was firmly attached; he would live.

The bloodied woman lying behind him was another matter. Her spirit swirled and writhed in its death throes. Melaia tugged off her cloak and pressed it to the woman's slashed belly. As the wagon crept ahead, the crowd surged in again, craning their necks to see, asking what happened.

"We'll know soon enough," Melaia snapped at them. "Let the wagons through." She looked around for Trevin, but then the woman moaned. Melaia refolded her bloody cloak and pushed the clean side against the wound. The woman's spirit pooled around Melaia's hands and then coiled up her arms, rising until it shrouded her in a dim mist.

A nightmarish vision bore down on Melaia, and she froze. A screaming child was wrenched from her arms. Her fists pounded on a man's broad back. Then he whirled toward her and shoved a dagger into her belly.

Melaia lurched, her hand to her stomach, as the woman's spirit drifted away, along with its final memories. Trembling Melaia rubbed her arms. She had merely glimpsed the attacker's face, but there was something familiar about him.

The children in the wagon shifted behind her, and a hand rested on her shoulder. "Melaia?"

"Trevin." She turned and buried herself in his arms.

"You're shaking," he said.

"The attack was terrible wasn't it?"

"Yes. Yes, it was."

Melaia pulled back and ran her hand over the streaks of dirt and dried blood on Trevin's face. "Are you wounded?"

He kissed her fingers. "Just scratches. We sent the Dregmoorians running or left them worse than the tavern maid." He nodded to the woman. "We arrived too late to save her – or the rest of Drywell. The town is in ruins. We brought back the survivors."

Melaia looked back at the three wagons following them. The king had expected Dregmoorian attacks to intensify with the return of warm weather, but he had insisted that fighting would be confined to the east along the Davernon River. This attack had upended that prediction.

"Drywell is less than a day's ride away," she said. "That's too close."

"The raiders attacked with a fairly small force," said Trevin, "but they had two advantages: surprise and an unprotected town. They never would have dared to strike Redcliff."

"Even so," said Melaia, "they came much too close." She turned back to the tavern maid, but the woman's spirit was gone.

❖❖❖

Melaia raised her leather shield, met the blow of Trevin's sword, and then lunged with her own blade. Trevin evaded and threw her a tantalizing half-smile before he struck again. Since the raid at Drywell the previous week, they had met every day on the practice field. With

Dregmoorians bold enough to attack close to Redcliff, she was determined to learn how to defend herself.

Up, down, left, right they sparred, swerving in and out of shadows cast by the palace towers. Every clack of the wooden blades jarred Melaia's shoulders, but she reveled in her growing skill. Two springs ago she was simply a priestess whose most pressing duty was learning herbs and chants. Now she could wield a sword – a wooden one, but a sword nonetheless.

She sliced left. "Are you sure you're not being easy on me?"

"I'm sure." Trevin whipped right.

Melaia angled to parry, but Trevin swerved his blade over and under hers. The dull-tipped wood halted a finger's breadth from her chest.

He smiled. "That, my lady, was a feint."

"Oh." Melaia let her shoulders slump and her arms fall. As Trevin eased back, she swung with all her might and sent his sword flying. His mouth fell open, and she grinned. "That, sir, was also a feint."

Scattered applause and laughter rose from servants and guards gathered at the edge of the field.

"Another bout!" cried the stableboy.

Melaia returned to a fighting stance as Trevin scooped up his sword, but he bowed and raised his eagle shield in a salute. "I admit defeat," he called to the spectators. When they cheered, he told her, "It seems our audience enjoys watching their princess best her favorite comain."

She lowered her sword and wiped sweat from her forehead. "How does my favorite comain feel about it?"

Trevin leaned in. "I feel that you're so advanced at swords, I should teach you hand to hand combat."

Melaia subdued a grin. "Mind your manners, sir." She nodded toward a balcony, where King Laetham's attendants carried him back indoors on his litter. Although she had not seen her father's face, she knew it held a scowl. The angels referred to people like her father as

Breakers. Like a sea wave his mood swung high and then crashed low. Unfortunately he tended toward the low, especially since losing the use of his legs in the earthquake at Qanreef.

Trevin looked up at the empty balcony and sighed. "I was too hasty to ask the king for your hand. Now he hates me."

"He doesn't hate you. He simply wants proof that you're the heir of the Eldarran throne."

"I'm not. Yet."

Melaia handed her wooden blade to Trevin, and they trudged toward a bench by the fieldgate, where her handmaid, Serai, stood with a flask of water, her copper hair gleaming in the sun and her wings hidden beneath her cloak.

"My father thinks you're trying to steal me away," said Melaia.

"I am." Trevin tossed the swords, hilt first, to a young armsman and peeled off his leather gloves.

Melaia sat on a bench and eased off her gloves, finger by finger. "I suspect my father's mood has something to do with the answer Windweaver gave when you asked for a sign from the Oracle. As I recall, Windweaver said, *You are that sign.*"

"But I never told your father." Trevin narrowed his eyes. "Did you?"

"No, but Windweaver said you wouldn't have to tell him – that he would just know." She laid aside her gloves and took a cup of water from Serai. "So maybe he senses it somehow."

"Maybe, but senses *what* exactly?" Trevin took a cup from Serai, dumped the water on his head, and eyed Melaia through the drips. "Whatever it is, it's something *I'm* not aware of."

Melaia swirled the water in her cup. She wished she could tell Trevin precisely what Windweaver had meant, but she didn't know either. The Archae tended to be aggravatingly inscrutable.

Serai refilled Trevin's cup. "A caravan of supplies arrived from Eldarra this morning," she said. "The journey-master said my mother plans to visit Redcliff soon."

"I look forward to seeing Livia again." Trevin swigged his water and wiped his mouth with the back of his hand.

Melaia could see his mind working. The arrival of a caravan from Eldarra meant that snow had finally melted in the mountain passes, and the way was clear for him to return to Eldarra. She had dreaded this moment.

Serai slipped a small scroll from her waist pouch and handed it to Trevin. "The Eldarrans brought this. From King Kedemeth."

Trevin broke the seal. As he read, he paced, and Melaia's stomach tightened. The previous summer, the king and queen of Eldarra proposed that they adopt Trevin, which would make him crown prince. In the fall he sent them a message accepting their proposal, but before the snows, he wrote a second message to make sure they understood that he had discovered that his true parents were alive in the Dregmoors. All winter he had worried that King Kedemeth would withdraw the proposal.

Trevin looked up grinning. "The offer stands. They request that I come as soon as possible to settle the appointment formally – which means I can bring your father proof of my inheritance. I'll ask him to grant me leave to travel right away."

Melaia dug at the ground with the toe of her boot. "You'd best wait until he's in a better mood."

"When will that be? Maybe never." Trevin tapped the scroll against his thigh. "Lord Beker might grant me permission."

Melaia pursed her lips. Lord Beker, the king's advisor, was the wisdom behind the throne, but would he go behind the king's back?

"Or you." Trevin pointed the scroll at her. "You could give me leave. It's no secret that, more and more, the decisions fall to you."

Melaia pried up a dirt clod. "Even if I could, I wouldn't be wise to allow you to travel to Eldarra. Not yet."

"Why not? Papers await my signature. Melaia, think of us." Trevin sat beside her. "As crown prince of Eldarra I'll be of rank to marry you."

Melaia didn't dare look into his dark, penetrating eyes, for Trevin always saw into her soul, and at the moment, her soul would betray what she felt obligated to say. She longed to go north with him, witness his appointment, and marry him in the courts of Eldarra, with or without her father's permission. If not for her allegiance to the Angelaeon, she would do exactly that.

She brought her heel down on the dirt clod, and it crumbled into dust. "I can't think of marriage yet."

"I know." He gently touched her arm. "That's why *I'm* thinking of it. I'll not pressure you, but I want to be ready when the time comes."

"I can't let you go to Eldarra, because I need you here, Trevin. For an entire season, I've been distracted by nursing my father –"

"– and sparring with swords and learning the game of Attacker/Defender."

She felt herself blush. "Your distractions are much more pleasant than my father's."

He grinned impishly. "Should I say, 'you're welcome' or should I apologize?"

Melaia sensed the golden pulse of Trevin's aura drawing her just as water drew a thirsty deer. Since their first kiss, she had not been able to get her fill of him. She couldn't count the sleepless nights she had spent wrestling with her desires, but she always arrived at the same irritating conclusion: Her first pledge was to the Angelaeon and to restoring their stairway to heaven. Trevin came second. Reversing the two could cause her to lose both.

She drank her last drop of water and said, "It's time we face reality. We should have gone into the Dregmoors weeks ago to win back the third harp."

"Can't it wait a while longer?" asked Trevin. "The stars are not yet aligned. You still have time."

"Do I? Each night the stars move closer into position, but I have only two harps, and who knows how long it will take to get the third?" She kicked at the dirt. "I've no one but myself to blame for the delay. I need to unite the harps – the sooner the better. Then the stairway will rise with its protective tree, and we'll be done with the whole mess the immortals have thrown us into."

"Do I sense some frustration?" Trevin tucked a strand of Melaia's hair behind her ear.

She stared into her empty cup with a sense of foreboding. "How can you be so glib about it? The woods and forests are dying. Every breeze carries moans from the trees. On top of that, the angels are restless and edgy."

"You mean Jarrod is restless and edgy," said Trevin. "That's nothing new."

"The other angels are anxious too," said Melaia. "Isn't that right, Serai?"

Serai shrugged her broad shoulders. She was an angel of the winged rank of the Erielyon, and Jarrod was a half-angel of the warrior rank Exousia. Soon they would announce their betrothal. If anyone knew Jarrod's mind, it was Serai.

"All of us are eager to cross the stairway to heaven," Serai said, "so it's only natural for us to grow agitated as the time draws near. As for Jarrod, he would restore the stairway himself if he could."

"I'm sure he would," said Trevin.

Melaia warmed at the smile that played at the corners of Trevin's mouth. He understood Jarrod, her half brother. They were, after all, in similar situations, both half-angel, half-immortal, and both waiting for the stairway to be restored before marrying. Jarrod and Serai had decided to couple, as they put it, after they crossed into the heavens, and Jarrod was not known for his patience.

Serai touched Melaia's shoulder. "Is that Peron?" She pointed overhead to a small black bird winging its way toward the palace.

Melaia shot off the bench and bounded through the gate like a cat after a mouse. "I'll not miss her this time," she called back.

Through the halls Melaia dashed, dodging startled servants. She sprinted up the stairs, through her apartment, and into the rooftop garden, where she snatched a handful of true-hearts, Peron's favorite flowers. As Melaia lifted the purple blossoms toward the sky, she eased down to a bench.

Melaia watched the circling drak and cursed Lord Rejius, immortal Firstborn, for transforming a dancing, laughing six-year-old into a spy-bird.

"Come," she crooned, motionless. "Come, Peron."

She heard Trevin and Serai step to the open doorway behind her, but they came no closer as, for the first time, the black bird's human hands settled on Melaia's outspread palm. The small fingers that should have been supple and smooth felt as callous as a goatherd's bare feet.

Melaia trembled slightly, and her throat tightened. "Peron," she murmured, searching the drak's ghost-gray eyes for some sign of the spirit of the fair-haired child within.

Peron pecked at the true-heart blooms, releasing a rosy scent. Then the breeze quickened and ruffled her feathers, and she flew.

"Bravo," said Trevin.

Melaia watched the little drak ride the wind currents eastward. "Why didn't she stay longer?"

"She'll be back," said Serai.

"I'll move a cage up here for you," said Trevin. "Once she trusts you, grasp her hands firmly and hold on. Speak to her gently –"

Melaia blinked at him through tears. "I couldn't cage Peron."

"Aren't you afraid someone spies through her eyes?" asked Serai.

"I can't think about that."

"You should," said Trevin. "She homes to the Dregmoors. No doubt Lord Rejius's spies are studying jars of oil-water at this very moment, scrying through draks' eyes. Whoever watches through Peron knows exactly where you are, what you're doing, and who you're with. At least with Peron caged you could control what she sees."

"But I couldn't endure seeing Peron in a cage day after day." Melaia dropped the true-heart petals into a marble birdbath and watched them float on the water. She wished all her cares would float away as easily, but they wouldn't. Not until she restored the stairway and its protective Tree.

She turned to Trevin. "Take me into the Dregmoors. To the Asp. If anyone can get the third harp for me, it's the Asp. Arelin." When Trevin looked east with a sad longing in his eyes, she felt a pinch of guilt for using his father as a lure. She softened. "The trip would benefit both of us."

"You're right about Arelin," said Trevin. "He's probably the only one who can get the harp, but *you* will not go into the Dregmoors."

"I have to." Melaia set her jaw and stared at him.

Trevin stared back.

Serai ducked indoors.

Trevin folded his arms. "Even if your father gave you permission – and you know he won't – I can't let you go into the Dregmoors. I brought you the second harp, and I'll bring you the third as well."

"I can help," said Melaia. "You've been teaching me swords."

"So you can defend yourself if Redcliff is attacked. Not so you can go swashbuckling into the Dregmoors. I'll take Dwin with me." Trevin extended his hand to help her rise from the bench.

Melaia rose on her own. "You're willing to take your brother but not me?"

Trevin dusted his hand on his tunic. "Melaia, it's dangerous."

She drew her cloak tight and tramped indoors past Trevin. "Why does everyone act as if I need to be protected?"

"Because you do." Trevin grabbed her arm. "It's not because you're weak. You're the strongest, most capable woman I know. I've watched you face danger without flinching, but you've seen the cruelty of the Firstborn. We protect you to ensure that you live long enough to unite the harps. I, for one, hope you live much longer than that."

Melaia pulled away and stared into the dwindling hearthfire, wishing she could leave Redcliff as easily as Trevin could. But unless she found a way around the objections of her 'protectors,' she would have to wait here. Either direction – north to Eldarra or east to the

Dregmoors – Trevin would go without her. She wanted to give him permission to go north. Instead she said, "Go to the Dregmoors. Bring me the third harp."

He set his jaw and nodded. "Very well. The sooner I leave, the sooner I return. If I recall, those are your words of wisdom."

Melaia's heart felt dull and heavy. She stared down at her feet.

Trevin placed a hand under her chin and lifted her face, his eyes intent on hers. "While I'm gone, don't even consider following me into the Dregmoors. Wait for me. I'll be back. With the harp this time."

"All right," Melaia whispered. Gazing into his eyes was dangerous. He didn't know how close she was to abandoning everything she ever stood for, to simply run away with him and leave the affairs of angels behind.

Chapter 2

Trevin stared at the ceiling as he lay on his mat in the room that he shared with his brother in the temple. "Are you saying you *won't* come to the Dregmoors with me, or you *can't* come?" he asked.

Shadows danced into the corners as Dwin lit an oil lamp with a twist of rushweed. "Can't and won't." He peered at Trevin through his dark curls. "Lord Beker wants me to spy for the king."

Trevin rose to one elbow. Dwin had spied for the Angelaeon in the Dregmoors, but for King Laetham? "General spywork, or something specific?"

"Specific." Dwin dropped the rushweed into a long-necked jar, leaving a rising tendril of smoke. "Have you noticed that our warriors are often sent to attack the Dregmoorians only to find abandoned camps, while the Dreggies always find a clear corridor to their prey?"

"As in Drywell," said Trevin, embarrassed that he had not noted that fact earlier, but his attention had been elsewhere. On Melaia to be exact.

"Lord Beker suspects someone is passing our plans to the Dregmoorians," said Dwin.

"Whoever he is, he walks a razor's edge. He'll be discovered sooner or later."

"Or she."

"Why didn't you tell me about this before?"

Dwin narrowed his eyes.

"I know you're a tight-lipped spy," said Trevin, "but you can trust *me*. I might be able to help you."

"That's why I told you. But keep it to yourself. If the turncoat finds out I'm after him – or her – the trail could suddenly lead nowhere."

"You're in grave danger if the informant thinks you've picked up his scent," said Trevin.

"That too." Dwin grinned. "But I'm not averse to danger."

"So why not take your search into the Dregmoors? Go with me. You know your way around. Help me retrieve the third harp, and I'll help you catch this informant."

"I may already be close to catching the fox." Dwin leaned back against the wall. "I received a message from Nuri today. In her new post at the temple in Treolli, she hears rumors, gossip, news. She thinks she may know who the informer is, but she wouldn't write it in the message. She says she'll tell me only in person."

Trevin smirked at his brother. Dwin and the priestess Nuri were themselves the subject of rumor, most of which was based on fact. They took any opportunity to spend time together.

"Come on." Dwin smirked back. "You know what it's like."

"At least your duty carries you toward the one you love." Trevin slipped the Eldarran scroll from his pouch, and reread it. He would have to send a message to request a delay in his appointment unless – he rerolled it, considering his options – unless he went to Eldarra first. He could make it a quick trip, only long enough to make his adoption legal. In fact a visit to Eldarra would provide a perfect diversion for Lord Rejius's spies. The immortal Firstborn never would expect him to enter the Dregmoors by way of Eldarra.

Jarrod tramped past the door, muttering. Trevin sensed his warm, brown aura. A moment later a crash echoed down the corridor. Then a curse.

"I wager he's angry about Drywell," said Dwin.

"He missed the fight," said Trevin. Not that he had expected Jarrod to be there. A trained strategist, Jarrod often rode out to coordinate Camrithian troop movements with the comains and other commanders. The surprise attack on Drywell surely stung him.

Dwin leaned out the door and called, "I have Eldarran barley beer fresh off the caravan. Bring your cup." He grabbed two mugs from the table and handed one to Trevin.

Jarrod appeared at the door, gaunt and sullen, his hay colored hair hanging long around his shoulders. He handed his cup to Dwin.

"Are the troops low on supplies?" asked Trevin.

"Until this caravan from Eldarra arrived," said Jarrod.

Trevin watched him gather his hair and rebind it at the nape of his neck. "The whole ordeal will be over soon."

Jarrod's eyebrows rose.

"I'm on the way to the Dregmoors to steal back the third harp. I prefer to go with someone who can sneak me in." Trevin cut his eyes toward Dwin.

Jarrod almost smiled. "Good luck with that."

Trevin held out his cup. "Maybe I can go by way of Eldarra."

Dwin snorted as he unstoppered a flask and poured Trevin's drink. "If you haven't noticed, Eldarra is the opposite direction."

"I know," said Trevin, formulating the plan as he talked. "But I'm sure I can make quick work of my appointment as heir. Then I'll ask Windweaver to walk me into the Dregmoors. He did it before, and it took very little time. This trip, I'll ask him to lead me directly to the Asp. Arelin can help me snatch the harp and escape safely."

"Does King Laetham know you're going to the Dregmoors?" asked Jarrod.

Trevin shook his head. "Melaia gave me the orders. Unfortunately the king is not inclined to give me audience. Even when he's in a good mood, he can hardly look at me without glaring."

Dwin eased down to his mat, balancing his full cup. "The king doesn't want to give his daughter to just anyone."

"I won't be just anyone if I can complete the adoption in Eldarra," said Trevin.

Jarrod rubbed his stubbly chin. "There may be another reason for King Laetham's coldness toward you. It may have to do with the fact that you saved his life. Twice."

"For that he hates me?"

"Think about it," said Jarrod. "When you saved his life at Alta-Qan, you publicly proved that he had been duped by a woman. Which made you, a lowly comain, appear wiser than the king."

"That wasn't my intent. He was about to marry a fraud." Trevin cringed at the memory. Crime of crimes. The lady, Stalia, was his own mother, queen of the Dregmoors, immortal, deceiver, betrayer. He couldn't begin to determine what that meant for him, but at least she was back in her lair and was no longer a threat to the king or Melaia. He never would choose Stalia's life. His life was in Eldarra and Camrithia.

"I think you're right to visit Eldarra first," said Jarrod, "but you'd be wise not to travel alone. Why don't you join the Eldarran caravan? They start the return trip tomorrow."

"Tomorrow?" Trevin's heart sank like stone.

"You wanted to make quick work of it," said Jarrod.

Trevin nodded. Jarrod was as impatient as ever, although he was right about traveling with company. But so soon? He sighed and drained his cup. "I'll tell Melaia tonight – but I'll say only that I'm going to the Dregmoors. She doesn't need to know I've gone by way of Eldarra."

"You can trust me not to tell her," said Jarrod.

Dwin scowled. "I don't like your idea of going to Eldarra first. Sounds like a great way to squander your time. You know how restless Melaia gets. She's likely to head to the Dregmoors to find you if you don't return soon."

"The king never would allow her to go," said Jarrod.

"You think that will stop her?" asked Dwin.

Trevin growled as he rummaged through his trunk, looking for his journey bag. Dwin was right. There was no time to waste. He would have to stay on track. "Urge Serai to keep Melaia busy," he said. "Assure her that I'll return as soon as possible."

"I'll do what I can," said Jarrod.

Trevin sat back on his haunches. "Meanwhile watch out for a turncoat."

Jarrod raised his eyebrows. "Turncoat?"

Dwin cleared his throat.

"An informer," said Trevin. "Lord Beker suspects that someone is compromising your plans. Surely you've thought the same."

"I considered that possibility," said Jarrod, "but I didn't know anyone else had. Thanks for the warning – and the barley beer." Grim faced he headed down the hall.

Dwin turned on Trevin. "Damn it! I told you not to tell anyone."

"Jarrod needs to know. Not only is he pledged to protect Melaia, but he also has to travel the roads. He needs to be wary." Trevin tugged out his coarse journey bag, and a tingle of anticipation wove through him. He had missed traveling. Of course he never would trade Melaia for the roads. And he was hesitant to leave her when a traitor was at large.

He frowned at Dwin. "Do you have reason to suspect Jarrod?"

"I have reason to suspect everyone. A person working both sides doesn't announce it."

"Do you suspect me?"

Dwin blew out the other lamp. "Should I?"

Trevin threw his journey bag onto his mat. "That's not worth an answer." He pulled on his cloak. "I'm going to make arrangements with the caravan master."

Down the curved, torchlit corridor he strode. Before he made arrangements with the caravan, he would speak with Melaia and tell her that he intended to leave for the Dregmoors at daybreak. He hoped they could say their farewells tonight so Melaia would not insist on watching him ride out in the morning. Otherwise he would have to head east and then circle back to meet the caravan on the northern route.

He stepped out of the temple's columned entrance into the moonlit courtyard and headed for the palace. Against the star-strewn sky its towers loomed dark. Lamplight flickered in only a few windows, which meant the hour was later than he had thought. Would he be admitted to the palace? What exactly would he say to

Melaia? His throat felt stuffed with wool. Perhaps he wouldn't say good-bye. He would simply assure her of his return.

"Soon," he whispered as he crossed the flagstones. "I'll return soon." He hoped he was right.

❖❖❖

Early morning was not yet warm enough for Melaia to make her ablutions a pleasant task, but raised as a priestess, she could not neglect washing before prayer, which she hoped would ease her troubled mind today. Serai had told her that the washmaid said that the porter said that Trevin was turned away from the palace the previous night, because the king and princess had retired early. Melaia had been discouraged by her father's pessimistic disposition at supper. Now she wanted to kick herself for retiring early.

She stood still in the temple's rear courtyard and tried to sense Trevin's golden presence, but it eluded her. Nor had she sensed him when she passed through the temple corridors, probably because she was agitated. Stilling her body did not mean she could still her mind enough to sense angels, and at the moment, her mind was far from still. She dreaded the loneliness she would feel after Trevin left for the Dregmoors, and she worried about the dangers he would face. To make matters worse, her father had sent word that he was too ill to give audience today. She would have to take his place. Again.

The courtyard brightened with morning light, and Melaia tried to settle her mind into a place of peace, goodness, connection with the divine. She closed her eyes and whispered the words around which her life centered, the prophecy of the harps carved from the wood of the kyparis tree that once held the stairway to heaven.

Three from one and one from three,
Music of the living tree,
One sleeps in stone, one touches skies,
One in the hands of mortals lies.
One shall wake, one shall shake,
Three shall light the way.

She tossed her cloak on a bench and rubbed the chill from her arms. The heart of today's prayer would concern Trevin and Dwin's upcoming journey to retrieve the third harp, the one sleeping in stone. She uncorked a vial of rose-scented oil, dribbled it into the font, and splashed the biting cold water on her face and arms. She was grateful that Hanni was now high priestess at Redcliff, for the previous priest had provided no scented oil.

As she patted dry with a towel, the water in the font darkened until it no longer reflected the brightening sky. Instead the irridescent swirls of oil snaked across the center of the basin, forming two parallel lines that eased apart like opening eyelids. Melaia pressed the towel to her mouth to keep from crying out. Gazing back at her was the immortal Firstborn, Lord Rejius. Trevin had told her that shape shifting had made Rejius more hawk than human, but she never had imagined him this grotesque. Matted black feathers served as hair, his nose curved like a beak, and instead of fingers, talons stroked the inky feathers of his cloak.

The hawkman grinned at her as the eyelid closed. Melaia barely breathed, but she could not look away until she heard footsteps behind her. She turned to see Hanni in her gold-trimmed, blue cloak.

"Mellie!" Hanni grabbed Melaia's cloak off the bench. "You're shaking like a stalk in the wind."

"I saw Lord Rejius," Melaia murmured. "In the oil-water."

Hanni peered into the font. "You were scrying?"

"Not on purpose. The image simply appeared."

"How could he enter here? Did you open some kind of gate?"

"I don't know."

Hanni took Melaia's towel and draped the cloak around her. "You can't scry unless there's a link."

"Could the link be Peron?" Even in the warmth of her cloak, Melaia shivered. "Peron came near yesterday."

"How near?"

"I held her. She perched on my hand."

"You're marked, then."

"But Iona has held Peron. Nuri has too." All of them had been young priestesses together before Peron was kidnaped. "We only want to hold her again. To comfort her in some way."

"In that case Iona and Nuri are marked as well, but they're not the ones who interest Lord Rejius. You're the one who holds the two harps he wants." Hanni took Melaia's arm and walked her indoors.

"He's waiting for me to make a move, isn't he?" Melaia asked. "So I will, but not the way he wants. I'll entice Peron to my garden, which is all Lord Rejius will see through her eyes. I'll bore him to distraction while Trevin and Dwin slip into the Dregmoors and steal the third harp out from under his wicked nose."

Hanni tossed the towel into a basket, and they strode down the curved corridor together. "You tell me if you see the hawkman in the font again," she said. "Rejius may think he's God, but this is not his temple, and I don't want word to spread that he has been seen here. I'm considering taking in novices, and I won't have them frightened away by that intruder."

"Novices!" Melaia gladly turned the conversation to a more pleasant topic. She had fond memories of Hanni's training. The high priestess was strict, but fair.

Hanni paused beside an archway that led to the altar room. "The midwife of Lowridge wants me to accept her daughter for training as soon as possible. It seems the girl's father is a drunkard and abusive. Do you think King Laetham would object to having novices in Redcliff?"

"No need to ask. My father can't give audience today, so he can't complain about my decisions. You have my permission."

"So your father trusts you with decisions now?"

"Not all, but most. Lord Beker advises me. It's a way for my father to train me as well as keep me occupied – and closely bound to him. I'll comply until Trevin and Dwin bring me the third harp. Then I'll have to leave my father's nest, because I intend to unite the harps in the Durenwoods."

"You might give your father some warning."

"I've tried." Melaia took a small incense bowl from the stack on a side table. "I've often reminded him of my duty to restore the Tree and its stairway, but he accuses *you* of filling my head full of ancient tales."

"Me?"

"He doesn't believe in angels. He thinks the stairway is simply a legend."

"That's no reason for him to keep you sequestered at Redcliff."

"What can I do? The guards who protect me from outside danger also serve to keep me within the city walls."

"Perhaps you can go to Lowridge to fetch my novice," said Hanni. "Take your guards with you, and accustom your father to allowing you a bit of freedom. Maybe his tether will loosen enough for you to leave for a while to unite the harps."

The high priestess placed seven pinches of pungent incense into Melaia's bowl. "Fresh," she said. "I ground it yesterday."

Melaia smiled. Seven pinches would fuel a long prayer.

"By the way," said Hanni. "You should know that Benasin is here."

The dim hallway shadowed Hanni's face, but Melaia knew the high priestess was blushing. Hanni was a worthy match for her long-time admirer. If only Benasin was not forced to constantly flee his brother Rejius, he and Hanni might have made a home together long ago.

"Benasin had best avoid showing his face outside the palace," said Melaia. "Otherwise Lord Rejius will track him here."

"He arrived under cover of night," said Hanni. "For now he's safe."

Melaia carried the incense bowl to the brazier near the altar. There she knelt, adding Benasin to her list of prayers.

Chapter 3

When Melaia left the altar room after prayers, Serai was waiting for her in the corridor. "Do you sense Trevin here?" asked Melaia. "I want to ask him to bring Dwin to a private supper tonight so we can discuss their travel plans."

"I passed his room as I was looking for Jarrod," said Serai. "All of them are out."

"Maybe they're at the market, purchasing supplies for their journey."

"Or they're at the stables or the guardhouse or the armory," said Serai.

They trudged back to the palace. In Melaia's room Serai sorted through gowns appropriate for Melaia's appearance in the throne room. "Dove gray or sea green today?"

"You choose. I don't care." Melaia strode to her bedroom window, leaned against the stone frame, and looked north over the walls of Redcliff. In the distance the tail of a caravan snaked around a curve in the road. "Already I miss Trevin, and he hasn't even left yet," she said. "I ache to be out in the world, traveling, camping among the trees beneath the stars."

"With Trevin." Serai spread both gowns across the bed.

"With Trevin." Melaia sighed. "Do you think I might yet persuade him to take me with him?"

"Even if Trevin agreed to take you along, your father would not allow it. The king will be the impasse."

"Unless I can find a way to maneuver around him."

"Don't count on it." Serai squinted at the gowns. "Green today, I think."

Melaia slipped her mother's palm size book from its snug hiding place beneath her waist sash. As she stroked the three-pronged sign of the Tree on the wooden cover, her heartbeat melded with its familiar life-pulse. She opened to one of the last pages, the one linked to the third harp. Like a window it revealed the harp's surroundings.

"The harp probably has not been moved since you checked it yesterday." Serai gathered up the gray gown.

"I want to make sure," said Melaia, "so I can tell Trevin and Dwin when we meet tonight."

As she stared at the page, lines swam across it and then settled and sharpened to reveal statues of entombed spirits standing in silhouette before an empty bench. The harp had not been moved, but Melaia's mouth went dry. The last time Trevin tried to retrieve the harp, he had been discovered and chained to that bench. She closed the book and pressed it between her palms, drawing courage from its pulse. This time Trevin would succeed. He now knew what and where the traps were. Besides, Dwin and Arelin would help him.

She set the book on the bed, and Serai helped her change into the sea green gown. Then they headed downstairs to the throne room, followed by two ever-present bodyguards.

"You seem agitated," Serai told her.

"That's why I'm going to the throne room early," said Melaia. "I want time to calm myself before I receive petitioners."

"Are you still bothered because you haven't seen Trevin yet this morning? I can send someone to find him and Dwin and invite them to supper for you."

"Yes, do." Melaia pulled her cloak tight against the draft that slipped through the latticed windows of the breezeway. "But right now I'm aggravated about having to take my father's place again."

"Lord Beker will be there."

"That's my one comfort." Melaia lowered her voice. "Actually I trust Lord Beker's insight more than my father's. As king he is too quick to appease people in order to avoid conflict. Not that he's a coward."

"He simply craves peace," said Serai.

"But in his desire for peace, he turns a blind eye to thorny problems. The truth is, if he resolved those problems early, he would minimize the very conflict he wants to sidestep. He doesn't see that."

As they passed an open window, Melaia looked across the courtyard at the aerie tower, hoping to see Peron in flight or Trevin peering out one of the windows, but she saw neither.

"You've eaten nothing since early this morning," said Serai. "I'll fetch some fruit and bring it to the throne room."

Before Melaia could protest, Serai ducked through an archway. Melaia smiled as she watched Serai stride down the corridor like a herald on official business. Then again, Serai probably considered it official business to mother the princess like a fussy hen.

Melaia continued her trek to the throne room. At the end of the breezeway she paused. The anteroom on the right fronted a stairway that led up to the king's quarters. For a moment she considered visiting him, but the echo of Benasin's voice drew her to the left. As she neared the library she heard Jarrod, too, sharp and caustic: " . . . thought it might interest you."

Melaia stopped a stride away from the open door.

"Where did you discover it?" asked Benasin.

Jarrod snorted. "At the scriptory in Aubendahl."

"You should have left it there. It's private information."

"And it explains why you never valued me."

"It has no such meaning." Benasin sounded weary.

"Then let me take over the job."

"No," barked Benasin. "You will not intervene."

Melaia bit her lip. The last time she had heard Benasin speak as sharply, he was confronting his brother, Lord Rejius, in the aerie.

Jarrod growled, "There's no reason –"

"There's every reason," hissed Benasin.

A bench scooted. "You never trusted me," said Jarrod. "Admit it. I'm a failure in your eyes."

"That's not so."

"You don't even *know* me." Sandaled footsteps slapped the floor, and Jarrod swept from the room, clutching a yellowed scroll bound with a tassled red cord.

He froze when he saw Melaia, and his eyes narrowed. "Eavesdropping?"

She recoiled as if he were about to burst into flame. "I'm on my way to the throne room," she said. "Don't worry. I heard only enough to know not to cross you today. You're in a foul mood."

Jarrod clenched his jaw and stormed down the hall.

Melaia peeked into the library and met the stony gaze of an ancient statue that ruled the room from the far corner. Carved like an eagle's head and torso atop a lion's haunches, it loomed in the shadows, its wings circling upward to support the ceiling, its claw-studded paws firmly on the floor. More than once she had shied away from the library, unnerved by the stern statue, but at the moment Benasin's staff leaned against its haunches, which made the beast appear somewhat tame, so she tiptoed in.

Benasin, Second-born immortal, sat on the corner of a desk by a tall window, head bowed, shoulders slumped, hands clasped in his lap. His chiseled profile resembled Jarrod's, but Benasin kept his dark hair cropped short.

He looked up with a sad smile. "I'm afraid my son inherited my surly disposition."

"I'd not call you surly."

"That's gracious of you." Benasin ambled to the winged column and retrieved his staff.

Melaia scanned the wall niches lined with scrolls. She would have read them all twice over by now if she had not spent every spare moment of the winter with Trevin. As it happened, she had not read any. "Do you know if these scrolls contain angel histories?" she asked.

"The Angelaeon keep their histories at the scriptory in Aubendahl," said Benasin. "This room holds only Camrithian writings, I think, but you would do well to acquaint yourself with them."

Melaia fingered the edges of one of the parchments. If she couldn't persuade Trevin to take her to the Dregmoors with him, reading would help pass the time. It might also serve to bore the Firstborn if he continued to spy on her.

She turned to Benasin. "I saw Lord Rejius this morning."

Benasin's eyebrows rose. "Here?"

"In the oil-water of the font at the temple. I think he watches me through Peron's eyes."

"Of course. My brother is not ignorant of the debt that must be paid. As for me, if there were any other way, any at all . . ." He looked down at the floor. "I'm sorry I involved you."

"Of my own free will I accepted my birthright as Breath of Angel, Blood of Man," said Melaia. "I'll not rest easy until I've united the harps and restored the stairway. I haven't pursued the task in months, but I haven't abandoned it either." She thought of Jarrod's narrowed eyes and clenched jaw. "That's what upsets Jarrod, isn't it? He questions my resolve."

Benasin looked up, startled. "How much did you hear?"

"Something about private information." Melaia sat on the sill of the window. "I know Jarrod is impatient. If you speak with him again, you can assure him that I'll soon have the third harp. I've engaged Trevin and Dwin to bring it back from the Dregmoors. As soon as they return I'll take all three harps to the Durenwoods and unite them them there."

Benasin stood taller. "I told Jarrod you had a plan. I'm glad it's true."

"If all goes well, I'll have the third harp in a matter of weeks," said Melaia. "Until then I have no qualms about distracting Lord Rejius. He'll see nothing interesting at Redcliff – as long as you keep yourself hidden."

Benasin grinned and shook a finger at her. "I wager Rejius greatly underestimates you – which is a lethal mistake in the game he plays."

Melaia forced a smile, but her chest tightened. Lethal for whom?

❖❖❖

The afternoon crawled past in the drafty throne room, but at last Lord Beker, holding his twisted left hand to his chest, ushered out the final petitioner. Melaia removed the gold circlet from her head and handed it to Serai. The king would be pleased to hear that the comains were making progress in their efforts to recruit and train men-at-arms. He would not be pleased to learn that they had failed to break the Dregmoorian blockade of the southern ports, including Qanreef, where the reconstruction of the palace had ground to a halt. And she hoped he would not make a fuss when he heard that she had given the merchant council permission to hold an autumn festival. The merchants claimed that even without an abundant harvest, a festival would lift the mood of the people, and she had agreed.

The truly disturbing news had come from Lord Beker, who suspected that a Dregmoorian spy lurked among the Camrithian troops and may have wormed his way into the king's court. Melaia had no idea what to do about such news, but she wasn't surprised. After all, Dwin spied in the Dregmoors. So did Arelin, known as the Asp. Why wouldn't Lord Rejius have spies among the Camrithians?

As Melaia stepped down from the throne, Benasin walked in and asked, "May I speak privately with you, my lady?"

Melaia nodded to Lord Beker, who bowed and left by the rear door.

Serai started to follow him, but Benasin called her back. "An Angelaeon viewpoint may be valuable. I wish to discuss strategy."

Melaia rubbed her forehead. She was on the verge of a headache, and strategy was a subject at which she felt completely inept.

Benasin leaned on his staff. "I've been mulling over what you said about uniting the harps in the Durenwoods, and I'm skeptical."

"About what?" Melaia sat on the bottom step that led to the throne.

"About where to unite the harps," said Benasin. "I can't shake the notion that the Tree should be restored where it was destroyed."

"Where is that?"

"Stone Grove. In the Dregmoors."

Melaia narrowed her eyes. Whose side was Benasin on? "Are you saying we should take the harps to the Dregmoors? Directly to Lord Rejius?"

"To the Dregmoors, yes," said Benasin. "To Rejius, no. That's why we need a strategy."

Melaia's heartbeat quickened. Take the harps into the Dregmoors? The thought frightened her and fueled her at the same time. Such a move would be risky. Dangerous. But it meant traveling with Trevin after all.

She turned to Serai. "Fetch Trevin and Dwin. They should be part of this discussion." As Serai left the room, Melaia strode to the map table. "Do you have a strategy in mind?"

Benasin scratched his beard. "The problem is getting the harps into the Dregmoors unnoticed when their warriors and raiders are swarming the border."

Melaia drummed her fingers on the map of Camrithia painted on the tabletop. "With the Dregmoorians blockading the southern coast, going by sea is out of the question, but we might cross the Davernon River if we can find a safe route." She ran her finger down the curve of the river. "Jarrod is the strategist. Surely he could find a way. Does he know you're speaking to me about this?"

"Not yet. He told me that most of your warriors went south to repel invaders. The attack at Drywell sent him scrambling to recall some of those troops. Now he plans to deploy the comains in separate groups to keep Rejius busy on several fronts."

"I see." Melaia felt as if she were playing the game Attacker Defender. Maybe Trevin had been teaching her strategy all along. "Dividing our troops keeps the Dregmoorians divided as well. Right?"

"We can hope so," said Benasin. "If we want to slip you and the harps into the Dregmoors, we'll need to draw their troops away from your entry point."

Melaia's stomach fluttered as she studied the map. At last she was moving forward.

"You wished to see me?" Dwin asked, as the doors shut behind him and Serai.

"Where's Trevin?" asked Melaia.

Dwin glanced at Serai, who pursed her lips. "I'm sorry," said Dwin, "but Trevin left Redcliff this morning."

Melaia put her hand to her belly. She felt as if the breath had been knocked out of her. "He left for the Dregmoors? Without you?" *Or me,* she thought.

"Trevin expects Windweaver to get him in." Dwin handed her a small scroll. "He tried to see you last night, but guards turned him away."

Melaia broke the seal on the scroll and opened it.

My Lady Love,

As Dwin could not accompany me, I thought it wise to join a band of travelers. They are set on leaving early. I hope to see you before I leave. If not, this is my farewell for now. I expect to reach the Dregmoors within a few days. With my father's help, I'll soon be back with the harp. I leave you with my heart. It shall always be yours.

Looking toward my return,

Trevin

He had drawn two harps side by side, which formed a heart like the one created by holding her harp pendant next to his.

She looked at Benasin. "In a few days Trevin will be in the Dregmoors. Do I recall him? Follow him?"

Benasin ran a hand through his hair and exhaled slowly. "At this point you'd best wait and let him bring you the harp. Maybe I'm wrong about where to unite them. I suppose we'll know as soon as the three are together."

Melaia pressed her hand to the pendant she wore and reread the message. Since she had commissioned Trevin to go, she couldn't be angry with him. The fact that he was finally on his way was reason enough to rejoice and be grateful, but she did not feel even a hint of joy. Instead she felt empty. Alone. Abandoned.

Chapter 4

Trevin settled his black stallion into a steady pace as he rode beside a wagon with a false floorboard that hid a strongbox of gold and gems, payment for Eldarran supplies. The journey master had been overjoyed to include an armed comain in the caravan, and Trevin was glad to make himself useful, although he doubted bandits would consider the scraggly looking travelers worth a second glance.

In his childhood he had watched caravans heading north loaded with kegs of coveted Lowridge cider, woven silkcloth from the southern ports, and grains from the western plain. These days the blight had whittled the goods from Camrithia down to a pitiful offering. From the midpoint of the caravan, he scanned the procession trailing him. Two loads of zilwood, a pack of donkeys in need of better pasturage, and a few wagons with an assortment of goods scraped together in hopes that they would fetch something more desirable in trade – namely food.

Satisfied that the last of the caravan was safely around a curve, Trevin turned back to the road ahead. High above, two dark birds spiraled. No doubt someone with a scrying glass watched through their eyes. Was the spy surveying the road in general or him in particular? The hair on Trevin's neck prickled. Blasted Dregmoorian spy-birds.

His stallion snorted and pulled at the reins, so he gave the horse some slack and galloped to the front of the caravan. Under his tunic his harp pendant jostled against his chest. He missed Melaia fiercely, but he had known the day would come when he would have to leave. He only wished he had insisted on bidding her farewell in person. He shifted in his saddle. As a comain, he had sworn allegiance to the kingdom of Camrithia. Was he deserting his post to go north? Was he betraying Melaia's trust?

Ahead the rounded heights of the Aubendahl Hills appeared as a line of dark knobs lurking along the horizon beneath the brilliant sky. Trevin shook off his doubts, squared his shoulders, and held his mount to a steady gait.

❖❖❖

Melaia paced around the sitting room of the king's apartment, waiting for him to appear. Yesterday's news about Trevin's departure had left her grumpy, careening back and forth between relief that Trevin was on his mission and grief over his absence. She paused at a window and threw the latticed shutters open to a fresh, cool breeze. With Trevin gone, the palace felt stifling, and she wanted it open to the world. No doubt her father would complain about the chill, but she was tired of pandering to him. If he was cold, he could sit by the lit brazier.

She moved to the next window and strained at a stubborn shutter latch. A zeal for action had always smoldered in her bones. Now it consumed her with the desire to complete her task. Unite the harps. Restore the Tree and its stairway. She would see it done. Soon.

The latch grudgingly gave, and she shoved out the shutter with a clack.

"My lady." Lord Beker bowed as two attendants entered, carrying King Laetham in his chair.

Melaia fought back the sense of despair that hit her every time she saw her father's frailness, his gaunt face, the rapid graying of his thick dark hair, and the melancholy in his eyes. She grieved over her inability to draw him out and give him hope, but he was a drowning man, and if she stayed in Redcliff, he would surely pull her under the waves with him.

"It's cold in here," said the king as his aides set his chair by the brazier. "Close those shutters." His attendants dashed toward the windows.

"Leave them open," said Melaia, "and be dismissed."

The attendants hesitated between the brazier and the unshuttered windows until Lord Beker nodded them toward the door. As they left he stationed himself behind King Laetham.

A breeze rippled the flame in the brazier, and the king scowled at Melaia. "Are you trying to kill me before my time?"

Melaia kissed him on the forehead. "I'm trying to awaken you to a long and prosperous reign. The fresh air will do you good." She sat on a footstool. "You've not given audience in a fortnight. Your people need to see you. They need to see you *rule*."

"What would they see?" He pulled his cloak snug. "An emaciated old cripple."

"Only if that's the way you present yourself. You have a choice."

"These legs give me no choice."

"It's not your legs that have failed you. It's your courage."

The king glared at the flames in the brazier. "The gods are against me."

"No one is against you but yourself." Melaia sighed. The conversation always followed the same path. She strode to the window and faced the breeze. *I, too, have a choice,* she thought.

She turned back to her father. "Remember when we first met in Qanreef? You said we could start over."

"I was whole then."

"Whole or not, let's start over from this day." She took a deep breath. "I'm going to Lowridge to fetch a novice for Hanni. Go with me. Lowridge is not that far. Show yourself to your people. Show them you're whole of mind."

"I'm not well enough."

Melaia clenched her fists at her side. "If you won't go with me, I'll go on my own."

"I will not allow you to trot around the countryside. I am not ignorant of the raids that plague us. Jarrod keeps me apprised."

"I'm not asking your permission."

"Good. Because I'm not giving it." The king waved to Lord Beker. "Call my attendants. I want to get out of this wind." He held his hand toward Melaia.

She kissed it and then stood back, her vision blurring with tears as the aides carried her father away.

Lord Beker paused at the door. "He's upset by a recurring dream that disturbs his sleep."

"What kind of dream?" Melaia wiped her eyes with the back of her hand.

"An eagle, my lady – an eagle swooping down on a lion." The arch of his eyebrows said, *Think about it.*

Melaia frowned. The lion adorned every flag and kingsman's cloak in the realm. "A white lion is the king's emblem," she said.

Lord Beker inclined his head. "And the eagle?"

Melaia sank to the bench where she had vowed to her father that she would marry no one but Trevin. The day after that, before Trevin was appointed comain, she had given him a gift. "Trevin's shield," she said. "I chose the eagle painted on it." Only two days ago he had hoisted his shield in the practice yard, triumphantly conceding defeat as her father looked on. "Is my father afraid of Trevin?"

"He suspects Trevin may be an informant working for the Dregmoorians."

Melaia gaped at Lord Beker. "Surely *you* don't believe that."

"No, I don't. I'm simply telling you why your father is upset." Lord Beker bowed out of the room and closed the door.

Melaia rubbed the back of her neck. The king's dream clearly grew out of melancholy and fear. An eagle swooping down on a lion – absurd. Unless . . . "The creature that stands in the library?" she murmured. She dashed out the door to the stairwell, where Serai waited with her guards.

Serai's eyebrows rose expectantly. "Did he agree to go to Lowridge?"

"He refused and forbade me to go." Melaia headed downstairs with Serai. Her guards followed at a discreet distance. Even so, Melaia lowered her voice. "My father holds a crazed notion that Trevin is an informant."

"Does he know Trevin has gone to the Dregmoors?"

"I don't know. *I* didn't tell him. He was in no mood to talk." Melaia explained the king's dream while they walked to the library.

The guards stationed themselves in the corridor as Melaia and Serai entered the musty room. A slanted swathe of sunlight drifted through an open window. Melaia pointed into the shadowed corner where the winged column stood. "What do you know about that creature?"

With her hands on her hips, Serai approached the stone figure. "Jarrod calls it the Gryphon," she said. "That's the extent of my wisdom on the matter, but I assume he knows its entire history. Shall I fetch him?"

"If you dare," said Melaia.

Serai turned with a mischievous spark in her eye. "I'm not one to refuse a dare." She headed out of the room, calling back, "*You'll* have to question him, though."

"If I dare," Melaia said to the shadowed column. The creature looked as if it might shake loose and stumble across the room, which stirred uneasy memories of Lord Rejius shifting into his hawk form.

"No need to fear a statue," she told herself. She had best make friends with this stone beast, because Benasin was right. She would do well to acquaint herself with the scrolls that lay under the Gryphon's gaze.

Melaia clenched her jaw and crept toward the column. At the height of her shoulders, the eagle's legs and feet protruded, forming the Gryphon's arms and hands, complete with outstretched claws. Defying her fear Melaia firmly touched the claws on the left. They yielded with a grating sound, and she jerked back. Then, firmly and carefully, she pushed on the claws again. The entire left arm slid into the torso, while the right arm lengthened and the beast's belly slid open. A cold draft wafted out.

Within the belly was a steep spiral stairway leading down. Melaia descended the steps, pressing her palms to the stone wall for support. She intended to go only as far as she could see by the library's light, but her eyes grew accustomed to the dim stairwell, and she took one more step, then another until she met a flicker of light trickling up. She picked up her pace but found the passage blocked by a lattice of iron worked in a pattern of leaves and branches. As Melaia looked through the lattice, she felt as if she were peering through a hedge.

Beyond the ironwork the stairway continued seven steps and ended at an open archway that stood over a small font containing the source of light: a bowl lamp with a flaming wick. She crouched to see farther. Past the arch and lamp an elaborately patterned mosaic floor extended toward shadowed columns that stood like a row of teeth, beyond which lay a gaping maw of darkness.

Out of the gloom came a low, undulating, cavernous thrum, the drone of deep, chanting voices. The sound lifted the hair on Melaia's neck. She raced up the stairs and stumbled back into the library, panting. Then she pushed on the right arm of the statue, and the creature's belly grated shut as its left arm elongated. Backing away she stared at the statue that stood sentinel over … what?

"Acquainting yourself with the Gryphon?" asked Jarrod as he stepped into the room with Serai.

"I think he has secrets," Melaia hinted, hoping Jarrod would mention the hidden stairway if he was aware of it. "Do you know anything about the statue?"

Jarrod shrugged. "He appears as half-eagle, half-lion."

Melaia rolled her eyes. "That's helpful."

Serai laughed. "Jarrod says the Gryphon was once one of the Archae – if I understand correctly?"

"In a way," said Jarrod.

Melaia eyed the figure again. Windweaver, Seaspinner, and Flametender were three angels ranked Archae. They looked strange, but not this strange. Even her mother, Dreia, another Archon, appeared in human form. "Is Earthbearer the Gryphon?" she asked.

Jarrod listed the Archae raising a finger for each. "Windweaver rules the air, Seaspinner the oceans and rivers, Flametender fire, and Dreia the plant world. Earthbearer is guardian of soil, rock, and earth elements. What's left?"

"Animals," said Melaia.

"And humans," said Serai.

"Impressive." Jarrod cocked an eyebrow. "You both have minds like fox traps."

Serai gave a satisfied smile.

"Why does no one speak of the Gryphon?" asked Melaia.

"How do you know they don't?" Jarrod scanned the scroll niches at the far end of the room.

"I've never heard of him," said Melaia.

"The Archae hold positions of guardianship." Jarrod pulled out a scroll, perused it, and slipped it back in. "The Gryphon is the symbol of a position held by people chosen to represent the human and animal realm."

"So there's no creature that really looks like the statue?" asked Melaia.

"Not that I know of." Jarrod selected another scroll. "As I understand it, two people at a time held the position of Gryphon. When one died, another was chosen. At the time the stairway to heaven was destroyed, no one had been named to replace the previous Gryphon."

"Has anyone been named since?" asked Melaia.

"Anyone who is chosen must be confirmed in Avellan." Jarrod unrolled the scroll and examined it. "With the loss of the stairway –"

"– the connection to Avellan was lost," Melaia finished.

"Exactly."

"What about the statue?" Melaia prodded. "Does it serve a purpose here?"

Jarrod looked the column up and down. "To support the ceiling?" He rerolled the scroll and returned it to its niche.

"Perhaps the statue was carved in memory of the Gryphon," said Serai, settling on a bench by the door.

"Maybe." Melaia frowned at the movable arms. Why the stairwell within? Why the font and flame, the mosaic chamber? She watched Jarrod scour the niches. Either he didn't know what the figure hid, or he wasn't telling. And if he wasn't telling, neither was she.

Jarrod saluted with a small scroll. "Here it is. A word about the Gryphon." He handed it to Melaia. "Don't get your hopes up. It's written in our mother's hand and contains all the clarity of her other writings."

"In other words, it's baffling." Melaia unrolled the papyrus. The first part was no puzzle. She read it aloud.

The Tree will only rise again

by breath of angel, blood of man,

Melaia shrugged. "That's me. Child of both angel and man, born to restore the Tree."

"So we've been told." Jarrod took a seat beside Serai.

"Listen to the rest," said Melaia.

but unity will not return

until the Gryphon dances.

"What does that mean?" asked Serai.

"I've never heard it before," said Melaia.

"Clear as mud." Jarrod rose and flicked his long tail of hair over his shoulder. "It's well past lunch time. Would you ladies care to join me?" He offered an arm to Serai, who crooked her elbow through his.

Melaia tucked the scroll into her waist pouch and bowed to the Gryphon. "We leave you, sir, to your solitary vigil."

She took Jarrod's other arm, but it was a poor substitute for the one she wanted, the one who now carried her heart into the Dregmoors.

Chapter 5

The sky had turned into a blanket of stars by the time Trevin settled his horse in a stall at the caravansary on the outskirts of Dahl, a fair size town at the foot of the Aubendahl Hills. Trevin took a piece of flatbread from his journey bag and wove through the milling group of travelers who were helping themselves to a savory smelling stew at the communal cauldron in the center of the dirt yard. He peeked into the pot and, glad to see meat, scooped a generous portion onto his bread.

The squat Eldarran journey master, Cyprian, sidled up, chewing vigorously, his bushy brows lowered in a scowl. "Meat's a good ways from tender," he said. "I wager they'll not be lending us fresh pack mules here. Seems they use them for another purpose." He swallowed with effort. "Care to try the tavern with me? See if they serve better fare?"

Trevin eyed the mixture topping his bread, which no longer appeared appetizing. "The tavern it is." He handed his meal to a young drover who seemed to appreciate the offering.

The west wall of the caravansary butted up to the east wall of Dahl, so the stroll into town proved short and pleasant in the cool of the evening. Trevin heard the jollity from the tavern before he saw it, which boded well for good food or good drink or both. He elbowed into the rustic room with Cyprian, and they took two seats at a corner table.

The tavern maid had just shoved bread and barley beer their way when a slur cut across the room in a voice that brought Trevin's head up from his drink. He locked eyes with a muscular, crooked nosed man wearing a russet cloak fastened with an emerald brooch the size of a walnut.

"Hesel," Trevin hissed. Gash running was obviously lucrative, but the vulture was a fool to wear his fortune. Or did everyone here know to stay out of his business?

Hesel's smile twisted as he continued to talk to his companions. ". . . dung digger," he said loudly and jerked his chin toward Trevin.

Cyprian set down his mug and tore into the bread. "You know the man?"

"He's a gash runner."

"Gash. Filthy drink, I hear. Does it really keep a person young?"

"Only on the outside," said Trevin. "It slowly hardens your vitals. Kills you from the inside out. And it's addictive. That fool gash runner was banished from Camrithia. I ought to drag him back to the dungeons at Redcliff."

"Seems to me you'd not take him without a stiff fight," said Cyprian.

"I've fought him before," said Trevin. *And won*, he thought, *or would have, if the prince of the Dregmoors had not intervened.* "A friend of his died after fighting me. Which was not my fault, but it would account for the man's malice."

The tavern maid set bowls of thick, steaming stew in front of them, and Cyprian sopped it with his bread. "I value your company in my 'van, Main Trevin. If you can see your way clear to avoid the man, I'd favor it."

Trevin forced his gaze away from Hesel and slurped a mouthful of salty stew. Hauling Hesel to Redcliff would be immensely satisfying, but it would delay his journey to the Dregmoors, which would disappoint Melaia. Besides which, she would learn that he was traveling to Eldarra first. She might see the wisdom of recruiting Windweaver's help, but explaining why he had headed to Flauren against her wishes might prove tricky.

"I'll stay with the caravan," said Trevin.

Across the room, Hesel scooted away from his table. He and his companions stood.

Trevin edged back his cloak to expose the hilt of his dagger. "I won't start a fight," he told Cyprian, "but I can't speak for the gash runner."

As Hesel and his friends wove out of the room, they shot threatening looks at Trevin, who glared back. Once the vipers were gone he ate heartily, but he drank only enough to quench his thirst in case he needed all his wits to defend himself on the short jaunt to the caravansary.

He and Cyprian walked back with daggers in hand. Cyprian was jumpy, but Trevin strode along easily, appreciating the ability to see in the dark. The gift did not make his judgment foolproof, but he could see down the dark alleys in town and across the fields once they left the city wall. He almost told Cyprian about his ability but then thought better of it. He didn't want the journey master to assign him more than his fair share of night watches.

Once they were safely within the walls of the caravansary, Trevin slipped up the inner stairs to the flat roof, where he could escape the smoke and the strongest odors and sleep beneath the stars. More important he could keep an eye on the yard and the gates, in case Hesel or one of his companions entered.

A lone guard stood on the opposite edge of the roof, his foot resting on the low parapet. Trevin nodded to him and removed his scabbard. Then he settled next to the parapet and positioned himself at the best vantage point to observe the movement below.

A breeze flapped the loose edge of Trevin's cloak and whispered, *Sciai eolin. Ciarai pyrin, Nai librein.*

Trevin drew his cloak tight and turned his face to the wind and the message it carried, the words of his naming, which Flametender had spoken over him.

Seed of wind, Heir of fire, Born to free.

Trevin looked at the guard, but the man showed no sign of having heard the shadowy voice. "Windweaver," Trevin murmured, picturing the Archon strolling the skies above. "I need you to meet me up north."

The guard glanced at Trevin and then turned back to the world beyond the walls.

"Windweaver?" Trevin whispered.

All was silent except for the snorts and scrapes of the animals and their drovers below.

Trevin leaned back against the parapet, wishing Windweaver had paused in his trek across the skies. They could have walked the wind together. The Archon could have taken him to Eldarra. At Windweaver's pace, they would be there by now.

Below, the gatekeeper bolted the caravansary doors. Trevin placed his hand to the harp pendant at his chest and knew who would meet him in his dreams.

Melaia blinked back tears as she cooed to Peron, who pecked seeds from her hand. She had fed Peron as a curly haired, red cheeked baby. This jerky bird-pecking cut like a knife at her heart, but she sat tall. Lord Rejius would see nothing through Peron's eyes but a peaceful morning in the rooftop garden. Peron hopped off her hand and along the parapet.

Serai leaned out the door and said, "Lord Beker is here."

Peron flew.

Melaia watched her disappear around the corner of a tower. Then she dusted her hands on her skirt and went indoors.

Lord Beker bowed. "You summoned me, my lady?"

Melaia motioned him to a desk. "I want you and Serai to sign a document." She spread out a scroll. "I expect us to keep this parchment a secret for now."

Lord Beker inclined his head. "I must warn you that I am bound to your father. If I deem your words important to him, I will be hard-pressed to keep it silent."

"I would not expect otherwise," said Melaia, "but I think you'll agree that my father need never know. His health declines, and as I'm heir to his throne but have no heir myself, I feel it's wise to leave a record of my wishes in case something should happen to both of us."

Lord Beker frowned. "Do you have a premonition of such?"

"This is simply a precaution," said Melaia.

"You're young yet, my lady," said Lord Beker. "You have good prospects for marriage. Should you not take this up with your father?"

"You know he would put me off." Melaia fingered a reed pen. "I can't ignore the possibilities. What if the Dregmoorians had not halted at Drywell? What if they had entered Redcliff? We should have a plan."

Lord Beker stroked his blonde beard with his twisted hand. "Do you propose to name an heir with this document?"

"I propose to name you," said Melaia.

Lord Beker opened his mouth, closed it, and ran his good hand through his hair.

"You already manage affairs in the shadow of the throne," said Melaia.

Lord Beker went to one knee, looking from Melaia to Serai and back. "I signed away Laetham's kingdom once –"

"Under torture," said Serai.

Lord Beker rubbed his twisted hand. "I'll never commit such an act again, tortured or not. Even so, I don't deserve to inherit the throne. Nor have I ever desired it. But there's a certain young man –"

"I thought about that, but my father perceives Trevin as a threat to his throne. If he should find this decree –"

"He'll not find it," said Serai. "You'll keep it safely hidden in your lockbox, to be opened only if necessary."

Melaia helped Lord Beker rise. "So you believe that Trevin is the right choice?"

"I do," said Lord Beker.

Melaia inked the pen. "What are the proper terms for this document?"

As Lord Beker dictated the words, Melaia copied them onto the scroll. With every line she felt more certain. Naming Trevin as heir made sense. He was already in line to inherit Eldarra and the

Dregmoors. Perhaps one day the three kingdoms would unite. Through marriage and not death, she prayed.

Melaia signed her name and handed the pen to Lord Beker.

"May we never need this paper." He scratched his name on the scroll and passed the pen to Serai. "Any news from Jarrod?" he asked.

"None." Serai penned her name. "I know only that he's headed to someplace in the vicinity of the Davernon. I don't think he knew exactly where."

"King Laetham will wish to see him immediately upon his return," said Lord Beker.

"I'll tell him." Serai cleared away the pen and ink as Lord Beker bowed and left.

Melaia set two bird-shaped weights on the scroll to keep it open while the ink dried. "*Now* I can go to Lowridge in good conscience," she said.

With fresh energy she strode around her quarters, making sure everything was in order – or a bit out of order. She didn't want the room to appear too neat, for the palace servants thought she and Serai were simply spending a few days in prayerful seclusion at the temple. Only Hanni knew they intended to leave Redcliff the next morning to fetch her new novice.

Melaia slipped her needle-knife into a sheath and tucked it into her waist pouch. "Did you find anyone to go with us?" she asked.

"Two Angelaeon: Xenio and Sorabus."

"Good. I'll be perfectly safe," said Melaia, defending herself to the grumble of her father in her head. She rolled the scroll, sealed it, and tucked it securely in her lockbox.

Serai lifted Melaia's cloak from its peg. "Shall we make our way to the temple for 'prayers?' I've already placed our journey packs there."

Melaia checked her waist pouch to make sure it held her mother's book, but she didn't pause to feel its pulse today, because her own surged with anticipation. "Ready," she said, taking her cloak from Serai. She swept it around her shoulders and strode out the door with a sense of adventure. At last she was waking from an overlong winter's nap.

❖❖❖

The late afternoon sun beat warm on the wagon rolling east, and Melaia shed her cloak to bask in it. No draks had crossed the sky since noon, so she felt safe uncloaked. She took a deep, satisfying breath of the grass-scented breeze. Was air in the countryside fresher than air at the palace, or did it seem fresher because she felt freer?

Of course freedom was relative, she mused, looking around at her protectors. She was practically wedged between two angels: on the right, broad shouldered Serai and on the left, driving the wagon, Xenio with his long dark braids. According to Serai, Xenio ranked as one of the Kuriotes, an expert leader. Sorabus, almond-eyed and soft-spoken, rode in the back of the wagon. He ranked as Thronos, a gifted negotiator.

Melaia sat taller. Escorts or no, she felt free now that she was outside the walls of Redcliff. The wide sky would be their tent tonight. Pure pleasure!

"Lowridge sits the horizon over this rise, my lady," said Xenio. "We'll arrive at the hind wall of the town. Main gates are on the other side."

Melaia eagerly peered ahead as they topped the hill. A squat, stone settlement came into view. So did a contingent of foot warriors with two horsemen in the lead.

Serai loosened her dagger. "I don't sense Angelaeon ahead, do you, Xenio?"

"No." He slowed the wagon.

"Malevolents?" asked Melaia.

"I think not," said Xenio, "but if they're common Dregmoorians, they may be gash warriors, and I'm none too eager to meet up with their kind."

It was too late to turn around or head south for the cover of the woods. Sorabus jumped from the back of the wagon and strode beside it, his cloak loose and open, exposing the hilt of his sword.

Ahead the warriors halted. Two loped toward Melaia's wagon, shields raised, a horseman following.

"They look Camrithian," said Sorabus. He called, "Greetings, friends!"

"Let's hope they're friends," muttered Xenio.

The two approaching warriors parted, and the horseman, a burly man with big ears, rode forward.

Melaia grinned. "They *are* friends." She waved and called, "Main Catellus!"

The comain dismounted, knelt in a bow, and motioned for his warriors to bow as well. "My lady!" he said. "I'm taken by surprise, seeing you here."

"And I'm surprised to see you," said Melaia. "We first thought your group was Dregmoorian."

"Could have been," said Catellus. "We skirmished with raiders southeast of here about this time yesterday – which made us wary enough to stop and check your wagon. Of course that's not necessary now." He nodded at her company and held three fingers over his heart in the angel greeting, the sign of the Tree. "What brings you this way?" he asked. "This whole area is less than safe."

"We've come to fetch a novice for the temple at Redcliff," said Melaia. "What about you?"

"We're on the way north to a spot where Jarrod says we'll find Dregmoorians. We hoped to catch them napping, but yesterday's skirmish delayed us, so they may have slipped our reach by now."

"Is Jarrod with you?" asked Serai.

"Haven't seen Jarrod in a while," said Catellus. "He sends messages by a runner."

Melaia felt Serai's shoulders sag.

Sorabus frowned at Catellus. "Jarrod sent no angels with you?"

"He doesn't expect malevolents up north," said Catellus. "Only gash warriors. Those, we can handle."

As Melaia watched the two discuss the locations where Jarrod anticipated the hottest conflict, she realized the enormity of Jarrod's task. Keep track of who moved where and when. Try to anticipate the enemy's every move. Spare the Angelaeon to fight where malevolents were involved, because only an angel could kill an angel. She felt a new respect for her half-brother. His job was difficult, and the stakes were too high to fail.

At a lull in the conversation, Serai called to Catellus, "Do you camp soon? We can provide angel company for the night."

"We'd welcome such company." Catellus shaded his eyes as the lowering sun shot a parting glare. "If you can stand the scent of journeying warriors."

"The smell of safety, I say." Xenio looked at Melaia. "My lady?"

Melaia agreed. As they followed Catellus and his men to the plains west of Lowridge, the cloudless sky darkened, and the air cooled. To the south a black bird flapped from a thicket, and once again Melaia donned her cloak.

That evening Melaia paced around a campfire, working out the stiffness from the day's ride. A small army surrounded her, their fires burning low across the field, mingling the smell of woodsmoke with sweat, stew, and the cider Serai poured.

Melaia took the cup Serai handed her, eased down to her pallet, and gazed through the spiced steam toward the back wall of Lowridge. Above, five stars formed a line, angling down toward three others. Melaia's heartbeat quickened. The beltway of stars was moving into position to receive the stairway to heaven. Such a formation of stars occurred only once every two hundred years. If the stars moved on before she united the harps, the chance to restore the stairway would vanish for the foreseeable future.

With the vast heavens above her and a sprawling encampment of men encircling her, Melaia felt as tiny as an ant, as weak as a worm. "Where has my mind been?" she murmured. "I can't save the world."

Serai sat down with a cup of cider. "You don't save the world with your mind. You save it with your heart." She placed a hand on Melaia's arm. "You can open the portal. That's all you need to do."

Melaia set aside her cup, took out her mother's book, and ran her hand across the etched wooden cover. Its peaceful thrum flowed through her, the same pulse of life she felt when she held the kyparis harps. She opened to the inscription on the first page, which always settled her: *For My Child.*

The next page remained an enigma.

I am the heart

that makes three one.

I am freedom,

the curse undone.

What confidence. *I am the heart. I am freedom.* If only she understood the riddle's meaning, maybe she would feel confident too.

She thumbed to the last page to check on the location of the third harp. If Trevin was with the harp, she might see him. Lines formed on the page, swam, and settled to reveal the silhouetted figures and the bench, which was empty. She let out the breath she didn't know she was holding. It was too soon for Trevin to have the harp. He was probably only now entering the Dregmoors.

As the flames of the campfire sank into glowing embers, Melaia slipped the book back into her waist pouch and lay down on her pallet, remembering other nights beneath the stars: Drover's Well where she saw a gash-drunk dying of his addiction, Caldarius where she bathed in hot springs, Caepio's camp where the actors laid plans to sneak into Qanreef. Trevin had been at each location, and it felt wrong to camp here without him. But until the stairway was restored, nothing in this world would be right and whole again, not even her bond with Trevin.

Melaia blinked heavily, the orange-red embers blurred, and she fell into a deep, dreamless sleep.

Until the silence was split by a scream.

CHAPTER 6

Jolted out of a deep sleep Melaia sat up on her mat, her heart racing. Black smoke boiled into the dawn sky over Lowridge, and she heard distant shouts. Camrithian warriors on every side were scrambling to their feet.

"Raiders!" The cry passed through the camp.

Melaia leaped up and dug into her pouch for the sheath containing her needle knife. Fumbling with the cords, she tied it onto her waist sash.

Serai dashed up with an armful of gear. "Catellus sent this." She stuffed a thick leather vest into Melaia's hands. While Melaia tugged it on, Serai fastened a sword belt around Melaia's waist.

"A sword, too?" asked Melaia. A thrill pulsed through her as Serai thrust the pommel into her hand.

"It's a short one, but take care. It's not dull-tipped wood." Serai shrugged on her vest. "Catellus's warriors will go ahead of us. You and I will follow in the wagon with Xenio and Sorabus. We will enter Lowridge only if we think we can reach the novice safely. Otherwise we turn back." She shot Melaia a look that said this was the final word on the matter.

Melaia nodded, shifting the hilt of the sword from one palm to the other as she had seen Trevin do. It was heavier, and its shape gave it a different feel from the wooden blade she was accustomed to. She thrust it into its scabbard, tingling from head to toe and marveling at Serai's calm. "You act as if you've seen battle before," she said.

"No." Serai slipped her dagger under her belt. "And I hope I'll not see it today."

The Camrithian warriors formed groups of twenty men each. As the first group loped past Melaia, heading for Lowridge, she saluted with her sword. "Lowridge is ours!" she called.

The passing warriors drew their swords and saluted. One shouted, "For the princess and Camrithia!" The second group took up the cry, then the third group and the fourth. "For the princess and Camrithia!"

Melaia stood tall, holding her sword high, but she wished her father were standing in her place. He should be urging his men into battle. They should be calling his name.

Xenio drove up in the wagon and insisted that Melaia ride in the back with Sorabus this time, while Serai sat in the front beside him. As they headed out, Melaia pressed a hand to her harp pendant, hoping she would remember Trevin's instructions if she had to use her sword. He had trained her for this moment. "Oh Most High," she murmured as her stomach clenched. "I hope I'm ready."

As the wagon bumped toward the town gate, Melaia craned her neck to see past Xenio and Serai. The rosy light of dawn edged the horizon north and south of Lowridge, but billows of smoke darkened the sky over the town, and now and then a tongue of flame flickered up.

Catellus led the first and second group of warriors through the postern gate. The following groups split, one sprinting north along the wall, the other heading south. By the time Melaia's wagon reached the city, Camrithians stood guard.

One saluted. "For now the battle is contained to the east section of town," he reported, "but you'd best be ready to leave if the fight spreads."

Xenio acknowledged the report with a nod, and the wagon rattled into Lowridge as clumps of townsfolk trudged out, lugging bundles.

"We need the midwife," Xenio called to them. "Who can show us the way?"

No one answered. They were busy herding each other or elbowing their way through.

Serai repeated the plea. "Where's the midwife?"

A prune-faced woman hobbled out of a hut with her bundle in a sling. "A poor day for birthin'," she told Serai as she trudged past, "but ye should be able to *smell* yer way to the gash house."

"The gash house?" asked Sorabus.

The woman paused. "Baize sells the stuff. Midwife's *his* wife."

"Baize," Melaia muttered. She knew the man only by sight. The last time she had seen him, he was selling gash openly in Qanreef. Most towns drove him out if they had any sense – which did not speak well of Lowridge.

The woman pointed a crooked finger down the street. "End of the road that runs along the west wall. House pretends to be rich. New tiled roof. Black hawk painted on the lintel."

Melaia gripped the side of the wagon as it lurched ahead. A black hawk, even painted, did nothing to quell her unease. The horses, too, were skittish. They were not accustomed to the sounds of battle, the cracks and crashes, shouts and screams funneling down the narrow streets. She could envision the fight, for she had survived the thick of the battle at Qanreef. Even so she was trembling like a plucked harp string, and with every breath of smoke-laced air, her chest tightened. She placed her hand over the bulk of the book in her waist pouch and tried to still herself.

Ahead a runner shot from a side street and hailed them. "Word from Main Catellus, sirs." He panted. "The Dregs have malevolents with them. Can you spare a couple of your angels?"

Xenio looked back at Melaia.

"Go on," she said. "You and Sorabus. Serai will stay with me."

Xenio handed the reins to Serai, leaped from the wagon, and dashed down the street with Sorabus and the runner. Melaia scrambled to the front seat beside Serai.

With effort they coaxed the horses to the road that fronted the town wall. The newly tiled roof was clearly visible at the end, and within moments, Serai was tethering the horses, while Melaia, shaking off a shudder, knocked on the door below the lintel adorned with a black hawk.

When no one answered, Melaia gently eased the door open, her hand on the hilt of her sword. Inside, the stench of landgash, akin to rotting eggs, was unmistakeable. The same odor had spewed from rifts in the ground outside of Redcliff the previous summer. Melaia swallowed a sour taste and entered a long, narrow anteroom painted an oppressive, dark red.

The only furniture in the hall was a bench along the far end, which was positioned an arm's length away from the back wall as if to provide a place to sit and contemplate the object that stood in a niche before it: a polished, black stone image of a hawk.

Melaia retreated, bumping into Serai who had just entered. As Serai steadied her, Melaia pointed to the image.

Serai hissed. "That's quite the welcome," she said. "Is no one here?"

"I've not seen anyone." Melaia took a deep breath and strode to an open door on the right. High windows in the room provided enough light to reveal a font, a trunk, and a low bed. As she turned back, Serai emerged from the opposite door.

"No one in the hearth room," Serai said.

Melaia headed for the door in the back wall. "Do you remember the novice's name?"

"Only the midwife's: Isma."

Melaia sidestepped the bench and crept through the far door into the back room, where threads of light seeped through cracks in the shutters. Shelves of jugs and jars lined the walls.

Serai stepped in, wrinkling her nose. "What's in here?"

"It's a stillroom," said Melaia. It reminded her of Hanni's stillroom in Navia, but instead of smelling like fresh herbs, this room stank of gash.

At the darker end of the room a full-length curtain shifted. Melaia's hand went to her sword, and Serai drew her dagger as a woman with mussed hair peeked out.

"Isma?" Melaia asked.

When the woman nodded, Serai sheathed her dagger.

"The high priestess of Redcliff sent us," said Melaia. "We're here for your daughter. It's a terrible time to come, I know, but –"

"No, please, it's all right," Isma said. "It's a good time. I barely got her away from the others." She disappeared behind the curtain, calling, "Claudia, fetch your things. Quick now."

Isma came back wringing her skirt. "Can you get her out safely?"

"Yes, but you said *others*. What others?" asked Melaia.

Isma lowered her voice. "The children. The ones to be sold to the raiders."

"The raiders who are fighting today?" asked Melaia.

Isma nodded. "There wasn't supposed to be fighting."

Melaia gaped at her. The fire, the smoke, the screams. Were they a child's screams? "Where are the others?" she asked.

Isma shook her head. "I don't know."

"I do." A girl with wide blue eyes edged around Isma. She looked about Peron's age. "I heard my da say the children were going to the storehouse, past the marketplace. It's not far. I can show you."

Isma shoved Claudia back. "You'll do no such thing."

Serai gripped Melaia's arm. "I know what you're thinking, but it's not possible. You're here for the novice. Besides, the other children may be gone already."

"And if they're not?" Melaia shook Serai off. "There's only one way to be certain. Claudia said it's not far." She headed into the entry hall. "Claudia can show me the way or not. The same goes for you, Serai." She knew Serai would follow. Claudia maybe.

Serai trotted up to Melaia, grabbed her arm and yanked her back. "*You* will stay here."

For a moment they faced each other, huffing and glaring. Then Serai said, "I'll go, but if I'm not back in a reasonable amount of time, leave Lowridge without me." She nudged Melaia away from the front door and ducked out of the house.

Melaia returned to the stillroom to find that Isma and Claudia had hidden themselves behind the curtain again. She paced the room, rubbing her arms. Raiders stole children to supply one of the ingredients of gash: young blood. That, she had known. But she had not heard that people were exchanging their children for a drink touted to keep them young.

She marched to the curtain and jerked it aside. Isma and Claudia looked up from where they sat on an elaborately carved bed. Baize was obviously well compensated for trading in gash and children.

Melaia glared at Isma. "What kind of people give away their children? What kind?"

"The kind that want the blight ended." Isma fumbled with the ties of Claudia's journey pack.

"What does the blight have to do with it?" snapped Melaia.

"They're giving their children to the hawk-god, hoping he'll lift the blight," said Isma.

"Hawk-god?" Melaia huffed. Only Lord Rejius would make such a claim.

"It's not my belief." Isma stroked Claudia's hair. "I want my daughter trained to serve of the Ancient, the Most High, but many people nowadays say the hawk-god created the blight in the Dregmoors and spread it through the world. They believe he'll repeal the blight if they can appease his anger."

"By sacrificing their children to him?" Melaia slumped into a chair carved to match the bed. "Only a cruel god would demand such a gift. You're right not to believe such rubbish."

"So I've told Baize," said Isma. "He's deaf to reason."

In strained silence Melaia stewed, drumming her fingers on the arms of the chair. Was there nothing she could do until Serai returned? When would that be? She grew more anxious by the minute. At last she rose and paced the stillroom again. *A reasonable amount of time.* What counted as a reasonable amount of time? What if she left without Serai and later discovered that something awful had happened, something she could have prevented by staying?

Footsteps echoed in the entry hall, and Melaia dashed out of the stillroom. "Serai!"

A brawny man with a shaved head staggered back, looking her up and down. "A lady warrior," he growled.

Isma stepped to the doorway of the stillroom. "Baize. You're home."

Keeping his eyes on Melaia, he drew his dagger.

"Don't Baize." Isma's bird-thin voice pleaded. "She's a priestess."

"You believe her?" Baize blinked heavily at Melaia over his dagger. "She's not dressed like a priestess." His brow lowered, and he wagged his dagger at Isma. "You! It's *you* who's handed us over." With a murderous glare, he started toward his wife.

Melaia darted between them, holding out her empty palms in an effort to calm the situation.

Baize paused, his jaw clenched, his face reddening.

"I *am* a priestess," said Melaia. "I'm here to receive your daughter as a novice for the temple at Redcliff. It's a great honor –"

"Liar!" Baize lunged at Melaia, who dodged as Isma shrieked.

While Baize recovered his balance, Melaia drew her sword, and Isma ducked into the stillroom. Before Melaia could take a defensive stance, Baize slashed crosswise. She deflected the blow, but awkwardly. Her sword felt unfamiliar, and the narrow entryway afforded little room to maneuver. Experienced and methodical, Baize forced her to work left and right, back and forth. She was lighter on her feet than he was, but she was unaccustomed to a sustained fight, and as she grew tired, Baize grew wild.

Although she met a good number of his swings, she had to duck time and again. Then, with a single stroke, he knocked the sword from her hand. She fumbled to yank out her needle-knife. As he stalked toward her, she pulled the knife free and thrust it out menacingly.

Baize chortled. He now had the greater reach. He jabbed, goaded, and stabbed toward her leather vest, never touching her, but driving her back the way a jester would direct a dancing bear. How long she could continue the deadly dance, she didn't know. She only hoped he would make a mistake and give her one moment to duck under his arm and strike.

Baize bared his teeth. "I'm done playing, girl," he said, slashing at her legs.

Melaia lurched back, forgetting that the bench stood behind her. It toppled, and she fell backward as Baize sliced down. She felt her body fold in as his dagger hit her vest and the book in the pouch beneath it. Gasping, she tried to rise, while Baize drew back to finish her off.

Then he grunted and arched, dropped his dagger, and tumbled forward.

Serai jerked her dagger from his back.

Melaia watched Baize's spirit writhe away from his body. Cold and moist it swirled around her before it gathered itself, snaked over the bench, and seeped through a crack in the floor.

Serai wiped her dagger on Baize's tunic, slipped it back in place beneath her belt, and extended a hand to Melaia. "You look awful," she said.

"It was harder –" Melaia grabbed Serai's hand and strained to rise. "Harder than the practice field. But I learned some new moves." She stood and bent forward to catch her breath, her hands on her knees. "The children?"

"Townsfolk were already freeing them when I arrived," said Serai. "That's what started the fight. Those opposed to the child trade lay in wait for the raiders and their neighbors who favored it."

Footsteps sounded outdoors, and Serai whirled, her dagger poised. Melaia straightened, gripping her needle knife.

Jarrod appeared and then retreated, his eyes wide. "Hold, ladies!"

Serai sheathed her dagger and ran to his arms. "I thought I sensed you, but I didn't trust myself."

"What are *you* doing here?" asked Melaia.

Jarrod eyed the body. "I'm apparently arriving too late for all the excitement."

"As exciting as a dagger in the belly," Melaia grumbled.

"I sensed *you*," Jarrod told Serai, holding her close. "I saw you helping with the children, but you ducked away before I could reach you. I followed you here."

Isma appeared in the stillroom doorway with Claudia clinging to her.

Melaia knelt by Baize's body. "I'm sorry," she said.

Isma nodded, her lips pressed in a thin line.

"The children were spared," Serai told her. "Do you still want Claudia to come to Redcliff?"

"Aye, I do," said Isma.

"Gather Claudia's belongings, then," said Serai. "And say your farewells."

Melaia trudged into the hearth room past Jarrod and Serai, who were still clutching each other. She plopped down on a stool to wait. Staring wearily at the cold fireplace, she wished she had someone to hold her close.

A frosty wind swept across patches of snow that spilled onto the mountain trail. Trevin held his impatient stallion to the caravan's plodding pace as they climbed toward the pass between looming peaks. He welcomed the sight. Only a day's ride more and they would arrive at Flauren, capitol city of Eldarra. Within a week he would walk the skies with Windweaver and make his way into the Dregmoors, where he would meet his father, Arelin. Together they would snatch the harp, and then he would lose no time returning it to Melaia. Within a fortnight the job would be done.

Little else had occupied Trevin's thoughts during the journey. His only other concern was the stranger that the caravan had picked up in Dahl. Cyprian didn't seem to be aware that the new traveler was an angel. Certainly the man, who called himself Ereph, never made such a claim, but Trevin sensed him the first moment he appeared.

A crop-haired, bulb-nosed fellow, Ereph seemed content to ride at the tail of the company. But Trevin felt uneasy about him. Every time he held three fingers over his heart in the sign of the Tree, Ereph returned the sign awkwardly, as if he were unused to such a greeting. What's more, Ereph's night-blue aura seemed off-color, although it was not as murky or oily as a malevolent's. Most likely Ereph was uncommitted like Paullus of Qanreef, who was neutral, allied with neither the Angelaeon nor the malevolents.

Trevin's horse tugged forward, but he held the stallion to the pace of the wagon carrying the gold. A pass was not the safest part of any trip. Perhaps it was good for Ereph to bring up the rear.

The pass funneled the wind into a frigid blast, and Trevin pulled his cloak tighter as the caravan snaked into the limestone corridor. Daggers of ice hung from the rock, but they were thawing, and the drips sounded like a steady rain.

Trevin's stallion stepped nervously, his ears swiveling, his nostrils flaring. The other horses seemed uneasy as well. Trevin patted his mount's neck. "It's only ice-melt," he said. "Just dripping water."

The stallion snorted and shivered but kept a steady pace, and before long, Cyprian led the head of the caravan out of the pass, raising his staff in salute to the Edgelands of Eldarra.

"Look ahead," Trevin crowed to his horse as they cleared the walls of the corridor. "We've almost reached –"

With a piercing cry a bandit leaped from a boulder onto the gold wagon. Others swarmed after him, dropping down, darting out, yelling, slashing.

Half the caravan continued to crawl through the pass. The other half scrambled to turn back to their aid. Caught in the middle Trevin drew his sword, jumped onto the gold wagon, and speared the first bandit. Three more clambered up. He struck down a man on his left. Another flew at him from the right but was speared by the driver of the wagon. Then Ereph bounded on board with a fierce grin, and Trevin was certain they would soon send the bandits running. But Ereph stabbed the driver, grabbed Trevin, and threw him off.

The horses pulling the gold wagon bolted, and Trevin rolled away from the wheels, dropping his sword in the process. He tumbled halfway down an embankment before he could stop himself.

As he scrambled back uphill to retrieve his sword, he growled at himself for trusting Ereph. The renegade was probably gloating over the easy haul. No doubt the bandits would scatter now that their booty was secure, but Trevin hoped he might capture one or two stragglers. He snatched his sword, topped the embankment, and was surprised to see the fight still raging. As he bolted toward the fray, Ereph blocked him. Trevin danced back from Ereph's blade, stunned that the traitor had returned.

Ereph attacked like a madman. Trevin met each strike, dodged and parried. At last he slashed Ereph's leg in a lucky hit, followed by several strong blows in succession, the last of which sent Ereph's sword flying. But Ereph dived at Trevin, grabbed his wrist, and slammed it against a boulder, knocking the sword from his hand. As Trevin tried to wrestle free, Ereph pressed into him, full force, clutching Trevin's neck, gouging his thumbs into Trevin's throat.

Trevin fought back, struggling for breath, trying to pry off the angel's hands. Black flecks speckled his vision as he wrestled to remain conscious. He heard a horse scream. Saw a flash of white. Then Ereph slammed him backward. Trevin's head hit rock, and with a bright slice of pain, the world went black.

CHAPTER 7

Before Melaia and Serai had taken two steps inside the palace, the steward met them with a message. "The king wishes to see you, Princess."

Melaia kept walking. "Tell him I'll come as soon as I clean up."

"Immediately," said the steward. "Your new bodyguards will escort you."

Melaia stopped and turned on the steward. "Where are my usual guards?"

"Sent to the battlefield," he said, as two brawny guards appeared behind him.

"A bad omen." Melaia handed her pack to Serai. "Go on. I'll see what this is about."

Serai squeezed her hand, and Melaia smiled weakly.

The two stone-faced guards ushered her to the king's apartment, one leading her, one following. She found her father in his bedroom, seated at a desk, a blanket covering his legs. He was picking through scrolls and did not look up.

"Father?" Melaia bowed. "You sent for me?"

"Yesterday. Which means you're late. Where were you?"

Melaia felt her face grow warm. "I went to Lowridge to fetch the novice for Hanni."

He swept aside the scrolls and glared at her. "The high priestess cannot fetch her own novices? If I recall, I forbade you to go to Lowridge. Did I not?"

Melaia shifted uncomfortably. Yesterday she had felt like a grown woman, a real leader. Now she felt as if she were a young novice caught eating the offering bread.

"Did I not forbid it?" The king spoke louder than he had in months.

"You did, Sire." She looked him in the eye. "But I can't stay within these walls forever, and your world will not fall apart if I take a short journey. You see? Here I am, returned safely."

"This was no social outing in the meadow. You led troops into Lowridge."

"I didn't lead troops. They would have gone into Lowridge without me."

The king leaned forward as if he intended to stand. Instead he gripped the desk and snarled, "I may have no legs, girl, but I have ears. 'For the princess and Camrithia.' Was that not the cry?"

"It was, but the cry should have been for you." Melaia folded her arms. "You should lead your troops once in a while. It's no wonder that the comains report entire towns too discouraged to take up arms. Why should people make the effort to fight for a kingdom whose king will not fight for them?"

"Look at me!" He threw back the blanket, uncovering his thin, twisted legs. "I cannot rise to greet you. I cannot walk across my own room. Surely you don't expect me to ride at the head of troops."

"There are other ways to lead."

"Being hauled from town to town! Here is your great king, carried like a baby?"

Melaia crossed the room. Hanging on the wall opposite the king's bed was his shield, embossed with the figure of a lion. She stroked the highly polished surface. "You never have used this, have you? Yet you came from a long line of warrior kings."

"I am a king of peace."

"So you have hung up your shield forever?"

He rubbed his forehead. "I do not wish to wage war."

"Lowridge is only a day's ride from here. Do you not know what that means? If Main Catellus and his men had not been in the vicinity of Lowridge, the Dregmoorians might have overrun the town. The enemy could be swarming our gates at this moment. Wouldn't you fight if they did?"

The king stared at his tumble of scrolls. "I'm a simple, uncomplicated man in a very complex world."

Melaia knelt at his side. "You are still the king, Father. You still have a country to rule."

He stroked her hair. "I desire only your safety, Melaia. I loved your mother, but I did not protect her as I should have. You are as headstrong as she was, with the same strange notions of angels and immortals. I fear to see her restlessness in you. Going to Lowridge was not only foolhardy but dangerous."

"I was well protected by . . . a group of seasoned warriors."

"And Trevin?"

"Trevin had nothing to do with this."

"If that's true, he is wiser than you. Once you leave the palace, you never know what perils await." He took her face in his hands, and his gaze softened. "Melaia, I have instructed Lord Beker to train you to rule. You are destined to be a great queen. But be careful. Be wise. I do not wish to outlive you."

❖ ❖ ❖

Melaia sat in the moonlight in her roof garden and studied the cracked cover of her mother's book. She regretted the damage, but she was grateful it had shielded her. If the book had not cushioned Baize's blow, she might not have returned to Redcliff. She ran her finger down the diagonal crack, which ran so deep that the wood was almost broken in two. Even so, it thrummed gently, and its pulse calmed her.

Serai stepped into the garden. "I'm on my way to the temple to return a bag of Claudia's belongings that I discovered with ours, and Dwin is here requesting a word with you."

Melaia nodded. "Send him in as you leave." She looked east toward the Dregmoors, hoping Dwin brought news from Trevin.

"My lady." Dwin sauntered into the garden.

"So my new guards let you in?"

"They did, but they'll have to stay alert." His eyes held a mischievous gleam. "They never would imagine all the ways I could enter."

"Spy that you are," Melaia teased. Dwin's half-smile looked so much like Trevin's that she missed him even more. "Any word from your brother?"

"None," said Dwin. "But it's early yet. Give him time." He strolled to the parapet and rapped on it with his fist as he stared into the night. At length, he turned to her. "I don't know how to say this."

Melaia folded her hands in her lap. "Straight out is usually best."

"All right. Keep an eye on Jarrod."

Melaia raised her eyebrows. "Jarrod? Why?"

"I find it strange that he was in Lowridge," said Dwin. "Xenio told me he saw Jarrod there, not fighting but standing back as if he were lording over the battle."

"He was probably creating some strategy," said Melaia. "Besides, Jarrod always looks as if he's lording over whatever is going on. It's his nature."

"And it's my nature to be suspicious," said Dwin. "I hope you're not offended."

"I'm grateful for your caution, but there's no need to worry about Jarrod. Serai tells me everything. She would know if there were a problem."

"I hope you're right. At any rate I may soon settle the issue of the turncloak once and for all. I've received a message from Nuri saying she has some information for me. She suspects a gash runner from the Dregmoors may be involved, but there's more she dared not put in writing. I intend to visit Treolli as soon as possible to find out what more she knows."

Jarrod appeared at the doorway, and Dwin stiffened. "I was looking for Serai," said Jarrod, "but I couldn't help overhearing the talk of Treolli. You may wish to go, too, Melaia. I know a book binder there who might be able to repair the cover of Dreia's book."

Dwin sauntered to a pot of white night-blooms. "Would you allow me to take some of your flowers to Nuri?" he asked.

"Of course." Melaia lightened her tone, hoping to alleviate the edginess she felt between Dwin and Jarrod. "I like the idea of taking my book to Treolli to be repaired. I could visit Nuri at the same time."

"You'd be welcome to come with me." Dwin bowed. "I'll take my leave. Thank you for your advice."

As Dwin strode out, Jarrod sat down beside Melaia. "Dwin sought advice?"

"Wooing Nuri," Melaia said. "Speaking of wooing, Serai is at the temple."

"No doubt looking for me," said Jarrod, but he made no move to leave.

Melaia fingered the crack in the book. "The truth is, I have very little chance of going to Treolli or anywhere else."

"Because of your father?"

"He learned that I went to Lowridge. To say he's upset would be an understatement."

"Perhaps I could take the book to Treolli for you."

Melaia stroked the book. She rarely let it out of her hands. What's more she was relying on its blank pages to reveal Trevin's progress as he retrieved the third harp and brought it to Redcliff. "I don't feel right releasing the book from my care," she said.

"In that case, perhaps I can take you to Treolli."

"You could sneak me away from my new guards?"

"There are ways," said Jarrod. "Then again, you may prefer that I sneak you into the Dregmoors instead. We could take the two harps and unite them with the third, right under the nose of the immortal Firstborn. Would that not be a coup?"

Melaia stepped to the parapet and looked down at the guarded inner gates of the castle. "It will be hard enough to travel to Treolli, much less the Dregmoors, without my father's knowledge."

"Are you never going to unite the harps?"

"Why do you think I sent Trevin to get the third harp?"

"But time is growing short."

"He'll be back in time. I trust him."

Jarrod rested his forearms on his knees, and his long tail of hair dangled over his shoulder. "I hope your trust is not ill-placed – in Trevin or Dwin."

"Trevin is trustworthy. So is Dwin. Isn't he?"

Jarrod shrugged. "Dwin says he's looking for an informant – which seems the perfect cover for *being* an informant."

❖❖❖

Trevin awoke to soft voices. *Melaia?* His head ached as he willed his mind to surface, but he felt weighted, dragged down, destined to sink into waves of stupor. His throat burned, and his ears roared as he tugged himself to the light. To the air. To Melaia.

A hand touched his forehead. "Bring water!"

Trevin recognized the voice – not Melaia's but Queen Ambria's. A thick twist of water-soaked cloth touched his mouth, and he parted his lips to let the cool moisture trickle across his tongue.

"Main Trevin?" Dio's voice lilted. "Can you stir yourself? Open your eyes? Enter the land of the living, so to say?"

Trevin almost smiled. The fragrance of flowers. The rich scent of wine. He was at the palace in Flauren.

He concentrated on his eyelids, which felt heavier than bags of coins. A slit of light came into view. Someone helped him sit up. Dio, he thought. He willed his eyes to open, blinked heavily, closed them, and opened them again, this time with greater success.

Queen Ambria sat on the right side of his bed, her hands folded in her lap, a pleased smile on her face. The jester Dio stood on the left, holding a pillow so large it hid his skinny body. Only his bushy hair and bright eyes showed above it. He plumped the pillow and shoved it behind Trevin.

Trevin grimaced. "Thank you. I think."

The queen pointed Dio to a flagon on a table by the window. Then she inclined her head toward Trevin. "We were worried about you. Quite."

Trevin gave her the best smile he could, trying not to groan. He suspected that 'worry' was too mild a term for her concern. She had lost her only son the previous year and expected Arelin's son to take his place.

Dio poured a cup of wine, handed it to the queen, and eyed Trevin. "We thought you had left us, had flown your physic, so to say."

"Which would have been most untimely." Queen Ambria held the cup to Trevin's lips, and he sipped the peppery wine. "King Kedemeth and I have eagerly awaited your return," she said. "Then this attack! On our very border!"

Trevin cleared his throat. "I'm surprised to be alive. How did I get here?"

"Almaron saved you." The queen gave him another sip.

Trevin raised his brow in question. The white stallion! He had left the horse in Eldarra the previous summer after discovering that Almaron was a flying horse whose wings had been severed by the Dregmoorians. "Why was Almaron at the pass?" he asked.

"He was carrying Livia to Redcliff to spend time with her daughter, Serai," said the queen. "Some of our best warriors were traveling with her. They plan to offer their aid to King Laetham in his fight against raiders."

Trevin took the cup from Queen Ambria and rested it on his lap, determined to drink it on his own, even if his weak hands trembled.

Dio drew a stool to the bedside and sat. "Livia told us about the bandits, set the stage, painted the picture, so to say. I'm already putting it to song." He leaned forward. "The journey master told how the attack began. Livia told how it ended, with Almaron rearing up to pummel your attacker, who wisely ran. Almaron turned his wrath on another of the bandits, though. The result was a sight..." He looked at the queen.

She paled and narrowed her eyes at Dio.

"...a sight that shall not be set to song," Dio finished, apparently disappointed. "Suffice it to say that Almaron took care of the brigand quickly enough, dispatched him, trampled him, sent his spirit to the other side."

"And Cyprian?" asked Trevin.

"Minor injuries," said Ambria.

With both hands Trevin brought his cup to his mouth.

The queen sat back with a satisfied smile. "Livia returned to Flauren with Almaron and the caravan."

"Or what was left of it," said Dio.

"I should thank Livia," said Trevin. "And Almaron. The stallion willingly left Eldarra?"

"Windwings are quite a brilliant breed," said the queen. "I think he understood that he was supposed to take Livia to Redcliff and return to Flauren with you." She leaned forward, her eyes sparkling. "I'm sure Almaron wants to introduce you to his Windwing foal."

"A foal?" Trevin handed Dio his cup and tried to rise, then sank beneath the pounding in his head.

"And there's the teensiest matter of your betrothal to princess Melaia of Camrithia," said the queen.

Trevin opened his mouth to ask what she had heard, but she shushed him.

"Livia told us what happened in Qanreef with the death of Princess Melaia's betrothed," she said. "We asked her if she thought we might approach King Laetham with a proposal to unite our two kingdoms, betrothing his daughter to our newly appointed heir. As you might imagine, the idea delighted Livia. So we shall propose a betrothal as soon as you are officially appointed. If you agree."

"I agree. No reservations." Trevin smiled. Success – at least for the first item on his list. He pressed his hand to the harp pendant that hung over his heart but felt only his heartbeat. He straightened, wincing. "Where's my pendant?"

Queen Ambria shot a questioning look at Dio, who shrugged and shook his head. "Check Trevin's journey bag," she said, "and the clothes he wore."

Dio rummaged through a trunk.

"It's a small wooden harp," said Trevin. "On a black cord."

Dio shook his head. "No pendant."

Trevin slumped back and closed his eyes. "It's probably on the trail near the pass, trampled to pieces."

The king's aide appeared, announcing the king. Dio went to one knee, and Queen Ambria rose. Trevin groaned as he tried to make some sign of obeisance at the entrance of King Kedemeth, a stalwart man, ruddy-faced with a red-brown beard.

"How is my heir?" asked the king.

"Trying to bow, Sire," croaked Trevin, envious of the king's rich voice.

"Lying prostrate before me suffices, even if it's on your back in bed," said the king. "Why did you not send word you were coming? We would have sent guards to accompany you."

"I had no time," said Trevin. "I was sent to the Dregmoors and must make quick work of it."

"To the Dregmoors?" The king's eyebrows rose. "You chose a roundabout route."

"I plan to ask Windweaver to take me, but I wish to discuss my adoption first."

"The papers are prepared," said the king. "We can arrange the ceremony for tomorrow if you like."

"He is recovering," said Queen Ambria. "It's much too soon for him to rise."

Trevin rubbed his forehead. "How long have I been here?"

"Two nights," said the king.

"Long enough." Trevin gritted his teeth, forced his legs over the side of the bed, and sat up.

Queen Ambria's eyes widened in alarm. "You *must* stay abed until you're stronger."

"Food will help," said Trevin, feeling lightheaded.

"Perhaps you could arrange a meal in the garden, Ambria," said the king. "Trevin might find fresh air as strengthening as food."

"Men! Always pushing the boundaries." Queen Ambria fluttered to the door and then turned and wagged her finger at Dio. "Since *our* son is determined to rise, *you* help him walk."

King Kedemeth grinned and nodded his approval at Trevin. "I'll meet you in the garden. After you've taken some food, you'll no doubt want to question the two bandits we captured." He strode out, followed by his aide.

Dio helped Trevin stand. "I'll fetch your clothes. Wouldn't do to go to the garden in your bedshirt."

Trevin scratched his chin. "I could do with a shave, too. At least a trim."

He tugged off his nightshirt and slumped back to the bed. Without the harp pendant he felt bare, body and soul. He rotated his sword arm and assessed his bruises, scratches, and cuts. They were nothing compared to the ache that came from missing Melaia.

The prison cell smelled like death to Trevin. In fact one of the bandits had already died, and the other, a listless, pock-faced man, lay as still as a corpse. No doubt his spirit would soon follow his comrade's into the Under-Realm.

The guard held a torch closer to the bandit, who roused. "We questioned both men, sir," said the guard. "They're Dregmoorian. Fought alongside the one named Ereph."

Trevin forced his weak legs to hold him upright. Food had strengthened him, but prison cells were not exactly uplifting. "He and his friend would have done better to follow the gold," Trevin said.

The guard nudged the man with the toe of his boot. "They expected payment in gold, but said you were their target."

"That I guessed," said Trevin. "The question is why." He tipped his sword to the dirt floor and angled it so the eye of the sword would reveal the man's true character. It showed only what Trevin already suspected. The man was a criminal through and through, and probably had been for most of his life.

The bandit's eyes flickered open and fixed on the sword. "Go ahead," he whispered. "Slay me."

"Not yet." Trevin knelt beside him, remembering the hours of agony he had spent in one of these cells, not dying, but wishing for death. "You can go to your grave an honest man if you want," he said. "Answer me true. Who hired you? And don't say Ereph. I want to know who ordered the attack."

The bandit said nothing as he strained to breathe.

"I've been told I was the target. Did you mean to rob me? Abduct me?"

The corners of the bandit's mouth twitched up.

"Does someone want me dead?" asked Trevin.

"Aye."

"Who?"

The pocked face smiled.

Trevin grabbed the bandit's collar. "Who, man?"

But the bandit had died. Grinning.

CHAPTER 8

In King Kedemeth's private sitting room, servants cleared the remains of the evening meal, while Trevin and the king arranged gray and white pebbles on a board at a gaming table. Hanging brass lamps threw patterned shadows across the room toward the hearthfire, where Queen Ambria and Livia sat, inspecting a collection of exquisitely painted perfume jars.

After a day of eating at the king's table and walking the palace grounds, Trevin felt stronger. "I've been teaching Melaia to play Attacker Defender," he announced.

"How novel." Queen Ambria opened a turquoise jar and sniffed.

Livia adjusted her cloak over her wings. "Melaia is an uncommon princess."

"So it seems." Queen Ambria handed the jar to Livia. "The wedding will be here, of course."

The fragrance of lavender drifted through the room, and Trevin's skin tingled. Lavender. Melaia's scent. He tried to keep his mind on the game board. "Melaia has a commitment to complete before she will consider a wedding," he said.

"I'm glad to hear you say so." Livia stoppered the jar. "I plan to nudge her into action when I visit Redcliff."

Queen Ambria waved another jar beneath her nose. A rosy smell joined the lavender. "The stars are definitely aligning," she said.

Trevin slipped a white pebble forward. King Kedemeth rubbed his nose as he studied the board and moved a gray pebble.

"I, too, have a commitment." Trevin moved a white pebble sideways. "I must find Windweaver as soon as possible and ask him to take me into the Dregmoors."

"To Arelin?" Queen Ambria opened a third jar. "He'll attend your wedding, won't he?"

Trevin looked up. The queen's cheeks seemed unusually red. Perhaps because she sat near the fire. Or because she had been breathing perfume. Or maybe she had blushed at the thought of seeing Arelin, whom she adored. Possibly all three.

"I've not thought much about the actual wedding," said Trevin.

King Kedemeth grinned. "Of course not."

"But," said the queen, "if you're marrying a princess, you'll not have one without the other."

King Kedemeth moved a gray pebble from the line of attack. "Let the young people complete their previous commitments first, Ambria. I'm sure they will then be happy to speak about a wedding - as well as discuss the responsibilities of the crown." Losing his smile, he locked eyes with Trevin. "I expect you to give serious consideration to your new position."

"I intend to," said Trevin.

"As soon as you complete your commitments," said the king. "That strikes me as the best strategy."

Trevin gave him a grateful nod. "In that case, after my appointing tomorrow, I must journey to Tabaitta Canyon to find Windweaver."

"So soon?" The queen handed another jar to Livia. The fragrance of sandalwood overpowered the other scents.

Trevin rubbed his watery eyes, pretending the perfumes irritated him. In truth, the scent of sandalwood pricked a wound only recently healed. Ollena had smelled of sandalwood. Ollena, the best swordmaster and bodyguard he'd ever had. Ollena, who died defending Melaia's father in Qanreef.

King Kedemeth waved a hand in front of his nose. "Are you ladies attempting to suffocate us with scent?"

Ambria sighed. "I suppose you must choose now, Livia. Which do you want for your daughter?"

Trevin jumped his white pebble over a gray and scooped the gray off the board. The king groaned.

Livia selected a jar and stood. "I'll leave you to your perfume and game. I've a day of travel tomorrow. Perhaps I'll make it through the pass this time."

"But you'll stay for the adoption ceremony?" Queen Ambria closed the jars.

"I'll leave immediately after." Livia bowed. "King Kedemeth. Queen Ambria." She turned to Trevin. "If I may be the first . . ." She bowed to him. "Prince Trevin."

Trevin felt his face grow warm at the title, which seemed presumptuous, but his father had chosen this path for him, and it would allow him to marry a certain princess.

Livia smiled. "Do you want me to carry a message to Melaia for you?"

Trevin hesitated. He would love to send a message to Melaia, but not from Eldarra. "I must ask you not to tell Melaia you saw me."

Livia's eyebrows arched, Queen Ambria bit her lip, and King Kedemeth eyed him with interest.

"Strategy." Trevin looked at the king, hoping for support. He explained how his plan to reach the Dregmoors differed from Melaia's expectations. "At any rate," said Trevin, "I think my strategy is a good one."

"You will know *that* only if it works," the king said and jumped Trevin's pebble.

Trevin hefted his journey pack over one shoulder as he left the rosy granite palace and crossed the courtyard, forcing his tired legs to match the long, lanky stride of King Kedemeth's brother, Haden. The adoption ceremony had required Trevin to stand longer than was comfortable, but he was determined not to look like a weakling. Besides he wanted to work strength into his legs in preparation for walking the skies with Windweaver. At the same time he was grateful that he could ride to the canyon on his black stallion, who had been found wandering near the wreck of the caravan.

As they neared the long, low stable, Haden pointed to the white stallion grazing in a fenced field that extended to the north wall of the city. "There's the one who saved your life."

Almaron trotted their direction.

"I've a mind to ride him to the canyon," said Trevin. "He's the most sure-footed of any horse I've ever ridden."

"Seems he heard you," said Haden. "I do believe he's smiling."

Trevin followed Haden into the field, and Almaron slowed to a walk. From his waist pouch Trevin plucked half an apple he had filched from the celebration table. "This isn't much," he said, "but you deserve a reward for saving me."

Almaron nipped the apple from Trevin's hand. "How about showing me that foal?" said Trevin.

With a proud grin Haden headed for the stable, and Trevin followed with Almaron.

"The little one is a true Windwing, and the mare has stayed with him," said Haden. "She keeps her distance from most folk, but she hasn't flown off yet."

"Will she take the foal with her when she does?"

"That remains to be seen."

"Does the mare let *you* come near?"

"Me and Almaron and the foal. When she sees how her mate sticks by you, she's likely to let you approach her too."

The sweet, pungent scent of hay and horse hung warm in the air of the stables. "Eldarra still has plenty of fodder?" Trevin asked.

"We're not generous with it, but we've not run out. Fields to the south yielded poorly last harvest, so we haul in feed from the north, but it doesn't take a bright eye to see that the blight's creeping that direction too." Haden pointed. "Last stall."

Quietly Trevin drew near. The foal, white like Almaron, stood alert in the center of the stall, his ears forward, his wings loosely folded against his sides.

Almaron whinnied. A whicker answered him from beyond a door that stood open to an outdoor pen. The foal bobbed his head and stepped lightly with his front hoofs. Then the mare appeared at the open door. She was more beautiful than Trevin had remembered. Her wings and mane gleamed white next to her gold body.

"The Golden," Trevin whispered.

"Aye, the Golden. Queen of Windwings," said Haden. He unlatched the gate to the stall and Almaron pranced in. The foal followed him out the back door with Haden and Trevin close behind. They leaned against the stable wall and watched the stallion and foal trot around the mare, a regal family of Windwings.

Almaron danced toward Trevin with the mare and foal following. Trevin thought the stallion was parading the Windwings to show them off, but then the mare paused and extended her left wing toward Trevin.

"What is she doing?" he asked.

Haden rubbed his ear as he studied the mare. "I've not seen her do that before."

The Golden folded her wing and trotted around the enclosure with the foal behind her. When she circled back to Trevin, she extended her left wing again and simply stood there.

"Great barn owls!" said Haden. "It looks like an invitation to ride."

A surge of energy pulsed through Trevin. Riding Almaron overland was ecstasy, but to soar through the air on a Windwing! He stroked the silky front edge of the Golden's wing, prepared for her to pull away.

Her round, dark eyes watched him closely, but she did not draw back.

The Windwings were a race owned by no one, and if their queen wanted him to mount, Trevin felt he should – but only with Almaron's permission. He looked up at the stallion.

Alert, Almaron dipped his head and then straightened, his neck high and proud.

Trevin approached the Golden and ran a hand along the leading edge of the wing to test its strength and find a place to mount. Though the feathers were soft, the bone and flesh beneath felt firm and flexible.

"I'll be 'swoggled," said Haden. "She's going to let you ride her."

Trevin stroked the Golden's neck, her cheek, her forehead. Then he extended his hand, and she nuzzled it with her soft nose. "You are a beauty," he said quietly. "Queen of Windwings. Almaron's mate. If you want me to ride, it will be my honor."

Haden studied the back edge of her wing. "Might this be the place to mount?"

Trevin walked around the wing, laughing. If only his brother could see him. Dwin was usually the one to forge the new path, to risk life and limb in pursuit of a thrill.

"I would step here." Haden stroked a thick webbing of skin that connected the wing to the horse's body. "Grab the mane and swing up. I wager the ride is smoother on air than on land, but lean close to her until you're accustomed to the feel."

Trevin tossed his pack aside, grabbed a fistful of the mare's long white mane, and set his left foot on the wing webbing. "I'm afraid I'm weak in the legs," he said.

"Here's a boost then." Haden supported Trevin until he tugged himself up and settled on the Golden's broad back.

Trevin adjusted his scabbard so that it wouldn't inhibit the Golden's wings. "With no reins, how shall I guide her?"

"I assume you use your legs and hips as with a regular horse," said Haden. "Then again you might be better off yielding to her sense of direction. She knows the paths of the wind better than you or I."

As Haden stepped away, the mare drew in her wing. She paced around the enclosure as if she was getting a feel for the weight on her back. Trevin leaned close to her, inhaling her warm, oily aroma. Then she began to trot, and he relaxed into her smooth gait. When she headed for a stone fence to the east of the field, he gently pressed her right side so she would turn. Instead she increased her speed, jumped the fence easily, and lengthened her stride into a full gallop, her muscles rippling beneath him.

Trevin clenched the Golden's mane and told himself to relax, lean in, be one with her. Never had he gone so fast before. She was so fast ... so fast ... so fast she was flying.

Over Flauren's walls the Golden soared, and the ground rapidly receded, along with Trevin's stomach. He swallowed hard and concentrated on breathing normally instead of gasping. The cold air whipped his cloak, but the mare's body beneath him pulsed warm. Her wide wings pumped with powerful strokes and then stretched to glide the wind and skim past wisps of cloud.

Trevin eased into the Windwing's rhythmic movements as she circled the palace, broadening her range as she flew. To the south, the peaks of the Eldarran Edgelands stretched like ridges in a plowed field, and he saw Livia's group heading into the mountains. For a moment he considered taking the Golden to the pass to search for his pendant, but the day was more than half over, he had a journey to take, and Haden, Almaron, and the foal were waiting.

When the Golden circled north, he saw Ledge Rock and the tree where he had discovered the second harp. Birds had shot out of the tree that day like a spray of arrows flying into the sky. He never had dreamed *he* would fly.

As they curved west he spied the glint of sunlight on the sea and realized that the Golden was ascending, gaining distance from the peaks of the Edgelands below. Then she angled north and east. A jagged mountain range came into view, its spine broken by the gap of Windsweep, which overlooked Tabaitta Canyon, where he had met Windweaver.

Instinctively Trevin urged the Golden on. At this rate she would reach Windsweep within the hour. He could hardly believe his good fortune. She could take him straight to Windweaver. As they tracked the backbone of the mountain, he sat taller and watched for the canyon to come into view. When it did, he pressed the Golden to cross the mountains and descend. "You can leave me with Windweaver," he told her.

The Golden simply pumped her wings, gained height, and continued to fly due east.

Trevin tried to turn her north toward the canyon, but she held to her course. "If you're not taking me to the canyon, it's time to head back to Flauren," he said, trying to circle her around. But he could not coax her to change her path.

A bitter wind whipped at them. Trevin leaned into the warmth of the Golden's body and watched the eastern mountains grow closer, their peaks catching the light of the setting sun.

"Montressi," Trevin whispered. For some reason the Golden was showing him the mountains along the eastern edge of Eldarra, where his father had lived before entering the Dregmoors to rescue Windwings.

The mare whipped her wings and ascended into a frosty fog that hid the mountain peaks, and still she climbed.

The wind grew wilder, the clouds thicker. Trevin squinted against the rush of ice crystals and inhaled the knife-cold air in short gasps. His chest stung with every breath. Just when he thought he would freeze to death, they rose from the clouds and soared among the highest peaks of the Montressi range.

The Golden angled right and rounded one peak. She angled left to skirt another. Then she folded her wings and plummeted toward the crags.

Trevin's stomach lurched. Freezing to death was not on the day's schedule. Falling to his death was.

The Golden veered right, avoiding a lance-sharp spike of stone. She swerved left, barely missing an overhanging boulder. Then she dived straight toward a massive outcropping of jagged, deadly rock.

Chapter 9

As the Golden plunged between mountain peaks, Trevin's thoughts whipped to Melaia, to his father, to his plans waylaid along with the caravan. How many years would pass before someone discovered his skeleton smashed into the rock face of some mountain in Montressi?

A dark gray ledge rose swiftly to meet them. Moments before impact, the Golden arched, beat her wings, and swooped upward. She landed on the ledge at a gallop and slowed as she headed into a pass. By the time they emerged from the dark stone corridor, she was at a walk.

Trevin relaxed his death-grip on her mane and looked around. They were in a high mountain meadow surrounded by cliffs. On one side a waterfall cascaded into a glimmering pool that in turn poured water into a rushing stream. The stream spilled into a ravine that disappeared in a gap in the south cliff.

The Golden walked to the pool. As she drank greedily, Trevin dismounted, wincing. The past few days had been less than kind to his body, and he felt bruised everywhere. He cupped his hands, scooped up a palmful of the icy water, and drank.

A voice splashed over him like rain. "Esteemed seeker."

Trevin shrank back as a pale blue spirit with short white hair rose, dripping, from the pool, her garment loosely draping her body in shimmering blue. He had seen her before, although only from a distance, as she strode the waves of the Southern Sea. "Seaspinner?" he asked.

She spread her bare, wet arms wide. "I see I don't need to introduce myself."

He bowed. "I owe you a great deal of thanks for helping me escape the Dregmoors last summer."

Seaspinner waved away the comment, flinging drops of water. "I simply spun the fog and soothed the sea. I'm satisfied with how the situation was settled." She waded to the Golden and said, "Bless you, Cherrim, for transporting my guest." The Windwing nuzzled her hand.

Trevin pulled his cloak tight. "Her name is Cherrim?" He wondered if she might have cooperated with him if he had called her by name.

"She graciously sailed you here for a momentous task," said Seaspinner.

"I don't wish to offend," said Trevin, "but I already have a pressing task. I'm on my way to the Dregmoors. Melaia – Dreia's daughter – expects me to bring her the third harp."

"In that case I shall send a message to Melaia. Shall I suggest that she expect you later rather than sooner?"

"No!" The sharpness of his answer surprised him. He cleared his throat. "She thinks I'm already in the Dregmoors. She doesn't know I went north."

Seaspinner's eyes narrowed. "You deceived her? Is that a habit we should address?"

"I didn't intend . . . I'm not . . ." All of his reasons sounded like withered excuses, but they led to a single conclusion. "I can't take on another task. I haven't time."

She shrugged. "Time with the Archae is fluid. In the spirit stream, we journey great distances in space and time and return in what seems only moments to you. Or hours or days, subject to where we enter and leave the flow." She slipped beneath the water.

Trevin watched her body undulate across the pool and growled, "Time is not fluid for me."

Seaspinner shot out the water, her arms held triumphantly high, as if she wanted Trevin to applaud.

He didn't. "I had hoped Windweaver would take me into the Dregmoors."

"No need. That's exactly where I'm to take you." She laughed with delight.

Trevin's shoulders relaxed, and he half smiled. Progress at last. "Shall we ride Cherrim?"

Seaspinner gaped at him as if he had lost his wits. "I? Ride a Windwing? Impossible. I'm guardian of waters, not skies. We shall follow streams all the way."

"Won't that take longer?" Trevin paced around the edge of the pool. "Cherrim or Windweaver could take me into the Dregmoors faster."

"Perhaps, but they were not selected to enlighten you. I was."

Trevin tried to keep a tone of courtesy in his voice, but he was growing frustrated. "Are you speaking of the task you referred to?"

Seaspinner swished across the water. "As soon as you returned to Eldarra and confirmed your choice, Windweaver and Flametender asked me to serve as your advisor."

"Does this have to do with my adoption?"

"Certainly that's part of it. You chose to accept your appointment as crown prince of Eldarra, but other choices remain. I shall facilitate."

"As long as it includes guiding me into the Dregmoors."

"So it does."

"When do we start?"

Behind him a warm, throaty voice answered, "After you have rested."

Trevin turned to see a dark-skinned woman with wild, fiery hair. Flametender. His hands grew hot at the memory of her searing touch in the naming ceremony. He bowed. "It's good to see you again."

Flametender glowed like an ember ready to flame. "I'm flattered you feel that way." She bent to the pool and dabbled her hands in the water. "I hear you've been convalescing, and your first flight on Cherrim no doubt fatigued you." The water steamed. "Perhaps a short respite in warm waters would help?"

"A *short* rest." Trevin took off his cloak, squatted at the edge of the pool, and splashed the heated water on his face.

"Don't be shy." Seaspinner waded into the pool. "Healing waters serve best when you immerse yourself."

Trevin eyed Seaspinner as he stripped to his leggings.

"My clothing is spun of water," said Seaspinner. "I'm always superbly wet."

"Horrifying." Flametender stirred the water, her gown glowing like molten metal.

Trevin tossed his clothing toward Cherrim, who grazed nearby. Then he waded in, hissing as he eased into the sizzling pool.

Flametender withdrew her hands, and Trevin closed his eyes as the tension in his aching muscles eased.

"Open your eyes!" Flametender's voice crackled.

Trevin blinked and sat straighter. On his first journey with Melaia, when they had camped at the hot springs at Caldarius, she warned him against falling asleep in the warm water.

"I've heated the entire stream you'll follow into the Dregmoors," said Flametender. "Don't let its warmth seduce you into complacency."

"If he does, I shall call Windweaver to gift us with an icy blast, yes?" said Seaspinner as she dribbled steaming water through her cupped hands. "Splendid," she said. "My thanks, sister."

"A service I would not offer to just anyone." Flametender reached toward the sky, swirled upward in flame, and vanished.

Trevin stared at the spot where she disappeared. "She's your sister?"

"Yes. Flashy, isn't she?"

"Is Windweaver your brother?"

Seaspinner shrugged. "In a way."

"What about Dreia, Melaia's mother?"

"A friend of ours. Inscrutible. Prone to dream. We've suffered for her indiscretion and will until her debt is paid."

"I thought it was Benasin's debt."

"His indeed, for he failed to meet her conditions. Yet he never would have been in such straits if Dreia had not given him the fruit of the Tree in the first place."

Trevin raised himself halfway out of the water, and the cold air jolted him to attention. "You know, then, why I must take the third harp from the Dregmoors. Melaia can pay her mother's debt by restoring the Tree. Which will happen only after Melaia gets that harp. Which will happen only if I go to the Dregmoors. Which is why I must move quickly. Melaia and I –"

"– have choices to make."

"My choice is to leave for the Dregmoors. Now."

"So we shall." Seaspinner slipped from the water and strode to Cherrim. She bent her forehead to Cherrim's, one hand on each side of the Windwing's cheeks, and closed her eyes.

Trevin eased out of the pool, tugged on his tunic, buckled his sword belt, and threw on his cloak to block the breeze that bit at his wet leggings.

As Seaspinner backed away from Cherrim, the Golden turned and headed back the way she had come. Trevin watched until the Windwing disappeared into the pass. "King Kedemeth will worry when Cherrim returns without me," he said. "Queen Ambria will be heartsick. Haden, too. They'll think I fell to my death."

"Queen Ambria is sensitive to the spirit realm," said Seaspinner. "Flametender or Windweaver will tell her where you are. Now come."

Trevin jerked on his boots and caught up to Seaspinner as she followed the flow of water into the ravine. She danced in the stream, kicking up sprays of water, while he trailed her, picking his way through the scree along the banks. Gnarled trees on the bluffs formed a canopy overhead, which filtered the waning light. For some time the two trekked in silence, accompanied only by the sound of rippling water, trilling birds, and scurrying rodents.

Trevin leaped a rivulet and grinned at the solid feel of his muscles. His soak in Flametender's hot water had strengthened him, as had the realization that he was finally headed into the Dregmoors.

Unfortunately they were entering from the north, far from the sea caves where the harp was held, but he felt as if he could trek all the way to the sea without stopping.

Through the narrowing ravine they followed the stream until it ended in a shallow pool at the foot of a cliff of dark gray rock. The water in the pool eddied around boulders and then spilled over a ledge into a low cave.

Seaspinner plopped into the pool and sat cross-legged, letting her skirts float around her like the water plants Trevin had seen in a royal pond in Qanreef. "We'll rest here for the night," she said. "At sunrise we'll enter the Dregmoors."

"But I can see in the dark." Trevin pointed to the cave entrance. "I can see where the stream leads, and I feel strong enough to walk for days."

"So save your strength for sunrise." Seaspinner scooped a handful of soggy leaves from the pool, broke off a stem for herself and offered the rest to Trevin. "Water greens."

Trevin wrinkled his nose, wishing for King Kedemeth's venison and fresh bread and one of Queen Ambria's honey cakes. He didn't even have his journey bag, which contained flatbread and a packet of dried fruits. As he removed his cloak and boots, his stomach growled. He waded through the pleasantly warm water to a rock that curved out of the stream like the back of a giant turtle.

Seaspinner plunked the mess of leaves into his hand. "Shall we discuss your destiny?"

Trevin munched on the leaves, which were pepper sweet and surprisingly tasty. "I can tell you that my destiny is entwined with Melaia's," he said.

"Truly?"

"Truly." He popped another sprig in his mouth. "What is my destiny without her?"

"Precisely the question." Seaspinner skimmed the water with her hands and gathered it into a ball, which she sculpted as if it were clay.

Trevin watched, fascinated as she raised the water into a column and shaped it into a sword, its tip aimed at the sky. "Is that . . . ?"

She nodded. It was an exact replica, in water, of his sword, the one he had inherited from Arelin. What's more, her watery sword was as highly polished as his father's. In its blade he saw his reflection, the same one he had first seen in the eye of the sword at Flauren – broad shoulders, long hair gathered at the neck in the fashion of a priest, and hands that glowed like embers, the right one raised in the sign of the Tree.

"You remember, yes?" asked Seaspinner.

"It shows my nature as Arelin's son," said Trevin, wishing he felt as confident and wise as the face reflected in the blade.

"And the hands?" asked Seaspinner.

Trevin raised three fingers in the sign of the Tree. "Committed to the Angelaeon."

"And?"

"Glowing with the gift given by Flametender when she spoke a naming over me."

"Sciai eolin, ciarrai pyrin, nai librein," quoted Seaspinner. "Seed of wind, heir of fire, born to free." She removed her hand from the sword, and it collapsed with a splash. "Did you ever wonder why Flametender spoke a naming over you?"

"I once asked Livia," said Trevin, "and she told me that Windweaver and Flametender graced me with their heritage. They spoke my destiny: born to free – which I fulfilled when I freed the comains."

"So it's no longer your destiny? That would be spectacularly short-sighted. Why do you suppose Windweaver and Flametender graced you with their heritage?"

"To honor my father, Arelin, for his bravery and faithfulness. He risked his life saving the Windwings."

"To honor Arelin, certainly." Seaspinner laughed and splashed Trevin. "They graced you with their heritage, because it's rightfully yours. Arelin is their son."

Trevin blinked through the drips. "Arelin is the son of two Archae?"

"They were displeased with Arelin's marriage to Stalia, but *you*, they cherished. You can imagine their distress when, in your infancy, you went missing."

"I'm their grandson?" Trevin pictured Flametender, his grandmother, warming the pool for him. Windweaver, his father's father, had walked the skies with him and had spoken to him on the wind.

"So you're my great-aunt." He grinned at Seaspinner. "Why didn't Windweaver tell me? Or Flametender? Why didn't they mention my true heritage?"

"Believe me, we discussed it." Seaspinner lay back in the shallows, halfway under water, and stared into the sky. "After you went missing, all of us searched for you. Flametender was the first to find you. She saw you from the campfire with Melaia at Caldarius, but you served the Firstborn, who could have easily corrupted you and used your knowledge of your heritage against you. We wanted to be certain that you were strong enough to choose your own path."

Trevin waded to the bank and leaned back against a tree trunk, his hands behind his head. A single star glowed in the slit of sky between the upper walls of the ravine. The scattered pieces of his life seemed to be fusing into a single bright point like that star.

"Flametender and Windweaver did not want their presence to sway or pressure you," said Seaspinner, "so they requested that I ask."

"Ask what?"

"Whether you will accept your destiny. Not your role as crown prince, but the destiny of your heritage among the Angelaeon."

Trevin watched her hair ripple in the current like waterweeds. "Will my destiny include Melaia?"

"I can't see the future. We angels have no way of knowing what humans will choose. Your choices are up to you."

Trevin stared at the star. He knew enough about the future to know that if he didn't take the third harp to Melaia soon, the entire world would suffer. Even the angels.

Seaspinner rose to one elbow. "Before we journey farther, I must ask: Do you choose your destiny?"

"Can I support Melaia?"

Seaspinner sighed. "That, I think, will be her choice. I suggest that you also ask whether she can support you."

The stream burbled and branches swayed. In the rippling water, the light from the single star reflected in a hundred sparks.

"Yes," Trevin whispered. He cleared his throat and spoke it aloud. "Yes. I accept my destiny."

"Yes!" Seaspinner rose, scooped water into her cupped hands, and poured it over Trevin's head. "It's a splendid word, is it not? Yes!"

Trevin sputtered and ran his hand through his dripping hair. The choice felt right, but would it take him closer to Melaia or carry him further away?

CHAPTER 10

Melaia kept her hood on as she peeked around the curtains of her carriage, which was old and less than royal, but sturdy enough to make the trip to Treolli and back. Xenio and Sorabus followed on horseback, and Dwin trotted ahead. She smiled. Trevin used to do that too, when they traveled. He would gallop ahead and trot back, over and over again the entire way, watching for danger.

Of course a good deal of Dwin's restlessness was due to the fact that he would soon see Nuri. The bouquet he had chosen for her filled the carriage with the sweet fragrance of purple true-hearts and cream white lilies. Because of the blight, flowers were rare, but these came from Melaia's garden, where they bloomed as if they sensed her link to her mother, guardian of trees and nature.

Dwin trotted to Melaia's window. "Draks are circling the town," he said, "but there's no sign of Dregmoorians."

Melaia nodded and leaned back, her hand over the book in her pouch. She had concocted her escape plan when a spoiled supper dish caused the entire court, including the king, to fall ill. She still felt weak and uninterested in food, and her body regretted not staying in bed under her handmaid's care, as Serai was pretending. What's more Melaia hated to be absent when her father was ill, for illness deepened his melancholy. Even so, she could not pass up this opportunity. Who knew when she would have another chance to personally carry her damaged book to the bookbinder?

The carriage rattled past the caravansary and through the gates of Treolli along with other carts and wagons. Townsfolk bustling about their daily tasks hardly looked at the carriage. A wistful reverie settled over Melaia. She'd once had the freedom to come and go as she pleased. She used to walk the streets of Navia alone. By herself she had searched for wild herbs in the fields outside its walls. At the time she hadn't appreciated such liberty. Now she measured the extent of her freedom by stolen hours that required her to travel cloaked and hidden from dangers darker than she cared to contemplate.

The carriage slowed to a stop, and Melaia heard Jarrod's voice as he gave instructions to the driver.

Dwin peered in the window, hardly able to contain a grin. "I'm off to the temple."

Melaia handed him the bouquet. "Tell Nuri I'll join you both there as soon as I'm done at the bookbinder's."

Dwin trotted off, and Melaia opened her door. Jarrod, sullen and distracted, helped her from the carriage.

"Your discussions went poorly?" she asked, wondering whom he had met and what they had talked about.

Jarrod stared down the street after Dwin, but his thoughts seemed much more distant.

"Did you discuss strategy?" asked Melaia.

Jarrod blinked at her, his mind obviously far away. Then he offered her his arm. "Strategy. Yes. I'm hopeful but uncertain."

They walked to a whitewashed shop with an ornately carved wooden door that stood open. The pungent smell of wood shavings drew Melaia in. The entry hall was empty, and with a shudder, she thought of Baize's house. However this hall was painted the color of cream, and the far door stood open to a sunny courtyard, where a stout man wearing a leather apron tapped delicately on a section of lattice that leaned against a table.

When the man saw them, he waved them into the yard, which was surrounded by a walkway jammed with a jumble of table legs, chairs, and chests. He bowed, holding three fingers to his heart.

Jarrod and Melaia did the same, and she breathed easier. She did not sense the man as an angel, but at least he was a friend of angels.

"Your Grace," he said. "Jarrod told me you were coming. A pleasure. A pleasure indeed. My name is Levret. How may I help?"

"I've brought an old book with a wooden cover recently damaged." Melaia slipped it from her pouch. "Jarrod said you might be able to repair it."

Levret's bushy brown eyebrows rose as he took the book. "Cracked, was it? There's a story in that, to be sure."

Melaia smiled courteously but chose not to relate the tale of her near-death for fear that her father might hear about it. What would he say if he heard her life had barely been saved, and by a book?

Levret carried the book to a bench and carefully untied the ribbon she had bound around it. The front cover bent along the crack as if it were hinged. He grunted, turned the book over. Grunted again. Studied it from one angle and then another. At last he set the book down and lovingly laid both hands on top. "It's heartwood."

Melaia frowned. "I thought it was kyparis wood."

Levret laughed. "I mean it's the heartwood of the tree. Comes from the very center."

"Does that make it difficult to repair?" asked Melaia.

"Not necessarily." Levret patted the book. "Any wood paste will fill this crack, but if you want a kyparis paste, I know of only a single kyparis that remains standing."

"Wodehall," said Melaia.

Levret nodded. "I'll have to send to the Durenwoods to request it. Or I can use zilwood. It's a near match."

"How long will it take?" asked Melaia. "I want the book back as soon as possible."

"If zilwood is your choice, I can stir the paste this afternoon and set it in this evening. It will have to dry, but overnight should do. I'll rub it smooth in the morning and have it ready for you before the sun's full up."

"Rub it smooth?" asked Melaia.

"I'll not rub off any of the design, to be sure," said Levret. "No, I'm careful as a gem-setter."

"I don't know," said Melaia. "I hate to leave it."

"I can vouch for Levret," said Jarrod. "He's a good man. He won't let anything happen to the book."

"Not at all," said Levret. "Not at all."

"In fact," said Jarrod, "I had already arranged to spend the night with Levret as a guard for the book. No offense to your honesty, master bookbinder."

"None taken, to be sure," said Levret.

"I'll bring the book to the temple tomorrow as soon as it's ready," said Jarrod.

"I suppose it must be done," said Melaia, already missing the feel of the book in her waist pouch.

"It's what you came for," said Jarrod.

"And to visit Nuri," Melaia said.

"Of course." Jarrod bowed like a nobleman and swept his arm toward the door. "Shall we?"

Melaia would have walked to the temple, but the carriage waited nearby, and Jarrod insisted on riding. As they wove through the crowded streets, Melaia peeked around the curtain of the carriage window and watched the people. *Her* people. She felt a responsibility that she never had known as a priestess in Navia. By restoring the Tree and its stairway, she could alleviate the blight and assure that their future was better than their past. She wanted to do it, and she would.

As the dome of the temple came into view, Melaia fully opened her curtain to see Nuri's home. A crowd of townspeople elbowed through the arched entrance. "I'm impressed so many gathered this early for evening prayers," she said. The carriage stopped, and she scooted to the door to climb out.

Jarrod pulled her back. "You give these folk too much credit. Something's astir. Stay here until I know what's happening." He jumped out and pushed through the throng, barking orders for people to stand aside.

As the crowd parted, Dwin emerged, carrying a limp figure wrapped in his cloak. He loped to the carriage, his face twisted with anger. Jarrod trailed him, asking what happened, but Dwin seemed not to hear.

Melaia went numb. "Nuri?"

Dwin eased the young priestess into Melaia's lap. Nuri's head lolled back, and dun colored gash trickled from her mouth.

"Ancient, have mercy!" whispered Melaia. She swiped the muck from Nuri's mouth, turned her face down, and pounded on her back.

Dwin climbed in and hovered over Nuri. "Is she alive?"

"She's breathing, but barely." Melaia could see Nuri's spirit wrestling to stay attached. She kept pounding. "Fetch the healer." Nuri coughed out gash and fought for breath.

"Nuri was the healer," said Dwin.

Jarrod cursed as he leaned into the carriage, wiping sweat from his forehead.

"Take us to Redcliff," Melaia ordered. "Now."

Jarrod climbed into the driver's seat, and they sped off faster than the old carriage had a right to go.

"Breathe, Nuri," said Melaia. "Breathe."

A ragged breath croaked its way in.

Melaia turned to Dwin. "Did anyone see who did this?"

"No one." Dwin glared. "She was at prayers. In private."

"She's not one for long prayers."

"I know, but I had given her plenty to pray about."

"Like what?"

"I had asked her . . ." Dwin buried his head in his hands. "I had asked her to marry me."

"Oh, Dwin." Melaia placed her hand on Dwin's arm. "I'm sorry."

"At the temple I waited for her as long as I dared. Then I went to her room and found her lying on the floor." Dwin's voice cracked. "I never should have involved her."

"You said she knew something?"

Dwin nodded. "Someone else must have known too. Someone who wanted to keep her quiet."

"Whoever did it," said Melaia, "I'll see them hang."

❖❖❖

Sorabus galloped ahead to alert Hanni. By the time the carriage clattered into the courtyard, a hushed crowd had gathered. Both Hanni and Serai dashed to the door of the carriage.

"How bad is it?" asked Hanni.

"She's alive," said Melaia. "I've cleared most of the gash, but she hasn't roused. I fear it was poisoned."

Dwin gently lifted Nuri from the carriage, and Hanni herded him to the temple with Jarrod at their heels.

Melaia climbed out and leaned into Serai's arms.

Serai brushed back Melaia's hair with her fingers. "I hate to tell you this, but your father is asking for you."

Melaia groaned. "Not now."

"I'm sorry," said Serai.

"Confound it!" Melaia wiped her eyes. A demanding father, a dying friend, a priceless book left behind at Treolli, and Trevin in the Dregmoors. "Confound it!"

She trudged to the palace and made her way to the king's quarters.

King Laetham sat in bed, sipping wine, strongly herbed by the smell of it.

"Father." Melaia knelt in a bow at the bedside.

The king grunted.

When she looked up she shivered. His gaze was distant, as if he were looking into himself instead of out.

She reached for the cup in his hand. "What's in your drink?"

He grabbed her wrist with surprising strength. "A pain killer," he said.

Melaia pulled back. "I was told you summoned me, but I can see this is a bad time."

"You think I'm a fool?" His face reddened. "You think I won't learn about your escapades? I expressly forbade you to leave Redcliff, and you blatantly disobeyed." He sipped his drink and grimaced. "Where did you go this time?"

"I think you know," said Melaia. "It seems you have someone reporting on my every movement."

He set his cup on the bedside table. "I'm giving you a chance to tell me yourself."

Melaia swallowed dryly, tempted to take a gulp of the pain killer. "I went to a bookbinder in Treolli to have a book repaired and to visit Nuri at the temple there."

From beneath the bedcovers the king drew a golden crossbow only a handsbreadth in size.

Melaia shrank back. "What is that for?"

King Laetham set a dart in the bow, drew it back, and let it fly. The dart hit the lion on the shield that hung on the opposite wall. He had clearly been practicing. It was pocked with dents.

He set the crossbow in his lap. "We were young stags, the three of us: Parrim, Beker, and I. Inseparable friends. Together we fought with my father's warriors, ambushed the enemy, covered each other."

He pinched the bridge of his nose, and closed his eyes. "The Battle of Gravium. The battle that won the war. Fiercest fighting I've ever seen. One moment Parrim and Beker fought at my side, and the next moment I had no idea where they were. I came upon a clump of warriors wrestling on the ground, one of our men holding his own against two of the enemy. I shot at the back of the enemy just as he rolled, and my arrow hit Parrim." Tears welled in the king's eyes. "I killed my friend."

"I'm sorry," Melaia whispered. "I didn't know."

"My father also died that day, and the kingdom passed into my hands. I vowed I never would fight again."

Melaia looked down at her clasped hands. "I understand your vow, but we're being invaded. The Dregmoorians are weakening our towns, one by one. If they decide to mount a full attack –"

"Precisely." He narrowed his eyes, and the tears rolled down his high cheekbones. "I do not want you prancing around the country."

"There were no Dregmoorians in Treolli. I knew that before I went."

"You do not know where the arrow might come from. How clearly must I say it? Stay within these walls."

"But –"

"Who am I to you?"

"You're my father."

"And?" He readied a dart in his bow.

Melaia felt the color rise to her cheeks. "You're my king."

The dart flew and hit the heart of the lion.

Lamp flames burned low, and the temple room was deep in shadows when Melaia roused from sleep at Nuri's bedside. The first kyparis harp still lay on Melaia's lap. She had played it for Nuri, hoping it would awaken her as it had once awakened the king, but after playing half the night to no effect, Melaia had fallen into a doze. Now she looked up to see Jarrod standing over Nuri, rubbing his chin. Melaia stretched, and he startled.

"Thanks for watching while I slept," she said.

"Don't thank me." He didn't take his eyes off Nuri.

"I see. Duty requires no thanks."

He clenched his jaw. "What does the death-prophet see?"

"I see that Nuri is alive, but struggling to remain so. I also see that you can stop suspecting Dwin. This proves he's not the informant. He never would have hurt Nuri."

"This proves only that someone is willing to go to great lengths to silence her."

"What are you saying?"

Jarrod folded his arms. "Think. Does it not seem like a strange coincidence? Who 'discovered' Nuri?"

Melaia felt the blood drain from her face. "Dwin."

Jarrod nodded.

"That's absurd."

"*That*, my sister, is exactly what the informant wants you to think."

CHAPTER 11

Trevin strode across the high mountain meadow beneath a sky salted with stars, taking care not to stumble over the dwarf-like angels called stargazers, who wore their long, black hair pulled severely back. They were scattered over the meadow, some lying on their backs, studying the sky, some sitting at flat rocks, writing on scrolls. He sensed their colors, muted yellows, greens, and blues.

A patch of white, star-shaped flowers bobbed in the night breeze, releasing their sweet scent, reminding him of Melaia. He plucked one. If only she were here, he would give her the sweet-scented blossom, and he would be content.

He took a deep, discontented breath and looked north over ridge after ridge. Which one held the hidden pool where Cherrim had left him? How far had he trekked with Seaspinner? The first day they had hiked through the ravine to reach the cave entrance. The second day they had trailed the stream through caves until they arrived at an underground lake fed by a spring. The third day they had followed the spring to a cascading freshet beside a stairway cut into the rock. After climbing the damp stone stairs, they had emerged in the stargazers' meadow to see the sun setting. Seaspinner had then explained his task and left him on his own.

"Three days," he muttered. "Three entire days." He clenched his jaw and crushed the flower in his fist. He was frustrated to the point of despair. If Windweaver had been his guide, he would have the harp by now and might be back in Redcliff with Melaia. The task at hand would further delay him. He was supposed to meet escapees from the Dregmoors here and lead them to safety, retracing the stream until they arrived at the waterfall in the mountain meadow. Seaspinner had said she would arrange for Windwings to meet them there and fly the people to Flauren.

Trevin tossed away the crushed flower. He would see the people safely to the Windwings, but then he would turn his full attention to finding the harp. Maybe in gratitude for his help, Seaspinner would instruct Cherrim to fly him into the Dregmoors. Or to Windweaver. Dash it! He would walk all the way to the harp on his own two feet if he had to. One way or another he would get there.

"My friend!" Ellias, the stargazers' overseer, waved from where he sat on the ground before a low stone table. "A refreshment, perhaps?" The little man held up a jug.

Trevin trudged to the stone and sat on the thick grass.

"Restless?" Ellias poured.

"Does my pacing disturb the peace here?" asked Trevin.

"It disturbs your peace." Ellias slid a cup to Trevin. "Your charges are on the way. You would do well to still your soul as you wait."

Trevin eyed the entrance to the stone stairway, watching for the lookout's signal. "What if they were discovered?"

"I'm told they're safe."

"Do you know who they are?" Trevin sipped the mountain water flavored with sweet berries.

"I know only that they have escaped from the Firstborn," said Ellias, as a lantern light flickered at the cave entrance. "You see?" he said. "Your charges are here."

"I hope they're ready to travel," Trevin growled. "I plan to leave tonight." He drained his cup and strode to the cave with Ellias trotting beside him.

At the cave entrance Ellias handed him a journey pack. "Seaspinner asked me to send provisions for your charges."

Trevin settled the pack on his shoulder. "Many thanks for your hospitality."

"We shall meet again." Ellias bowed. "Perhaps in Avellan."

"Most certainly in Avellan." Trevin gave a respectful nod, entered the cave, and descended the damp stone stairwell as fast as he dared. Lantern light glowed from below, but he heard nothing. How many refugees were there? A small group, he hoped.

As he neared the bottom step, someone raised a single lantern, and he saw them. Dirty-faced, wide-eyed, and huddled together, they were indeed a small group. Small in stature.

"Children," he whispered. No doubt children stolen and sold for their blood.

They stared at Trevin, and he stared back, counting. Twelve, maybe a few more if some had ducked behind the others. The tallest held the lantern. She looked a couple of years younger than Dwin.

Trevin took a deep breath. "Well, then, are you ready to travel?" He took a step toward them, and the entire huddle shrank back against the wall.

Trevin retreated. "Do you have a spokesman?"

They blinked at him. The tall one murmured and pointed to the hilt of Trevin's sword.

He flipped his cloak over the sword and called up the stairway, "Ellias? Is Ellias still nearby?"

The little man peered down from the top step. "We meet again."

"Yes, well, I could use some help." Trevin motioned to the huddle.

Ellias pattered down the stairs, slowing when he saw the children. "Bless me!" he said. "Most are no taller than I."

"I think they're afraid of me," said Trevin. "How can I lead them when they fear me?" He hoped Ellias would offer to lead them out. Then he could follow the tunnels south, deeper into the Dregmoors.

Ellias tugged the pack of provisions off Trevin's shoulder and opened it. He laid out bread and dried fruit, speaking to the children in a low, musical voice.

The tallest child crept to the food, keeping a wary eye on Trevin. When Trevin retreated into the shadows and sat on a boulder, the other children ventured out and joined the tall one. While they ate, Ellias went to refill the pack.

Trevin waited in the shadows. By the time Ellias returned, several children were dozing. So much for a night journey, he thought. In fact all hopes for a fast journey, day or night, had vanished.

Ellias talked with the children who were awake and reported to Trevin, "The tall one, Judith, seems to be the leader by default. I told her she can trust you, but she's wary."

"They seem to trust *you*," he hinted.

"Of course." Ellias chuckled. "I'm their size, and I don't look dangerous."

"And I do?"

Ellias shrugged. "I advise keeping your dagger sheathed and your sword in its scabbard."

Trevin sighed. "I can do that unless I have to defend them. Do you think they're being followed? Who showed them the way?"

"Judith said the ghost lady brought them as far as she could and pointed out the tunnel to take."

Trevin eyed the tunnel that led south. The ghost lady. Seaspinner? No, she had gone for the Windwings. Flametender? He doubted that anyone would describe her as a ghost. No matter. The real question was not who she was, but why hadn't she led the children all the way to Seaspinner and the waterfall?

Trevin turned back to Ellias, who obviously did not intend to volunteer to take his place. "The children will have to follow me tomorrow," Trevin said. "How do I persuade them to trust me?"

"I'll introduce you, but as far as trust . . ." Ellias rubbed his chin. "Don't children enjoy a song or two before bedtime?"

"I'm not the man for that," said Trevin. "Melaia is the singer, not me." But he followed Ellias to the group of children. The ones who were awake watched him intently. He sat cross-legged and tried to look as non-threatening as possible, while Ellias introduced him. Then Ellias returned to his meadow.

Trevin tried to recall his childhood. He had been the sole caregiver for his little brother, who was not only scared of strangers but also of dogs and unfamiliar noises. At night to comfort Dwin, he told stories, but he hadn't thought about those tales in years.

He cleared his throat. Which was Dwin's favorite? "Have you heard the story of the magic cloak?"

Those who were awake looked at each other and shook their heads.

"It all started with a boy named . . . Dwin." Trevin frowned as he told the story, trying to remember the details, but perfect recall obviously didn't matter. Before the tale was done, all the children were asleep, and the only sound was the freshet burbling down the rocks and into the spring. He recounted the children. Fourteen of them. Tomorrow he would lead fourteen children toward safety.

As soon as morning trickled down the stone stairway, Trevin handed out bread, informed the children that they would eat while they walked, and pointed out the spring they would follow. After Judith assured them that the ghost lady would want them to follow this man, the group gathered behind Trevin, munching their breakfast.

Trevin soon realized that his normal pace was too fast for children, even when he and the older children carried the youngest on their backs. So he walked at a frustrating, leisurely pace and often looked back over his shoulder to make sure his charges were not straggling.

Although the children were slow they followed all day without complaint, and by the time they stopped for the night at the underground lake, they were talking in hushed voices. When Trevin set out the provisions, they needed no invitation to join him, and his heart felt lighter. Born to free. That was his destiny, and no, it had not been completed at Qanreef.

As he watched the children settle around him, he sat taller with his heart expanding and his world enlarging. Their tentative glances held a glimmer of hope, and he did not want to disappoint them. He wished he could build a wall of protection around them the way he had tried to do for Dwin. That night when he told the story of Dwin and the magic cloak, he smiled.

❖❖❖

With Serai at her side, Melaia trudged across the courtyard from the temple to the palace, led by a torchbearer and flanked by the double guard ordered by her father. She huffed. It was ridiculous to amass such an entourage simply to walk to and from the temple.

"Claudia is adjusting well to her new position as novice," said Serai.

Melaia recognized the comment as benign chatter meant to distract her from the aggravation of the guards. "Yes, Claudia learns quickly," said Melaia. So had Nuri, when she was a novice. Nuri, who was slowly failing. Melaia's stomach curdled at the thought of Nuri's spirit slipping into Lord Rejius's realm. Nuri had to stay alive at least until the stairway and Tree were restored. After that if she died, her spirit could cross into Avellan.

A guard approached from the inner court gate. "My lady?"

Melaia wiped her eyes. "Yes?"

The guard bowed. "A youth arrived before the gates closed. He's been asking for audience with you. We turned him down and questioned him about his business, but he's leeched onto us, insisting that he speak to you and you alone."

By the light of a torch ensconced near the gate, Melaia saw two Redcliff guards standing by the young man, all three looking expectantly in her direction. The youth wore the patched tunic and breeches of a field worker and held a cap that he twisted in his hands.

Jarrod approached. "What's this about?"

"A young man insists he has a message for me," said Melaia. "Maybe a child in his family has been abducted. No doubt he promised to present the case directly to me, poor man. I see no danger in hearing him out. I'm well guarded."

Jarrod beckoned to the young man, who stepped over, bobbing his head, twisting his cap. He bowed low, three fingers over his heart.

Melaia returned the greeting. "What is your name?"

"Innery."

"Do you have a request of me?"

"A missage, if you please." Innery's glance darted from the guards to Jarrod to Serai. "It's a spoken missage, and I was told it's for your ears alone."

Melaia nodded to her escorts, who retreated a few paces. The guards drew their swords, and Innery's eyes grew wide.

"It's all right," said Melaia. "As long as you don't attack me."

"Oh, no, m'lady, I'd n'er do any sich thing. It's jist a missage I bring." Innery dug into his waist pouch, withdrew something in his fist, and held it toward Melaia. "The missage is from the one who give me this."

When Melaia extended her hand, Innery gave her a black cord looped through a small, carved harp. She could hardly breathe. "He sent this?"

Innery's voice dropped to a murmur. "He says meet him in Navia." He twisted his cap.

"Nothing more?"

"That's all, m'lady." Innery bowed.

Melaia felt light enough to fly. "Tell him I'll be there before the week is out."

Innery nodded, shifting uneasily.

"You may go." Melaia closed her hand around the pendant as he scuttled away.

Serai sidled up to her. "What is it?"

Melaia took Serai's arm, and they hurried back to the palace, with Jarrod and her guards following.

When Melaia, Serai, and Jarrod were safely within her apartment, Melaia blurted, "Trevin is in Navia." She held out the pendant.

Serai fingered the small harp. "You're sure?"

"I am." Melaia's heart danced. "The messenger said that the one who wore this pendant wants me to meet him in Navia. This is Trevin's pendant. The wait is over. Trevin is three days away. Only three days!"

Jarrod closed the latticed shutters. "Did you send a return message?"

"Of course. I said I would come before the week is out."

"Hen's teeth." Serai folded her arms. "Your father explicitly prohibited travel. What's more he placed a double guard on you. Tell me how you plan to sneak around that."

"With your help, I hope." Melaia plopped down on a floor cushion.

Serai rolled her eyes. "I helped you last time. I am highly suspect."

Jarrod leaned against the wall and finger-combed the end of his tail of hair. "I'll help you."

"You, too, helped her last time," said Serai.

"Dwin, then." Melaia looked at Jarrod, who kept combing, but raised his eyebrows. "Dwin said he can enter my quarters in ways my guards never dreamed of. Surely that means he knows how to sneak me out."

"That's frightening," said Jarrod, "but I wager it's a bald boast. Let me cover for you and Serai. I'm sure I can find some holy week that will require your presence at the temple in Navia."

"You would persuade my father?" asked Melaia.

Jarrod shrugged. "I can try. I have some influence with him."

Melaia leaped to her feet and hugged Jarrod. "You're a perfect brother."

He scowled. "I'm not a perfect anything."

"I think you are." Melaia hugged Serai. "To Navia!"

"You'll accompany us, won't you, Jarrod?" asked Serai.

"I'm needed here and in the field," he said. "Besides I promised to fetch Dreia's mended book from Treolli."

"The book!" said Melaia. In her excitement she had forgotten the book and the fact that Jarrod had volunteered to retrieve it. "When you get the book, bring it to Navia."

"Why?" asked Jarrod. "Don't you want it locked up here with the harps?"

Melaia spoke near a whisper. "The harps won't be here."

Jarrod narrowed his eyes. "Where will they be?"

"In Navia," said Melaia. "Trevin obviously has the third harp with him. We can unite all three in *Navia*. Perhaps that's where Dreia intended to unite the harps all along. After all, that's where she sent me the first message about Breath of Angel, Blood of Man. Trevin must have discovered that –"

"Wait." Jarrod held up his hand. "Did the young man specifically say Trevin had the third harp?"

"Trevin is too smart to send such a message outright. Instead I have this." She let the harp pendant swing from her hand. "I'm sure it's meant as a sign. He has one harp. I'm to bring the other two. Why else would he want me in Navia?"

Jarrod rubbed his eyes. "Most High, have mercy."

"What's wrong?" asked Melaia.

Serai stared at Jarrod as if she were reading his mind. "It's too great a risk to remove the harps from Redcliff."

"We'll conceal them," said Melaia. "No one needs to know."

Jarrod exhaled slowly. "In that case, I insist on coming with you."

"I thought you were needed here." Melaia returned to her cushion, certain that Jarrod was responding from his guilt. He had always blamed himself for failing to protect their mother who had been traveling with one of the harps when malevolents attacked.

"If you're carrying those harps, the more protection the better," he said.

"How will I get my book back from Treolli?" asked Melaia.

"I'll retrieve it after you're safe in Navia." Jarrod strode to the door, his face in a dark frown. "On the morrow, ladies."

As the door shut Melaia turned to Serai. "I'm sorry. I distracted Jarrod tonight. I know you usually spend the evenings together."

"It's all right." Serai laughed. "You curved his road somewhat. Jarrod lays plans and likes to follow them exactly. A trip to Navia was obviously not in his plans."

"He doesn't have to go with me." Melaia slipped Trevin's pendant onto her neck and matched it to hers, forming a heart. "I'll find my way to Navia, even if I have to walk."

Chapter 12

"Navia ahead!" The shout passed from wagon to cart, drover to driver along the caravan.

Melaia roused in the back of Jarrod's wagon, where she had been dozing against two stacked cushions, each containing a harp and plenty of wool padding. After three and a half days of travel, they had almost reached their destination. She edged to the front of the wagon bed and peered between Jarrod and Serai as the wagons ahead disappeared, one by one, around the bend.

Serai glanced at Melaia. "Navia is over the next hill."

Jarrod grunted and urged the horses ahead. Terse and tense at the start of the journey, he had become more irritable as the days passed. Melaia couldn't blame him. He should have been directing troop movements, discussing strategy, and whatever else he did in the field. No doubt he felt anxious about the duties he postponed in order to make this trip.

Melaia considered it a miracle that Jarrod had persuaded her father to allow her to travel, and she had told Jarrod so. After profusely thanking him to the point that he reddened with embarrassment, she had swallowed her praises, but she was truly impressed with her half-brother's persuasive powers. He had taken advantage of the news that the temple in Navia, ravaged by raiders more than a year ago, had finally been restored to full use. He told King Laetham that the royal family should be represented at the dedication of the temple, where Melaia's friend Iona served as high priestess. The king had agreed to send Melaia, but only after Jarrod promised to personally escort her. In a caravan. Accompanied by Camrithian guards.

The dedication of the temple had been Jarrod's idea. Iona did not yet know about it, but Melaia was certain she would not object. After all, it would be the grandest celebration in memory, for she would unite the three harps and restore the angelic stairway with its protective Tree.

"There's Navia." Serai leaned away from Jarrod so Melaia could see better as their wagon crested the hill.

Across the valley on the next rise, the city stood solid and steadfast on a trade route to the coast. Even at this distance, Melaia could see reminders of the raid in the charred streaks that scarred the outer walls. In contrast the familiar dome of the temple appeared freshly whitewashed, a welcome sight curving gracefully above the town's flat roofs. Beyond it loomed the overlord's tower, its parapet adorned with dark stones that looked like hands beseeching the sky.

Jarrod waved a signal to the Camrithian guards who flanked the wagon. They turned their mounts and galloped north, returning to Redcliff. Melaia smiled as she watched them disappear over a hill behind her. Jarrod had been right when he told the king that the road to Navia was completely safe. This morning he arranged to send the guards home, insisting that they were needed closer to enemy-threatened territory.

On the outskirts of Navia the caravan left the road to camp in a field. Jarrod shouted his thanks to the journey master and drove on to the city, where guards at the rebuilt gate waved them in. The streets looked both familiar and strange to Melaia. Newly painted buildings butted up against dilapidated, stained houses or empty dark lots where houses had once stood.

As Jarrod turned down a back road that led to the overlord's villa, Melaia looked down a side street, trying to glimpse the temple. They had argued about where Trevin might be. She assumed he would wait for her at the temple. Jarrod thought he would be with the overlord. Serai said he would probably stay at the inn. Jarrod won by insisting that the overlord, who kept his fingers on the pulse of the city, would be able to tell them where Trevin was staying.

Jarrod pulled the wagon to a halt in the villa's stable yard and hailed two servants. "We're guests from Redcliff, here for the temple dedication. I sent word ahead."

One of the servants, a jowly man, took the reins as Jarrod climbed down. "Aye, we were told to expect you. You'll want to enter by the rear door, where you'll find the secure storage room you asked for."

The other servant helped Melaia from the wagon and reached for the journey packs, but Jarrod waved him away. Serai took one cushioned harp, Melaia took the other, and they headed for the rear entrance of the villa.

Again Melaia was impressed that Jarrod had thought of everything, including a secure storage room, which no doubt locked with a key. The third harp might be here already – or in the secure room at the temple. Either way, she would soon see the third harp – and Trevin.

A stern-faced servant held the rear door open for them. Melaia recognized him as the man who had ushered her to Lord Silas's chambers the day she first met Trevin. The servant now led them to the storage room.

Jarrod ducked in, motioning for Serai and Melaia to follow. "Cushions in the far corner," he said.

Melaia stood in the center of the room, letting her eyes adjust to the trickle of light entering from a high, narrow window. Casks and chests lined the walls. If the third harp was here, it was well hidden."You're sure the harps will be safe here?" she asked.

"I'll see to it," said Jarrod.

As Melaia settled her cushion on top of the one Serai had set down, she heard the door click shut behind her.

Serai grabbed Melaia's arm and said, "Jarrod?"

Melaia turned to see a crooked nosed, heavyset man blocking the door. He wore a russet cloak fastened with a large brooch. When he folded his arms across his chest, his cloak conveniently parted to display both his sword and dagger. She stiffened. He was the attacker she had seen through the spirit of the dying woman from Drywell. No wonder he had looked familiar that day. She knew him as a companion of Prince Varic of the Dregmoors. Hesel. A gash runner.

"What are you doing here?" Jarrod asked him.

Hesel grunted. "I know, I know, I was supposed to meet you at the stables, but I had business here at the villa."

"What business?" snapped Jarrod.

"You really want to discuss it in front of your lady friends?"

Jarrod's jaw clenched, and his fists tightened.

The look that passed between Jarrod and Hesel set Melaia on edge, and she eased back toward the harps. If it came to a fight, Hesel was outnumbered, two angels to none. Did he know that?

Jarrod placed a hand at Serai's back as if to usher her out. "I'll settle the ladies first."

"The way we did in Treolli?" asked Hesel.

"Shut up," said Jarrod.

"I brought gash," said Hesel. "It'll be as easy to silence these two as it was to take care of the girl."

Melaia's breath caught in her throat. She glared at Hesel and growled, "If you had anything to do with the attack on Nuri, I'll see you hang."

"Here's my neck." Hesel ran a finger across his throat. "Come and get me."

Serai stepped in front of Melaia, drawing her dagger, but Jarrod plucked it from her hand. "No need to incite the snake," he hissed. "I'll take care of him. Let's get you two to safety."

"What about our cushions?" Melaia asked.

"I will personally lock the room," said Jarrod, drawing Serai toward the door. Melaia followed close behind.

With a mocking flourish Hesel opened the door and stepped into the corridor. The stern-faced servant, waiting there, handed the key to Jarrod and took his leave. After locking the door, Jarrod turned to Melaia, showed her the key, and tucked it into his waist pouch. "Shall we find your guest room?" he asked.

"I'd rather speak to the overlord and find out where Trevin is," said Melaia.

"Patience." Jarrod took Serai's arm. "First things first."

Hesel took Melaia's arm.

Jarrod's dagger was in his hand before Melaia saw him reach for it. "You touch her, and I'll have your head on a platter."

Hesel laughed. "No you won't. You need me." But he backed off, raising his hands. "Put the dagger away, grim one. I'm here only to assist."

"You can assist by going peacefully with us to the overlord's cells," Melaia said. "I'm having you jailed for assault. Maybe murder."

"You're having me jailed?" Grinning, Hesel looked her up and down. "How much does a princess sell for these days, Jarrod?"

"I don't deal in people," said Jarrod.

"I do." Hesel swaggered away down the hall, calling back, "You'll find me in the stable, where I'll be counting my coins."

"Jackal," Jarrod muttered, heading upstairs with Serai.

"You're letting him go?" asked Melaia. "He's guilty of gash running, kidnaping, assault, possibly murder, and who knows what else."

"And I will see him hang. I can promise you that," said Jarrod. "But all in good time. Hesel serves me, and he knows he has to cooperate or he's dead. It's that simple."

Melaia huffed and grudgingly followed.

"I don't like it," said Serai. "Are you sure you can control him?"

"I just did, didn't I?"

Through an arched door on the first landing, Melaia spied the walkway that led to the overlord's quarters. "Can't we stop at Lord Silas's room?" she asked.

"He's ill today," said Jarrod. "The servant told me."

Melaia tried to still herself and sense Trevin's presence, but she sensed only Serai and Jarrod, who obviously had a strategy. One that she wasn't sure she agreed with. Hesel working for Jarrod? It curdled her stomach.

The next landing opened onto the roof-walk of the main villa, but Jarrod kept climbing. As they ascended higher and higher, Melaia realized that they were in the overlord's tower. Which made sense if, as a safety precaution, Jarrod wanted to use the tower as a lookout to keep an eye on the countryside.

Through an open door at the top of the stairway, they entered a square stone room with lattice-shuttered windows on the east and west walls. The light of the setting sun drifted through the lattice on the west, breaking into golden, laced patterns on the floor. The room contained only two rolled mats, a lidded chamber pot, and a small table with an unlit bowl lamp.

Jarrod toed one of the mats. "Fools! I sent ahead and told them the princess was coming. This cell looks as if they were expecting prisoners."

"Iona will have room for us at the temple," said Melaia. "Maybe Trevin is there."

Jarrod shut the door and leaned back against it. "Look, Trevin is not in Navia. Neither is the third harp."

"What about this?" Melaia drew out the harp pendants from beneath her tunic. "The messenger who brought Trevin's pendant said he was here in Navia."

Jarrod looked down his nose at her. "Did he?"

She frowned. "He said the message was from the one who gave him this pendant."

"It wasn't Trevin," said Jarrod. "The truth is, when Trevin left Redcliff, he went north by caravan to Eldarra, hoping to ask Windweaver to take him into the Dregmoors. Hesel reported that bandits attacked the caravan. When I asked about Trevin, he simply showed me the pendant."

Melaia sank to one of the rolled mats. "Did he steal it from Trevin or –" She covered her mouth.

"I don't know," said Jarrod, "but Trevin is not here."

"Wait," said Serai. "Hesel lured us to Navia? Why?"

Jarrod trudged to the east window, rubbing his forehead. "I'm sorry. It wasn't supposed to happen this way. I intended for both of you to come to Navia, stay at the temple, and celebrate with Iona. I didn't mean to accompany you. But you had to take the harps."

"I thought King Laetham insisted that you travel with us," said Serai.

"Travel with you, yes, but that's all I would have done. If you hadn't taken the harps, I would have seen you safely here and then returned to Redcliff."

"So you're staying to protect me and the harps?" asked Melaia.

"That's a good way to look at it," he said. "Except that I'm not staying. You'll be guests of the overlord for a few days, during which time, for your protection, you'll be in this room. I simply ask that you be patient. When I return –"

"Return from where?" asked Melaia. "If we're to stay here willingly, we need to know exactly what's going on, and I don't want Hesel lurking around."

"Hesel will go with me," said Jarrod. "Believe me, I planned to do this from Redcliff while you two were having a wonderful time in Navia with Iona."

"Do what?" Serai huffed. "You're dancing around the truth, and I'm growing tired of it."

"I'm taking the two harps to the Dregmoors to unite them with the third," said Jarrod. "It would have been easier to take them from Redcliff."

Melaia rose to her feet, her hands in fists at her side. "Steal them, you mean?"

"They're not yours," said Jarrod. "They don't belong to anyone."

"But only I can unite them."

"When?" Jarrod's voice rose. "You're taking your pretty princess time about it. Time we don't have."

"I sent Trevin –"

"Has he returned?" Jarrod shook his head. "Who knows where Trevin is?"

Melaia's eyes grew moist, her throat thick.

Jarrod sighed. "Remember when you first learned I was Dreia's son? You asked me why I couldn't restore the Tree. It was a good question, one that hounded me until I realized that I *could* restore the Tree. And I will."

"What about the prophecy?" asked Melaia. "*The Tree will only rise again by breath of angel, blood of man.* That's me. You're breath of angel, blood of *immortal.* You told me that yourself."

"Hang the prophecy," said Jarrod. "How much breath has been stifled and stolen since the fall of the Tree? How much blood has been shed? *That's* the price of the Tree. *That's* the breath and blood. When I was a young child, Dreia told me that restoring the Tree was my destiny. How disappointed she and Benasin were when 'the harps did not live' in my hands. They apologized. They were mistaken. I was not the one. They sent me to the temple and expected me to support the Angelaeon, while Dreia went off to try again for her dream-child, this time with King Laetham. It was a grand slap in my face. I became the disappointment, the failure. But I'm no longer a child. I now understand that Dreia sent me down a false trail."

He took Serai's hands in his. "The one who will succeed is the one who is bold enough. I am that one. I promise I'll return as soon as the harps are united. Meanwhile you two will stay here, protected."

"I don't need protection," Melaia said. "Take me into the Dregmoors with you."

"Dreia claimed she needed no protection," said Jarrod. "That miscalculation cost not only her life but also the lives of everyone traveling with her. I couldn't protect her, but I can protect you – by leaving you here."

Melaia opened her mouth to protest, but Jarrod held up a hand. "I'm traveling with Hesel. He will slip me into the Dregmoors and provide passage to the third harp."

"Traveling with Hesel." Serai rubbed her arms. "That's absolutely no comfort."

Jarrod stroked her cheek. "Don't forget that I'm half-angel and Hesel is not. I can sever his brains from his brawn in less time than he can yelp, and he knows it."

As he kissed Serai, Melaia strode to the west window. Obviously Jarrod had been scheming about this for some time, strategizing about the harps while he was planning troop movements – with Hesel? *It's as easy to silence these two as to take care of the girl in Treolli.* Jarrod had been at Treolli. He had been at the gash house in Lowridge. He had sent Catellus to battlefronts where the enemy had moved on. Time and again Camrithian troops were misled, while the Dregmoorians found unobstructed access to defenseless towns like Drywell, where Hesel had struck down the tavern maid. Did Hesel receive safe passage for enemy troops in exchange for Jarrod's safe passage to the third harp?

Melaia whirled to face Jarrod. "It's you, isn't it?"

Jarrod and Serai looked up, startled.

"*You* are the informant. Nuri knew it." Melaia narrowed her eyes. "*You* silenced her."

Serai pulled away from him. "Jarrod?"

"That was Hesel's doing," said Jarrod.

Melaia darted to him and shoved him back. "Traitor! You ordered it done."

"Hush!" Jarrod grabbed her wrists and shook her. "I did *not* order it done. Hesel and I occasionally met in the temple library at Treolli. On one of those occasions, Nuri happened to overhear us, but silencing her with gash was not part of my plan, and I had nothing to do with it."

"You met to discuss troop movements, didn't you?" said Melaia. "You sent our warriors to fight at places where there was no enemy, while Dregmoorians attacked our unprotected towns."

Jarrod clamped both her wrists in his left hand. With his right he slipped her needle knife from her waist pouch. "Only keeping you safe." He released her.

"Jarrod?" Serai backed away. "People have died. *Our* people."

"Serai, we're Angelaeon," said Jarrod. "We have no people. The few who die are the price of freeing the thousands imprisoned in the

Under-Realm. The cost is worth it. The stairway will soon rise and those dying souls will cross to Avellan with us."

Serai folded her arms and turned her back to him.

"You might try to see it my way," said Jarrod. "You two are well away from danger here."

Melaia rubbed her wrists. "You're witless if you think we're going to stay here."

"You're witless if you try to leave," said Jarrod. "Yareth guaranteed Iona's safety only as long you give him no trouble."

"Yareth? He was banished as a traitor," Melaia muttered. "I'd not trust him with anyone's safety."

Jarrod pulled Dreia's book from his pouch. "You can have this. I thought perhaps it held some clues about where to unite the harps, but it was completely useless." He tossed it to Melaia

She examined the front. The crack was barely visible, and the wood still thrummed. "How long have you had this?" she asked.

Jarrod shot her a glare, strode out of the room, and shoved the door shut. The bolt shot into place with a thud.

"Confound it, Jarrod!" she yelled. "I hope bandits attack *you*. I hope they send me your horse tail of hair!"

CHAPTER 13

Melaia threw open the shutters on the east side of the tower room. The window was unbarred, but the roof walk lay too far below to provide a way of escape. She could yell for help, but she didn't want to risk endangering Iona. Even so, when Melaia spied Jarrod and Hesel riding toward the city gates under the light of the full moon, she was tempted to scream. That would shock Jarrod and bring him galloping back. Or would it?

She turned to Serai, who sat on the rolled mats, staring at nothing. "Did you not know about this? Didn't you suspect something was wrong?"

"Didn't you?" Serai squeezed her eyes closed. "I'm a fool."

Melaia fingered Trevin's pendant. She never had seen Serai look this defeated. "I'm sorry," she said. "You're no worse a fool than I am. I wanted so badly to believe that Trevin was in Navia with the third harp." She dug his note from her waist pouch and unrolled it, but her vision was too blurred to read. Her mother had been killed when her caravan was attacked. "Do you think Trevin is – "

"No," said Serai. "No. Don't say it, don't believe it. Not until you have proof."

The door bolt scraped, and a servant girl entered with a tray of supper. Yareth swaggered in behind her, moon-pale and sly-eyed. The girl slid the tray onto the table and scurried out.

As Yareth shut the door Melaia stuffed the note into her pouch and wiped her eyes.

Yareth clucked his tongue. "So the lady does have feelings after all."

Melaia swallowed a stinging retort. "I wish to see Iona," she said.

"Iona is not to know you're here." Yareth cocked a single, straw-thin eyebrow as he strolled to Melaia. "But her safety does depend on you."

Melaia backed away. "Does your father know I'm here? Surely Lord Silas did not agree to lock me in his tower."

"My father is in no position to know anything. He will soon leave the land of the living."

"I'm sorry to hear that." Melaia stepped back again and bumped into the wall.

"I'm sure you are." Yareth grinned as he stepped closer. "His departure makes me overlord."

"If you're overlord," said Melaia, "you would be wise to show your support for the king. My imprisonment here is Jarrod's doing. Don't hang because of him." From the corner of her eye, she saw Serai rise. "Set us free, and I'll see that you're completely pardoned. Returned to full citizenship."

Yareth leaned nose to nose with her, his breath hot on her face. "I'd rather be rich."

"In that case return me to my father," Melaia said. "He'll pay."

"I'm not sure he can afford it." Yareth mouthed her lips in a wide, sloppy kiss.

Serai leaped at him and bit his forearm, and he jerked back, flinging Serai across the room. She landed hard, sprawling across the floor.

As Melaia darted to her, Yareth stomped to the door, gripping his arm and snarling, "Rot you both!"

"Wait!" Melaia tugged Serai to her feet. "Let us walk out with you. I'll make sure you're pardoned and paid well."

Yareth glared. "*If* you walk out, it will be only *after* I'm paid – by Lord Rejius. You are going to make me a very rich man." He stormed out, slammed the door, and banged the bolt into place.

Melaia's chest tightened, and she shouted at the door. "Why would Lord Rejius pay?"

Yareth didn't answer.

"Because he wants the harps," muttered Serai, rubbing her arm.

"But I don't have the harps."

"A fact we'd best keep to ourselves," said Serai. "As long as Lord Rejius thinks he can use you to procure the harps, he'll keep you alive."

Melaia exhaled slowly. "Compared with Lord Rejius, death sounds more appealing."

"That is not an option."

"But escape is." Melaia opened the shutters on the west window and looked out. She saw only storehouses, a couple of dark alleyways, and the rear wall of the city, but the drop went straight down to the yard below. Trying to escape through this window meant certain death. Unless...

She turned to Serai. "You're going to fly from here."

Serai's eyebrows rose. "I most certainly am not."

"There's a full moon, but this is the shadowed side of the villa. I think you can escape unseen."

"I will not leave you here alone with Yareth. Besides I think my arm is broken." Serai pulled back her cloak.

Melaia tenderly felt Serai's swollen left arm. Sprained? Broken? She didn't know. "What about your wings?" she asked.

Serai rolled her shoulders. "The left one is sore."

"But not broken? In that case we'll bind your arm. Your mother flew holding me."

"Only the distance of a stone's throw. Not even she could carry you from here safely."

"I'm not asking you to carry me. I'm simply saying that if your mother flew holding me, surely you can fly without the use of one arm. You're to fly straight to Benasin or to your mother. Ask them to send help."

Serai shook her head. "Who knows how long that will take? Meanwhile what happens when Yareth discovers I'm gone?"

"He won't know. I'll bundle our cloaks across your mat and make it look as though you're huddled there. I'll tell him you were injured when he tossed you aside. Or I'll say you've taken ill."

Serai inspected the food on the supper tray. "Have you considered the law of the Erielyon?"

Melaia bit her lip. The first part of the law said Erielyon could fly outside their own territory only if doing so would save a life. In this case flying would save at least one life: Serai's. But the rest of the law required those who flew outside their land to return home at once. The law was intended to protect the Erielyon, but it would require Serai to go home after she flew. Who knew when she might be allowed to return?

"Supper is cold and not terribly tempting," said Serai, "but we should eat." She handed Melaia a piece of barley bread and poured her a cup of thin cabbage soup.

Melaia sat on the floor. "You don't have to serve my food tonight."

"Of course I do." Serai slipped a packet from her waist pouch and carefully folded back the cloth. A variety of plump dried fruits lay in the middle. "I brought these from Redcliff."

Melaia fingered a dried apricot. If she sent Serai for help, she would be alone in the tower to face whatever lay ahead, but she saw no other choice. She cleared her throat. "Do you believe Jarrod? About Trevin?"

"I think Jarrod told you everything he knows." Serai placed her hand on Melaia's arm. "Hesel gave Jarrod a pendant, which tells us nothing about Trevin except that his pendant was stolen."

Melaia nodded. She would miss Serai's calm reason. "Before you fly home –"

"I'm not flying."

"It's not your decision. I am your mistress, and I am ordering you to fly."

Serai clenched her jaw and scowled at Melaia.

"You have to," said Melaia. "Not only to send help, but also to learn the truth about Trevin. Find a way to let me know. Please."

Serai sighed. "All right. I'll do what I can."

After picking at the meal Melaia helped Serai bind her wounded arm close to her body. Then she extinguished the lamp flame so no one would see their silhouettes in the window.

Serai slipped off her cloak and flexed her cloud white wings. Then Melaia helped her climb onto the window ledge, where Serai crouched, clasping Melaia's hand and scanning the sleepy city and the fields beyond.

"You were wrong," said Serai.

"About what?" asked Melaia.

"You're not my mistress. You're my friend." Serai squeezed Melaia's hand. Then she leaped out.

Melaia clenched the window ledge, barely breathing as Serai's wings unfolded. For a moment Serai angled, unsteady, and then she regained her balance, pulsed her wings evenly on the air, and rose rapidly. Soon she was merely a speck of white disappearing into the night.

Long after Serai was gone, Melaia continued to gaze into the sky. Then she sank to her knees before the window in the cold, moonlit room. "Farewell, Serai," she whispered.

Trevin stood on a high stone ledge that overlooked the mountain meadow and the waterfall where he had first met Seaspinner. She was in the pool, splashing with the children, but he was watching five dark spots that had appeared in the sky over the northern horizon. He said nothing until he was certain that they were not simply a flock of geese. When he saw that they were truly Windwings, he whooped.

"They're here," he called. As he scrambled down the rock, Seaspinner shooed the children out of the pool, and by the time the Windwings trotted into the meadow through the stone corridor, the children were dry and dressed. A gray Windwing entered first, followed by a red, a dark brown, a sleek black, and the Golden. The children grew quiet and gathered around Seaspinner, eying the winged horses that would carry them to Flauren.

As the Windwings headed for the pool to drink, Trevin carefully approached Cherrim and stroked her. "I'll settle the children on the other horses," he said, hoping she could understand him. "They'll go to Flauren, but I want you to take me to the Dregmoors. You won't have to stay there. Simply drop me off in Stone Grove, and you can fly back to Flauren."

Cherrim snorted and drank from the pool before following the other Windwings across the meadow to graze.

As Seaspinner arranged the children into groups, she called to Trevin, "Three to a horse, do you think?"

"Let's try four." Trevin waved the children to the horses, but the children didn't move. "It's all right," he said. "The horses won't hurt you. They'll fly you to Flauren. You'll like it."

The smallest girl ran to Trevin. "I want to ride with you."

"I need to ride alone," said Trevin. "I'm going a different direction."

Seaspinner folded her arms and narrowed her eyes.

"I need to get to the Dregmoors," he said.

The little girl put her thumb in her mouth and ran to Judith, who picked her up.

"Don't leave us," said Judith.

A freckle-faced boy scowled at Trevin. "We won't go without you."

Cherrim nudged Trevin with her nose and extended her wing.

He gave her a brief nod. "All right," he said. "I understand." He felt as if he were the rope in a tug of war, but he managed a smile. Taking the youngest girl in his arms, he said, "You'll ride with me." Then he patted the freckled boy's head. "You, too." Pointing to the four tallest children, he said, "Each of you will ride a Windwing with two of the others seated in front of you. I'll show you how it's done. Follow me."

With a few tears, a few giggles, and a lot of help from Trevin and Seaspinner, the children mounted. When everyone was settled Trevin nudged Cherrim, and they led the other Windwings, trotting single file across the meadow. As they entered the stone corridor they picked up speed and headed toward the edge of the cliff.

Trevin wondered if he should have warned the children, but it was too late. In another few paces the Golden galloped off the cliff and launched into the sky. He looked back as, one by one, the Windwings ascended. Some children ducked their heads, some squealed, and others grinned, but all hunkered, wide-eyed, over their Windwings. He trusted that they would cling as tightly as they could – exactly as he was doing.

He leaned protectively over the boy and girl who sat in front of him and resisted the urge to glance south toward the Dregmoors. But he had not given up on finding the harp, and he hoped Melaia had not given up on him.

Cherrim and the Windwings circled Flauren in a wide, descending spiral. Below townspeople ran into the streets, pointed to the sky, and shouted. King Kedemeth watched from his balcony, and Queen Ambria hurried down the front steps of the palace with her attendants. Almaron and the foal raced across the field outside the stables. By the time the Golden began her final descent, it looked as if the entire town had gathered at the fence.

The Golden hit the ground at a gallop. Trevin heard the other Windwings land behind her as she raced toward Almaron and the foal, who joined her as she circled the field, slowing to a walk. The other Windwings followed her lead.

Haden strode out of the stables with his stableboys. They stood at the edge of the field, admiring the Windwings. As Trevin slid off Cherrim's back, Haden called, "I would send my boys to help the children down, but I'd not want them to spook the mounts. You'd best do the job."

Trevin lifted down his small traveling companions. "You don't sound surprised to see us. I thought you would be astonished, not only at seeing the Windwings, but at their riders, too."

"They're a sight, that's sure, but Queen Ambria heard they were coming. From Windweaver, I think. She posted a lookout, who spread the word as soon as you were spotted."

The oldest children were already climbing off their mounts, but Trevin made the rounds to ensure that everyone dismounted safely. From Windwing to Windwing the children followed him. He strode back to Haden with the smallest girl in his arms and the others bunched around him.

Queen Ambria swept into the field, beaming a motherly smile. "Welcome to Flauren."

The children turned questioning faces to Trevin, who nodded. "You're safe here, and I'm sure you'll find food waiting for you."

"Honey cakes." The queen extended her arms to the little girl, who only clung tighter to Trevin.

He whispered to the girl, "You must try Queen Ambria's honey cakes. They're the sweetest in the world. Will you save one for me?" She nodded, and he slipped her into the queen's arms.

As Queen Ambria led the children toward the palace, Trevin asked Haden, "What happens to them now?"

"They'll be fed and bathed and given warm beds. Kedemeth will do his best to locate their families and return the children." Haden leaned back against the fence, watching the Windwings. "Do you think one of them would take me for a jaunt?"

"I wouldn't risk it unless you're willing to go wherever the Windwing has a mind to take you and stay as long as she wants to keep you."

"So the Golden didn't follow your lead?"

"Hardly." Trevin watched Cherrim nuzzle her foal. "I've not yet been to the Dregmoors."

"You expected the Golden to take you there?"

"I had hoped she would take me to Windweaver." Trevin unlatched the gate and shoved his way out. "I'll ride to Tabaitta Canyon first thing in the morning." He headed for the palace.

Haden called after him. "You should know we have a visitor from Redcliff. He rode in yesterday afternoon."

Trevin waved his thanks and broke into a jog, his heart pounding. Had Melaia found him out? Had she sent a messenger to recall him? Shades! How he craved her. Under any other circumstance he would jump at the chance to return to Redcliff. As it was, he dreaded facing her disappointment. Worse, her wrath. She had every right to be furious.

As soon as he entered the palace, the steward directed him to the council hall. He dashed up two flights of stairs and emerged into the broad chamber, where King Kedemeth and a weary looking Benasin sat at the main table, their heads bent over an assortment of scrolls.

A breeze from the tall, unshuttered windows cooled the sweat on Trevin's brow. As his footsteps echoed across the mosaic floor, the king and Benasin rose. Trevin bowed.

"Welcome, son." King Kedemeth motioned to Benasin. "I believe you know our visitor."

"I do." Trevin clapped a hand on Benasin's shoulder. "It's good to see you."

"And you," said Benasin. He and the king returned to their seats.

Trevin scanned the open scrolls, detailed maps of Eldarra and Camrithia. Perhaps this was not about Melaia after all. "Is your brother on the hunt for you again?" he asked.

"Rejius is indeed on the hunt," said Benasin. "He unleashed all his ambitions this time. The Dregmoorians have attacked Redcliff in full force."

Chapter 14

After supper – and a bedtime story told by special request – Trevin made his way to the library. A servant was lighting the lamps when he entered munching on the honey cake that his little friend had saved for him. He pulled a stool to the table where he and King Kedemeth had often played Attacker Defender. This time Benasin sat with them, the game board was a map of Camrithia, and the game was real.

The king nodded at Trevin. "I just received news that raiders attacked an Eldarran caravan en route to Redcliff. Obviously the Dregmoorians intend to prevent supplies from reaching the Camrithian capitol, but an attack on Eldarran caravans is an act of war against our country. We are fully involved now."

Trevin stared at the circle marked *Redcliff.* No doubt Melaia was helping the wounded and encouraging the king. He hoped she would stay out of harm's way. "Jarrod sent most of Redcliff's forces to fight in the east," he said. "Has he recalled them?"

Benasin shook his head. "He stripped the city's defenses to a minimum and was away when the Dregmoorians attacked."

"What will his strategy be now?" asked the king, scooting aside the map to make room for an ink bowl and parchment that his scribe laid out.

"Since Jarrod was in Navia at the time of the attack, he's probably scrambling to return Camrithian forces to Redcliff," said Benasin.

"No doubt." Trevin finished his last bite and licked his fingers. "Why was Jarrod in Navia?"

"He accompanied the princess there for a dedication of the restored temple," said Benasin. "As I heard it King Laetham allowed the trip only because Jarrod went along to ensure Melaia's safety."

"In that case she's safe." Relieved, Trevin shifted his attention to the section marked *Dregmoors.* While he hated to think of Redcliff under siege, the attack might distract the enemy long enough to allow him to slip into the Dregmoors, snatch the harp, and escape before Lord Rejius knew what was happening.

King Kedemeth selected a stylus from a writing box. "We need a clear strategy. Redcliff is a critical position, and I don't want to see it fall to the Dregmoorians. My troops are gathering to march south, with the first group leaving tomorrow. Others will follow close behind." He looked at Benasin. "What do we know of the enemy?"

"Most of the attacking troops are gash warriors," said Benasin, "meaning they're addicted to gash and will certainly have barrels of the stuff located along their supply lines."

Trevin stood to stretch his legs. "Maybe you could sneak in and slash the barrels. Empty them of gash."

"Perhaps," said Benasin. "I suspect we'll also find malevolents among the gash warriors."

The king inked his stylus. "Do you expect Lord Rejius to be there as well?"

"That I don't know," said Benasin, "but you can be sure he's behind the attack."

The king began writing. "What's his objective?"

"Two kyparis harps." Trevin strode to the west window and looked down into the burial garden. "The harps are locked in a trunk in Melaia's room at the palace. Only a handful of people know their true value. Lord Rejius is one."

Benasin leaned back from the table and stroked his beard. "With Jarrod and Melaia in Navia – and Serai as well – the harps are less than safe."

"Livia knows to protect the harps," Trevin pointed out. "Isn't she at Redcliff?"

"Not to my knowledge," said Benasin.

King Kedemeth looked up, frowning. "Livia left us several days ago, headed to Redcliff with a group of my best warriors."

"They hadn't arrived when I left," said Benasin.

Trevin drummed his fingers on the smooth marble of the window ledge. What if he returned with the third harp only to find that Lord Rejius had stolen the first two? Who else knew to protect the harps? "What about Dwin?"

"He was at Redcliff," said Benasin, "but he was giving most of his attention to Nuri." He explained that Melaia had rushed back from Treolli with Nuri near death. Then he had to explain why Melaia was in Treolli, which led to an account of how Dreia's book had been cracked in Lowridge.

With each account of her escapades, Trevin's tension knotted until his hands were in fists. "Lowridge? Treolli?" He marched back to the table. "Who allows Melaia to put herself in such danger?" But he knew the answer: no one. Melaia always found a way to pursue the path she thought right, never mind danger. He planted his palms on the table, leaned straight-armed over the map, and stared at the Dregmoors. Is that where she intended to go next?

"The greatest danger seems to be at Redcliff," said King Kedemeth. "My scouts will report the Dregmoorians' positions and their strength, but with Redcliff under siege, we'll need to either draw off the enemy or fight our way through." He handed the parchment to his attendant. "This is a message I'm sending north, requesting help from the Erielyon."

Trevin nodded, but he was haunted by the fact that Melaia had slipped King Laetham's grip more than once. She might truly think she could travel to the Dregmoors – and not only think about it but do it, believing that he was there. Or if she had discovered that he had gone north, she might very well go after the third harp by herself. The Angelaeon would not stop her. On the contrary they would encourage her.

While the king and Benasin talked, Trevin kept his eyes on the map, but he could not keep his mind on the discussion, and as soon as the king adjourned the meeting, he retired to his room. He sat on the bed, drew Arelin's sword from its scabbard, and gazed at his reflection. Son of Arelin, grandson of Flametender and Windweaver, heir of the

Eldarran and Dregmoorian thrones, he was well worthy of Melaia in rank. But his record of fulfilling his word was lackluster at best. He had failed to retrieve the third harp once before. This time, he hadn't even stepped into the Dregmoors.

Calls and footfalls echoed across the courtyard below as men prepared for tomorrow's ride toward battle. Trevin wandered to the window, sat on the wide sill, and watched them as he fought a battle in his mind. Where should he go on the morrow – to Tabaitta Canyon and the Dregmoors? Or to Redcliff and Navia? On the surface it seemed a simple choice. In reality it felt agonizing. Great stars, how he missed Melaia. But did he dare return without the third harp?

A firm hand clasped his shoulder. Only then did he realize that King Kedemeth had entered the room. The king's ruddy, care-worn face held a confident, expectant smile. "You'll ride with us tomorrow?"

"Us? You're going too?"

"Whatever you command others to do, you must be willing to do yourself. It has been a long time since Eldarrans have gathered to fight, and I'm asking them to do so on Camrithian soil. I mean to go along to foster their trust and courage." He leaned against the windowsill, surveying his torchlit city. "I'll ride as far as the foothills and await the troops gathering from outlying areas. A select group of riders, including Haden, will continue through the pass as our vanguard. They'll advance as close to Redcliff as possible."

The king folded his arms and studied Trevin. "I know I've supported your prior commitments, but the attack on Redcliff has required me to rethink my position. What's more, if you're interested in protecting Melaia's harps, it's to your advantage to help prevent the fall of Redcliff. In short I would like you to lead troops into Camrithia with Haden. I'll follow in the next group."

Trevin returned his sword to its scabbard. "Will my presence help?"

"It's a good opportunity to show your adopted countrymen what their next king is made of."

"What *am* I made of?"

"Go with us and find out." The king gave Trevin a tight-lipped smile. "We leave at first light." With a nod he strode out of the room.

Trevin flopped onto the bed and stared at the ceiling, where the flicker of lamplight skirmished with shadows. His destiny seemed to be drawing him south at the head of Eldarran troops, which would require him to abandon his quest for the third harp. He squeezed his eyes closed. He had come to Eldarra with the best intentions, hoping to smooth the way for Melaia to be with him forever. Would she understand that? Or had he pushed his luck too far? Did pursuing his destiny mean leaving Melaia to pursue hers alone?

At dawn the next morning, Trevin galloped south with King Kedemeth, Benasin, and a score of Eldarran horsemen, including Haden. Since fodder was scarce in Camrithia, they carried what feed they could, and a wagon of supplies trailed them.

After leaving the king in the foothills where other warriors were gathering, Trevin and Benasin, with Haden and his men, rode up the mountain trail to the pass. While scouts climbed boulders and crept through the pass to flush out any bandits, Trevin searched the ground for a small wooden harp on a black cord. The scouts found no bandits, and he found no pendant. Haden and his men offered to wait while Trevin broadened his search, but he knew they were eager to clear the pass and make good time down the other side of the mountain.

After one last, quick look Trevin admitted that he would probably never see the pendant again. "Add that to my list of confessions for Melaia," he muttered to his horse. He mounted and led Haden's men through the limestone corridor.

The journey from Flauren to Redcliff usually took five days. Trevin and his group pressed themselves and their mounts to make it in four. As they neared Redcliff, draks appeared, circling overhead, and a lone rider approached from the south. Benasin pulled his hood down over his forehead.

Trevin loosened his sword and squared his shoulders. He had left Camrithia as a comain. He returned as Prince of Eldarra.

"We've a score of men," said Haden. "We can take a lone rider."

"Unless he's not alone," said Trevin. "Others may be waiting to ambush us after he distracts us." That's the way Dreia had died. In fact she was ambushed on this exact road. Trevin himself had reported her location to the hawkman. It would be fitting for the arrows to turn on him this time. "Watch your flanks," he called back.

But the rider was an Eldarran scout headed home. He reported that Dregmoorians patrolled all roads south and east of Redcliff. The capitol city was indeed under siege, but its gates were not yet breached.

Trevin scanned the horizon, wondering where his group could camp safely. Perhaps in the Durenwoods, which lay ahead to the southwest. Earth-angels called sylvans lived there and hosted groups of Angelaeon on occasion, but they were a protective clan and, according to Melaia, they rarely allowed visitors.

He caught Benasin's eye. "Might the sylvans welcome us?"

"They're allies of the Angelaeon," said Benasin, "a fact we can use to our advantage."

"If they allow us to explain ourselves before they shoot," said Trevin.

"Is it true that sylvan arrows turn their victims into bushes?" Haden asked.

"It is," said Benasin.

"Which means we can't risk entering the woods looking like attackers," said Trevin. "Tell the men to keep their weapons sheathed and their empty hands in sight."

Haden looked skeptical. "Our men will not be happy keeping their weapons hidden in the face of danger."

"Even so, we should greet the sylvans as allies, not enemies," said Trevin. "If they allow us to enter, we can count on their protection tonight."

"To the Durenwoods, then." Haden turned his mount and rode back to spread the word.

Trevin led the horsemen west across the field, and in the late afternoon they entered the woods, passing first through a section scorched by Lord Rejius's men in search of Melaia's book. Beyond the charred sentinels, the trees that had escaped the flames had succumbed to the blight. Though it was spring, they stood as leafless as timberland in the winter. Trevin could only imagine how grand this forest had looked at one time and how beautiful it might be someday, when the stairway was restored and the blight reversed.

Warbles echoed through the treetops, and Trevin halted his men. Pale green, thin-limbed sylvans sat among the branches, their deadly arrows aimed at the intruders. He held three fingers to his heart and called, "We come as friends of the Angelaeon and allies from Eldarra. We seek only refuge for the night."

The sylvans did not budge.

"We request the counsel of Noll at Wodehall," Benasin called.

Two sylvans dropped to the floor of the woods and motioned Trevin's group forward, while the other sylvans followed overhead through the branches, whistling their signals from tree to tree and keeping their arrows trained. When the leading sylvan halted at a laurel hedge, a reedy, light green man emerged from the branches. He tucked the end of his long, gray-green beard beneath his waist sash.

Trevin dismounted and bowed, three fingers to his chest. Haden, Benasin, and the other men followed suit.

"You come in peace?" the bearded man asked.

"We do," said Trevin. "I'm a Camrithian comain, here in service to princess Melaia. These are our allies, the Eldarrans. We plan to join the fight to defend King Laetham at Redcliff."

"I'm the Second-born immortal," said Benasin, "also allied with the Angelaeon."

The sylvan held up three twiggy fingers as his pale green eyes studied Trevin. "You are yourself Angelaeon?"

"Son of Arelin," said Trevin, relieved that the man could sense him. "My name is Trevin."

The man nodded, his eyes crinkling into a smile. "I'm Noll, steward of the Durenwoods. I should have known you, but ill news blows through the forest these days, and I make it my business to turn over every leaf. So I ask your pardon if you've felt less than welcome. We'll soon remedy that."

Noll sent some of his archers back to their posts and directed others to lead the Eldarrans to a guarded grove where they could camp. Then he led Trevin and Benasin through the laurel hedge and into a wide, round common room that smelled of the fresh, sharp scent of kyparis wood. A curved staircase hugged the back wall and disappeared into the upper reaches of the tree.

"Wodehall," Trevin mused. "Exactly as Melaia described it."

"When the others arrived, we were disappointed that Melaia was not with them," said Noll.

Trevin looked around the room. "What others?"

Noll beckoned to Trevin and Benasin, and they followed him up the curved staircase lit by glow-lichen in box-shaped lanterns. The stairs spiraled up the red-brown inner trunk as far as Trevin could see. Noll ushered them to the second level and across a landing to an open door, where he stood aside and waved them in.

As Trevin and Benasin crept into the dim room, a plump, pale green woman with moon-white hair looked up from a table, where she was crushing herbs in a mortar. From Melaia's description Trevin recognized her as Noll's wife, Esper. The person he did not expect to see was Dwin, who rose from the bedside, his dark curls matted to his forehead.

Dwin's face broke into a smile. "Trevin! Benasin!"

Trevin marveled that he stood eye to eye with his brother, who had thinned into a lean man in need of a shave. "I thought you were at Redcliff," he said.

As Dwin raked back his curls, his smile disappeared. "I *was* at Redcliff." His voice cracked, and he turned back to the bed.

Trevin knew who lay there before he looked, and when he did, his heart sank. Nuri was propped on pillows and blankets, half-sitting, but she was ashen and still. She reminded him of the children he had rescued.

Benasin stepped to the end of the bed. "I told Trevin about Nuri."

Dwin sank to a stool. "Hanni thought Esper's healing herbs might help, so I brought her here shortly after Benasin left Redcliff."

"Bless us, we're trying to help Nuri," said Esper, "but my herbs are only holding her this side of life, not bringing her back to health. Not yet." She shook her head. "And her so young."

Trevin drew up a stool and sat beside Dwin, and there they stayed through the night, each telling the other their experiences of the past weeks. Trevin didn't know when he fell asleep, but it was Nuri who woke both him and Dwin.

"I'm thirsty," she croaked.

Trevin roused to see Dwin scrambling to the table, where he poured a cup of Esper's spice-scented potion.

Sunlight was spilling through the open window, and Nuri blinked into it, whispering, "Where am I?"

"Wodehall," said Dwin. "In the Durenwoods." He sat on the edge of the bed and held the cup to her lips. "Don't worry. You're safe."

She sipped and then in a raspy voice asked, "Who's here?"

"In this room only Trevin and me," said Dwin. "Esper's been nursing you."

"No one listening?" she asked.

"None but us," said Trevin as Dwin gave Nuri another sip.

She swallowed and licked her lips. "Jarrod," she said. "Jarrod's the traitor."

Trevin stiffened. "Are you sure?"

Nuri nodded. "And another man."

Trevin sprinted out the door and down the stairs.

As he neared the bottom of the staircase, Esper looked up, startled, from her kneading bowl. "Nuri?"

"Awake," said Trevin, "but –"

"I'll go see about her." Esper headed for the stairs. As she passed Trevin, she waved a floured hand toward the brazier on the far side of the room. "We've more visitors, newly arrived."

Only then did Trevin sense the warm green presence and the blue. Serai sat on a bench by the brazier, her eyes red and swollen. Her mother, Livia, was binding her left arm.

Serai gave Trevin a pained smile and started to rise, but Livia drew her back.

"What happened to your arm?" asked Trevin, looking around for Melaia. He didn't sense her silver presence. "Where is she?"

Serai looked down at her clasped hands. "A messenger gave her your pendant."

Trevin's hand flew to his chest as if the small harp still hung there.

"We feared you had been killed by bandits," said Serai, "but Mother told me what happened."

"At least the way we understood it in Flauren," said Livia, tying off the binding.

"How did Melaia get my pendant?" asked Trevin. "Where is she now? With Jarrod?"

Serai fingered the binding on her arm. "Jarrod has gone to the Dregmoors."

"With Melaia?"

Serai shook her head. Staring into the brazier, she told the whole story, pausing now and then to wipe her eyes or blow her nose.

Trevin paced as he listened – until Serai repeated Yareth's boast: Lord Rejius would pay him well in exchange for Melaia.

"Blast!" Trevin's fist came down on Esper's table, rattling the kneading trough.

"It may be a meaningless boast," said Livia.

"I would have stayed with Melaia," said Serai, "but she ordered me to fly for help. I tried to reach Redcliff, but I couldn't get in, so I flew to Aubendahl. That's where I found Mother."

"I couldn't reach Redcliff either," said Livia.

"Let me guess. Dregmoorians blocked the way." Trevin rubbed his forehead. "Was that Jarrod's strategy?"

"Jarrod's not evil." Serai cradled her bound arm. "He's not like the malevolents, not like Lord Rejius."

"Whose side is he on?" Trevin paced again. "Don't answer that. Angelaeon are on their own side. The fall of kings and kingdoms makes no difference to you."

"It does now," said Livia. "Melaia chose to accept her father. We'll help her as best we can." She stroked Serai's hair. "My Eldarran guards left me safe at Aubendahl and headed east to join Camrithians fighting under the comains. They hope to bring them to the aid of Redcliff."

"Mother and I decided the fastest help for Melaia would come from the Durenwoods," said Serai, "so we came here. Noll sent some archers to Navia, but how they'll reach Melaia, I don't know, and by the law of the Erielyon, I must fly home now."

"Couldn't you stay?" asked Trevin. "King Kedemeth sent a messenger to the Erielyon requesting aid for Camrithia. You could be one of their number."

"Not without permission from our governor," said Livia, with a sly smile. "He happens to be my husband and Serai's father."

Serai nodded. "I'll fly north and report everything to my father. I'll also confirm Eldarra's request for help."

"I expect her to return leading a group of Erielyon," said Livia.

Trevin knew without a doubt that Serai would be back. She did not easily accept defeat, and she would not rest until she knew Melaia was safe. Neither would he.

Livia rose, adjusting the dagger at her waist. "Trevin, may I accompany you to Navia?"

Trevin half smiled, for she had read his intentions. "I welcome your company," he said. "Let's hope Yareth's threat to involve Lord Rejius was simply a warped wish."

Within the hour Serai flew north to find King Kedemeth on her way home and tell him Trevin's plans. Meanwhile Trevin, Benasin, and Livia led Haden and his men south to Navia. They arrived two days later at sundown and camped quietly, hidden in the woods outside the city.

A sylvan scout located the archers Noll had sent previously, and their leader, Eigel, joined Trevin over a cold supper. With his twiggy finger Eigel drew a square in the dirt. "Navia's walls are guarded here, here, here." Eigel placed pebbles at the appropriate spots.

Trevin studied the etched dirt as if he were playing Attacker Defender with King Kedemeth. "Any malevolents?" he asked.

"All the wall guards are malevolents. And there's one other." Eigel plunked down a small rock. "A swaggerer who rules the main gate."

Trevin eyed the rock. "Can your archers take him?"

"After we dispose of the wall guards." Eigel pointed to the arrows in his quiver. "By sunrise the parapets will be lined with sylvan-made trees."

Haden squatted and refilled Eigel's cup. "I advise holding your arrows until the gates open. If the gatekeepers panic, they'll close up tight."

"Then we'll wait for the gates to open," said Eigel, "but I'm told that'll happen early on the morrow because of the overlord's death. Seems they open early and close late to allow folk from the countryside to come for the mourning."

Benasin, who had been resting against a tree trunk, leaned into the conversation. "Lord Silas died? I served him as advisor for a time. Lived in his villa."

"I met the old man once," said Trevin. "He was a good man. Loyal to King Laetham. I can't say the same for his son, Yareth."

"Aye and it's Yareth who's overlord now," said Eigel. "They say he's been asserting his authority there for some time and grew impatient."

"You mean he murdered his own father?" asked Benasin.

"That's the rumor," said Eigel.

Benasin grunted and sat back. "No doubt it's true."

Trevin palmed the hilt of his dagger. He would welcome the opportunity to come face to face with Yareth. He turned to Haden. "As soon as we've secured the main gates, bring in your men, but not on the attack unless we're forced to it."

"You've read my thoughts," said Haden.

"One more thing." Benasin looked at the sketch in the dirt. "I'm told Jarrod is far away by now, but if he's found in Navia . . ." His voice cracked. "Be easy on him. Spare him for my sake. Allow me to speak to him."

Trevin nodded but thought, *If that's your wish, Jarrod had best be found by someone besides me.*

Sylvan archers crept out of camp before dawn. By the time Trevin, Benasin, and Livia rode toward the city the gates were open, and the sylvan archers were at work. As Trevin watched, arrows felled the gash-guards on the parapet and turned them into dark, leafless saplings. The sylvans moved so silently, no one raised a cry.

Before the transformation was discovered, Trevin, Benasin, and Livia cantered to the gate. One of the gatekeepers recognized Benasin and greeted him. After they spoke condolences to each other, the man waved the three travelers through.

"Where is the bully who's supposed to rule the gate?" Trevin asked.

Livia nodded toward a man a stone's throw down the road. He was eying wagons and foot traffic. Immediately Trevin sensed his oily green aura.

As alert as a dog scenting a fox, the malevolent turned toward them. "Halt!" he ordered, swaggering their direction. He took only five steps before a sylvan arrow slammed into his chest. As he stumbled back, he reached for his dagger, but his feet rooted, his legs and torso hardened into black bark, and his arms twisted upward, forming branches.

The sight transfixed Trevin. He heard Livia tell Benasin, "You take care of the plump gatekeeper. I'll manage the tall one." By the time he tore his gaze from the malevolent-turned-tree, the gatekeepers had been disarmed and sylvans had appeared on the parapets, their arrows aimed toward the streets. Townspeople backed away or disappeared into the nearest doorways as Haden and his men trotted into town.

Trevin, Livia, and Benasin turned their horses toward the overlord's villa. Trevin studied the tower with the strange cornerstones jutting into the morning sky. According to Serai that's where Melaia was being held. The highest window looked like a blank, open eye. Was Melaia watching? Did she sense his approach?

The porter at the overlord's gate brightened when he recognized Lord Silas's former advisor. He saluted Benasin by name and welcomed Trevin and Livia. As they dismounted he called for a stableboy to help with the horses.

Trevin and Livia followed Benasin through the gate and into the atrium. Stands of flickering oil lamps encircled the area, and on a bier in the center lay the body of Lord Silas, draped in black, his face the color of his wispy white hair. Servants hurried quietly along the surrounding columned walkways. Many nodded to Benasin or spoke a brief greeting, but no one questioned his presence.

Trevin would have marched straight to one of the servants and summoned Yareth, but Livia caught his arm and held him back. "One moment," she said. "For respect."

Benasin approached the bier and bowed his head.

Trevin scanned the walkways, ready for Yareth to strut out in mourning garb, maybe make a show of grief. Did Melaia know about the overlord's death? He was an old friend of hers. Had Yareth allowed her to visit the bier?

After a respectful moment Trevin sidled up to Benasin and murmured, "Point me to the tower stairs."

Benasin looked up and blinked as if he were waking from a dream.

"The tower?" asked Trevin.

Benasin nodded. "This way."

Trevin beckoned to Livia, and they followed Benasin to the second level of the villa. They drew their daggers and crept along the shadowed side of the second-floor walkway to stairs that were strangely unguarded. With Benasin in the lead they ascended, alert for movement below and above.

At the top landing Benasin hissed and pointed to an open door. With daggers poised they entered. Sunlight streamed into the sparsely furnished room through unshuttered windows. Serai's cloak lay heaped in a corner, an upturned mat sprawled against one wall, and Melaia's cloak draped the table as if someone in a hurry had flung it aside.

"What happened here?" Trevin muttered, trembling with anger. He grabbed Melaia's cloak and shouted, "What happened? Damnation! Where is she?" He darted out the door and practically flew down the stairs, yelling, "Yareth! You blasted devil!"

"Restraint!" said Benasin at Trevin's heels.

"We'll find her," called Livia, following.

But Trevin was done with restraint. He dashed along walkways, flinging every door wide, and eying whoever or whatever was inside. "Yareth!" he shouted. "Show yourself, fiend."

He stormed into the atrium, where he turned full circle, yelling at the galleries he had just prowled. "Where is that snake? Where is Yareth?"

Livia grabbed a servant boy as he tried to duck behind a column. As she spoke to him, Benasin grabbed Trevin. "Calm yourself," he said. "Try reason first."

Trevin shook him off and yelled to the hidden household, "I'm the Prince of Eldarra with warriors at my command. You will loosen your tongues for me."

A stooped, wrinkled woman emerged from the shadows of the colonnade and set down a basket of laundry. She shot a warning glare at Trevin and then shuffled to Benasin, holding three fingers over her heart.

Benasin made the sign of the Tree as he bent to listen to her. As she talked, his hands balled into fists.

"Can she show us to Yareth?" asked Trevin.

The woman padded away, and Benasin shook his head. "She doesn't know where Yareth is, but she confirmed that he smothered his own father to make himself overlord."

Livia approached with the servant boy and nudged him.

"I know, sir." The boy bowed. "Lord Yareth called for a wagon at dawn, sir. He left in haste, headed for the postern gate, I heard."

"Did he take anyone with him?" asked Trevin. "Where did he go?"

"I don't know, sir," said the boy.

Benasin ran a hand through his hair. "Too bad he left town. I could have sent him out in a shroud."

Trevin was on the verge of demanding the presence of all servants for questioning, when Haden strode in.

"The city is secure, for the most part," said Haden. "Did you find the princess?"

Trevin scowled his answer.

Livia placed a calm hand on Trevin's shoulder and told Haden, "We're afraid Yareth has taken Melaia somewhere."

"We heard that a few folk left the city this morning by the postern gate," said Haden. "I sent men after them. One returned to report they'd found something noteworthy. I intend to ride out and take a look, but I thought I'd check with you first."

Trevin flexed his hands and took a deep breath in an effort to calm himself. Haden's appearance reminded him that as Prince of

Eldarra, he represented an entire kingdom. His response to this crisis carried weight. "Lead the way," he said.

Within moments Trevin was galloping out the back gate of Navia with Haden, Benasin, and Livia. The trail took them west across a bridge spanning the Tuarin River. Then it wove around knolls and groves before curving sharply southward. As they rounded the curve, they found the road blocked by a group of Eldarran warriors.

The warriors parted to reveal an overturned wagon. One side of the rig tilted up, resting on two wooden chests that had split open. Gold pieces and gems lay scattered across the dirt.

"Melaia!" Trevin dismounted, ran to the wreck, and grabbed the side of the wagon. "Help me right it," he shouted.

Haden and his men muscled the rig right side up. Someone *was* underneath, and for a moment Trevin's heart lodged in his throat, but it was Yareth, alone, crushed beneath his treasure.

Trevin felt weak with relief. He glanced at the surrounding hills and asked the Eldarrans, "Did you search the area for anyone else?"

One of them laughed. "If there was anyone else, they snatched what they could carry and ran."

Benasin stared at Yareth. "I doubt anyone could have walked away unhurt," he said. "Crawled away maybe."

"Search the area," Haden barked to his men.

Trevin wanted to believe that they would find Melaia wandering, trying to make her way back to Navia, but he knew in his gut they wouldn't. Yareth hadn't inherited chests of jewels and gold from his father.

He looked up at Livia astride her horse. "Yareth made the trade with Lord Rejius."

Livia nodded, her face somber.

"Let's go back to Navia," said Benasin, mounting his horse. "I must attend the funeral of a friend. Perhaps we'll find Melaia in the city."

Trevin scanned the hills once more and then mounted his horse and followed Livia and Benasin. He knew they wouldn't find Melaia in

Navia. She was with Lord Rejius, the Firstborn immortal, the hawkman. As for Yareth, in a way he had gotten exactly what he wanted. He had died a rich man.

CHAPTER 16

Melaia stood on tiptoe in her cave cell and peered through a crack in the wall toward her homeland across the Davernon River. From this height in the cliffs, Camrithia looked like a strip of scraggly woods, giving way to brown-green fields that stretched to the horizon. In contrast the roiling whitewater below made the Davernon look alive. To the ungifted eye, the spray rising from the foam was simply river mist, but Melaia saw spirits of the dead within it and wondered why they had not been entombed in the Under-Realm.

Although she had been imprisoned only a few days, she had made a habit of studying the mist daily, straining to see Trevin's spirit. Individual features were difficult to discern from this distance, but she could not stop looking. *Not* seeing him gave her hope that he was alive and well. Somewhere.

It still galled her that Yareth had sold her to Lord Rejius, whom she had not yet seen. The hawkman had sent malevolents to fetch her in Navia. They, along with a taciturn woman, had hauled her into the Dregmoors, straight to her cell. Fortunately they had not taken her waist pack, which held her mother's book and Trevin's note.

She reread it now, holding the note to the light that filtered through the crack. Though she had memorized every word, she wanted to read it again just to see Trevin's handwriting. Without him, her heart felt like an empty chasm, and seeing his words made her feel a bit less lonely. *Looking toward my return.*

Melaia squeezed her eyes closed. This entire situation was her fault and hers alone, because the responsibility for the harps was hers, not Trevin's. If only she had entered the Dregmoors months ago and taken back the harp herself. Instead she had delayed, and now everyone was paying the price for her negligence.

Footfalls echoed down the stone corridor along with a deep, smooth voice that made Melaia's skin crawl. She quickly stuffed the note into her waist pouch. The light of the guard's lantern bobbed into view outside the bars of her cell, illuminating Lord Rejius.

Melaia recoiled. The vision of the hawkman in the oil-water at the temple had been bad enough. The sight of him in person turned her stomach. Feathered head, beaked nose, mottled face, jerky motions – was he human at all? His round, yellow eyes studied her as his talons motioned to the lock. The guard opened it, and the immortal Firstborn strutted in. Melaia forced herself to stand tall.

"Dreia's daughter." The hawkman's human mouth grinned. "You pay me a visit at last."

Melaia raised her chin defiantly. "You welcome me with cell bars?"

Lord Rejius placed his fingertips together at his mouth and tapped the talons of his forefingers as he studied her. "If I recall, Stalia arranged an easy way for you to get here. You could have come willingly as Varic's bride."

"Stalia was not interested in me," said Melaia. "Nor was Varic. Nor are you. You want only the harps, but I don't have them."

"Of course you don't, my dear. However I intend to barter your life for them. Your father doesn't believe they're of any value. He'll be quite willing to make the trade."

"My father doesn't have the harps either. They were stolen."

"In that case your father will find them." The hawkman cocked his head. "Who stole the harps, pray tell?"

Melaia hesitated. She dared not put Lord Rejius on Jarrod's trail. "If I knew who stole them, I would know where to look for them," she said, "but I have no notion of where to look."

"If I believed you, my dear, I would be foolish indeed, but it matters not who holds the harps. Anyone who values you will bring them to me." He motioned to the guard, who brought in a jug and pottery cup. "I've brought you an exceptional drink."

As the guard poured a thick, dun-colored liquid into the cup, Melaia covered her nose. The rotten egg odor of gash was almost overpowering. "I prefer water," she said. "Clean, clear water."

"Come now. You never have tried gash, have you?" He took the cup from the guard and offered it to her.

"I know about gash," she said. "It's addictive, hardens drinkers from the inside out, and makes them barren."

"That's common gash, my dear. I'm offering you the enhanced potion, a gift for Dreia's daughter. It will keep you young in every aspect. Go ahead."

"I know about the enhancements." She swallowed back the sour taste rising in her throat.

"Young blood?" He laughed as he took her hand and curled her fingers around the cup. "Not for those I deem worthy of everlasting life. *This* gash is enhanced with ashes from the burning of the Wisdom Tree. Drink this and live, young and whole, forever."

"Young and whole like you?" She thrust the cup back into his taloned hands.

"You can't afford to be difficult, my dear." He narrowed his eyes. "Who values you?"

A sultry voice answered. "Trevin does." Stalia swept into the cell in a flowing white robe. Her dark hair seductively framed her heart-shaped face and the dark, alluring eyes that King Laetham had fallen for. "I suppose you're prepared for Trevin to come after her?" she asked.

"Ah, yes," Lord Rejius hissed. "I have unfinished business with him."

Stalia snatched the cup of gash from Lord Rejius, muttering, "Don't waste this on *her.*"

"Jealous?" He laughed. "Of course you are. You're afraid I might feel fatherly toward her." He stroked Melaia's cheek with the smooth side of a talon. "Or perhaps you're afraid my intent is more than fatherly?"

"If you intend to prevent her escape, you're a fool to keep her here in the upper quarters," said Stalia. "If she's so valuable to you, the lower cell block will be more secure."

"Then take her deeper." Lord Rejius pointed a talon at Stalia's face. "See that she lives. She will procure the harps for us."

"Deeper then." Stalia grabbed Melaia's arm and marched her out of the cell, along a corridor, and down a stairwell that disappeared into darkness so deep that Melaia felt as if she were descending into the throat of the night.

Trevin and Benasin crept to the top of the southern hill across the valley from Redcliff's mass of ruddy, square towers. As the sun set Dregmoorian campfires sprang to light in fields on both sides of the valley highway, which became a bridge rising to the top of the red clay bluff where the city of Redcliff stood. Gash warriors wheeled a battering ram down the bridge.

Benasin huffed. "As Redcliff's first defensive move, King Laetham was supposed to destroy the section of bridge that led to the city gate."

"Maybe he had no time to destroy it." Trevin eyed Benasin. "Do you sense your brother's presence?"

"I'm not close enough," said Benasin, "and if I were, he would likely sense me."

Trevin scratched his stubbled chin. In Navia he had spent his time questioning the overlord's servants. Only two knew that Melaia had been taken away, though neither knew her destination. Trevin's first guess was that Lord Rejius believed the harps were at Redcliff and was holding Melaia somewhere nearby, but now he had second thoughts.

"I'm questioning my strategy," said Trevin. "Why would Rejius batter the gates if holding the princess hostage would open them within moments?"

"Logical," said Benasin, "except that in Rejius's game, logic often twists back on itself. What he could not take by more peaceful means, he will now take by destruction." Haden eased down beside them.

"Everyone is in place. Catellus and his men are ready to ride in from the east, the sylvans from the west, and King Kedemeth from the north."

Benasin watched draks circle the valley. "I hope they keep themselves hidden."

"I've no doubt they will," said Haden. "And the moonless night is on our side."

Livia quietly joined them. Under her cloak she was dressed in a man's tunic and leggings, with a sword at her side. "The runner is here," she said.

A lean young man stepped up, tightening his waist sash. "I'm ready to take word to the sylvans whenever you say."

Trevin pursed his lips. His word would give the sylvans permission to signal the start of the attack. "Wait until I return from searching the Dregmoorian camp," he said. "I don't want to attack until I know exactly where Melaia is – if she's here."

"The longer we wait, the greater the risk that we'll be discovered," said Haden.

"If I don't return soon enough for your liking, consult Benasin and Livia. If you three agree, send the runner." Trevin headed down the hillside, plotting a course that skirted each group of enemy tents. If he found Melaia, he would try to release her. If she was too well guarded, he would bring Livia and Benasin back to free her when the fighting began.

As he slipped into the camp, the Dregmoorians lit a bonfire near the bridge. All eyes were on Redcliff as he crept from shadow to shadow, tent to tent. But he didn't find Melaia. He didn't even sense her. His legs felt as heavy as logs as he forced himself to return to Benasin's side without her. There was only one other place she would be. The Dregmoors.

"We should move in," said Haden. "They've made the ram into a giant torch. The gates will burn tonight."

Trevin nodded to the runner. As the young man sprinted away, he crouched in a thicket with Benasin, Livia, and Haden, whose men were fanned out along the ridge with a group from Navia. In tense silence they watched as the ram hit the gates again and again, setting the wooden sections ablaze.

At last the sylvans' flaming signal arrow arced high overhead, trailing sparks into the night. Shouting for battle the defenders of Camrithia swarmed out of the hills and woods, setting fire to enemy tents as they surged toward Redcliff. A stunned cry rose from the Dregmoorians on the bridge. A sizable force stayed with the ram, but the rest raced back toward their burning tents as their attackers closed in on the valley.

From the west sylvan archers aimed, precise and deadly. From the east Catellus struck with formidable forces, including a number of Angelaeon. King Kedemeth's Eldarrans pushed in from the north. Advancing from the southern hills, Trevin feared his contingent was the weakest, for Livia was the only Angelaeon among them, but Haden and his men were well-disciplined and fought fiercely. Fires flared everywhere. Shouts and screams filled the night.

Then the ram hit its mark with one final, splitting crash, and a triumphant cry rose from the Dregmoorians. Trevin glanced up at the broken, burning gates of the beseiged city for a moment too long. His horse sidestepped, and a blade bit into his right arm.

Trevin swerved to strike back, but his attacker was already tumbling to the ground.

Dwin saluted with a bloody sword. "If your horse hadn't danced away, it would have been your head," he cried and galloped after Benasin, who bore down on the last knot of Dregmoorians barring the way to the bridge.

Gritting his teeth against the rising pain, Trevin rode after Dwin as Dregmoorians flowed into Redcliff like a breaking wave. Catellus and a score of his men pursued them, while Trevin, Benasin, and Dwin fought their way across the bridge. By the time the three entered Redcliff, the Dregmoorians had spread out, and skirmishes blocked every route to the palace.

Trevin, Benasin, and Dwin battled their way to the courtyard. The palace guards, outnumbered, had scattered and were fighting singly and desperately, leaving the palace entrance unguarded.

"Look to the sky!" shouted Benasin.

Trevin glanced up only long enough to see Erielyon descending through the smoke-filled night, their swords drawn, their white wings streaked with reflections of golden red firelight. With renewed hope he fought toward the palace steps with Dwin and Benasin at his side, but he was tiring, and his wounded arm ached.

"Behind you!" yelled Dwin.

Trevin turned to face a hulking gash warrior, who drove at him, slashing two-handed, fast and furious. He knocked Trevin's sword from his hand and had drawn back to run him through when a gold dart speared the gash man in the neck, and he fell.

Trevin looked up to see King Laetham sitting on the balcony of the council room, aiming a small crossbow at another attacker. But he also sensed malevolents. Surely Lord Beker was covering the king's back, but who else? Trevin grabbed his sword and ran for the palace.

Benasin was already at the door, struggling with a gash warrior. Trevin skewered the man, Benasin swept inside, and Trevin sprinted after him. They ducked around skirmishes and dashed past Erielyon who were securing the corridors. When they arrived at the stairway that led to the council room, they found it littered with dead and wounded Camrithian guards. They stumbled up and burst into the king's chambers as a malevolent slammed Lord Beker into a wall and turned to the king.

King Laetham trained his crossbow on the assassin, and his dart flew at close range, stabbing the malevolent's heart.

The assassin snorted and shoved his dagger into King Laetham's chest. "No mortal can kill me," he said.

"Then face an immortal," growled Benasin. As the assassin whirled toward him, Benasin struck him down.

Trevin fell to his knees beside King Laetham.

"Tell Melaia," rasped the king. "Tell her I died . . . defending . . ."
He gasped.

"Her throne," murmured Trevin as the king shuddered his last
breath.

Someone had set Melaia's gold crown on the empty seat of the throne.
Trevin sank to the footstool and rested his head on the seat cushion.
He had just returned from a walk through the courtyard, where he
had tried to encourage the wounded who awaited their turn for help
from palace staff and townsfolk. Little good it had done for his own
wound. His right arm throbbed, and his whole body begged for rest.

Hanni bustled in with her bag of healing supplies. "Benasin said I
would find you here. I heard your arm took the sharp end of a blade."

"It's not deep." Trevin shrugged and winced at the burn. "You've
tended to Lord Beker?" He hissed as Hanni eased his slashed sleeve
away from the wound.

"I have. He took a blow to his head, but with a bit of care he'll be
fine. He ordered Dwin and Benasin to carry him to the council
chamber, and he's asking for you."

Trevin started to rise, but Hanni tugged him back. "After I've
bound your wound."

"But Melaia –"

"Benasin told me." Hanni cleaned the slash. "Melaia is strong-
spirited."

"I've failed her."

"You're quick to pass judgment on yourself. You cannot save
Melaia from what she alone must face." Hanni swabbed a stinging
ointment on the wound.

Trevin gritted his teeth. "I can face it with her."

"Perhaps." Hanni bandaged his arm. "You would do well to hold
your hopes with a loose hand. There may come a time when you'll
have to let Melaia go."

"But I love her."

"That's what love does, Trevin. Love lets go."

All the way to the council room, Trevin wrestled with Hanni's words. *Let go.* But how? Melaia was his hope, his inspiration. She was the silver to his gold.

The council room thrummed with tension. Lord Beker sat sideways on a bench, his legs stretched out, his back against the wall. Dwin stood beside him, a scroll in hand. Benasin paced the room.

Lord Beker motioned to Trevin with his twisted hand. "I asked Dwin to fetch this scroll." He paused, clearly in pain. "I'll not rest easy until you've read it."

Dwin handed the scroll to Trevin.

"It's sealed," said Trevin. "With Melaia's signet." He had no right to break the wax, but Lord Beker nodded, so he carefully tore away the seal and unrolled the papyrus.

His throat tightened at the sight of Melaia's handwriting, and he blinked to clear his eyes as he read. Then he frowned and reread it. "She appointed me heir in the event of her death." He was unable to keep an edge of panic from his voice. He stared at Lord Beker. "But she's not dead. Unless you know something I don't."

Lord Beker closed his eyes. "She's missing."

"Melaia is now the queen," said Benasin, "but since she is not here, someone must make decisions in her absence. Her writ points to you."

"We don't intend to spread the news that Melaia is gone," said Lord Beker. "As far as her subjects know, she has been in Navia. We'll announce her return but say she's in mourning and has appointed you, the heir of Eldarra and her betrothed, as her spokesman."

"Betrothed," Trevin said numbly. "Is betrothal what Melaia would want, or will she think I'm taking advantage of the circumstances?"

Lord Beker rubbed his forehead. "These are dire circumstances, and the people *must* accept a leader they trust. They'll easily believe you and Melaia are betrothed." "Will they believe she's here if they don't see her?" asked Trevin.

"Serai returned with the Erielyon," said Benasin. "If she's here, people will assume that Melaia has returned as well."

A knock sounded at the door. Dwin opened it, and a servant popped in. "I'm sorry to interrupt, sirs," he said, "but the guards are holding a messenger at the main gate. A Dregmoorian. He says he'll give his message only to the one in charge."

Benasin looked at Trevin.

Trevin looked at Lord Beker.

Lord Beker nodded. "You."

Trevin tossed the scroll to Dwin and strode out, his fists clenched. The one in charge was ready to choke a Dregmoorian. Any Dregmoorian. A messenger would do.

But in the courtyard Trevin saw Haden tending wounded Eldarrans, men who would judge their future king by his words and actions. He took a deep breath, unclenched his fists, and tried to look like a man in charge.

At the main gate two guards held their swords to the chest of the messenger, whose arms bore feathered etchings, the sign of servitude to the hawkman.

Trevin stood tall. "I'm Prince Trevin." How awkward it sounded.

The messenger handed Trevin a scroll, bearing the seal of a hawk.

Trevin snapped off the seal, opened the scroll, and silently read.

Your princess is a guest in the Dregmoors.

In exchange for her life, you will send

the two kyparis harps to Lord Rejius

within a fortnight.

Trevin glared at the messenger. "How do I know this is true?"

The etched man inclined his head. "As I've not read the message, I cannot vouch for its truth, but I was told it deals with a trade, and that the risk is far too great for you to believe the message a lie. I'm to carry back a reply."

"Reply that I will make the trade, but I require proof that what's offered in trade is in good condition." Trevin motioned to the guards.

"Hold this man until I can send my own envoy to get proof that he tells the truth."

Trevin tramped to the palace, clenching the scroll as though it were Lord Rejius's neck. Surely the hawkman would not harm Melaia. Not yet. But his stomach knotted at the thought of Melaia in the caverns of the Dregmoors.

Halfway across the courtyard he stopped in his tracks and slapped the scroll against his fist. "Blast!" he said. He had no harps.

CHAPTER 17

Melaia rubbed her arms as she paced the uneven stone floor of her new, windowless cave-cell. Five paces wide, five paces long. The heavy iron door helped to diminish the sulfurous odor of the Under-Realm, but a cold draft crept in from somewhere. While it carried a welcome breath of untainted air, it also chilled her and fluttered the single lamp flame, creating fingerlike shadows that fidgeted across the curve of the ceiling.

Weary and shivering Melaia lay down on a straw-filled mat and drew out the two pendants from beneath her tunic. Clenching the small harps in her fist, she fell asleep.

Sometime in the night a whisper roused her. "Melaia?"

She rose to one elbow. The lamp flame had died, drowning the cell in thick funeral black. Without windows she had no way to tell when morning came, but her groggy head told her she had not yet slept a full night.

"Melaia?" The voice sounded a bit like Trevin.

She rose to a crouch and backed against a wall, staring into darkness. Was she awake or dreaming?

"Melaia, it's safe. Come up."

A flickering, thread-thin line of light shot halfway up the center of the back wall. She crawled across the floor, ran her hand up the line, and discovered that it was a crack that allowed light to seep through, along with the slightest breath of air.

"Melaia, do you hear me?"

The voice was Trevin's, yet not Trevin's. Was it his spirit? Was it a trap?

"Melaia, wake up."

"I'm awake," she murmured into the crack.

"Come up," the voice repeated. "Slide the stone aside."

Melaia edged her fingers around the lip of the crack and tugged. The stone slid sideways with a scraping sound. She stopped for fear a guard would hear.

"Keep going. A little farther."

Melaia felt along the base of the stone and discovered a carved groove that it slid across, which obviously went unnoticed in the dim light of the cave. She gripped the edge of the stone and heaved it along the groove with all her might.

The slab of rock shifted, widening the crack enough to see light filtering down an ascending stairway crudely carved out of stone. Again she tugged at the slab. When the crack grew wide enough, Melaia eased through the opening and squinted into the glare of a lantern at the top of the stairs.

Its owner's face was in shadow, but the lantern bobbed as if it were pleased. "I'll not come down, but you can climb up."

The light invited her, the fresh air drew her, and the voice hooked the core of her heart. She climbed.

As Melaia neared the top of the steep stairs, she sensed the man as Angelaeon, a rich, dark purple. He hung the lantern on a rock that jutted from the wall and then grasped two crutches, fitted them under his armpits, and retreated, giving her room to enter. He wore a neatly trimmed beard and mustache, but he was bald on top. The rest of his brown hair, salted with white, hung to his shoulders, but it was his eyes that arrested Melaia. They were Trevin's. Older, yet Trevin's just the same. She opened her mouth, but words fled her.

He bowed as far as his crutches allowed. "I'm Arelin."

"Trevin's father," she murmured. "The Asp."

"As some call me." He strode quickly and steadily on his crutches to the far side of the room. "Come in."

Swathes of fresh night air flowed through a waist high, unshuttered window. The moonless view lay cloaked in darkness, but she could hear the rush of the river below and suspected that daylight would reveal the same scene she had spied from the crack in her previous cell. All the windows in this cave realm seemed to open on the cliff side, overlooking the Davernon toward a forested Camrithia on the far shore.

Melaia inhaled deeply, waking to the hope of escape. The Asp would help her leave the Dregmoors. Maybe tonight. She followed him past shelves that contained a good number of scrolls and a variety of strange relics: a bone, a painted ball, a mortar and pestle, a long, white plume.

Arelin lowered himself to a chair beyond a glowing brazier. He nodded at a low table beside him. "Water is in the pitcher, bread in the basket, fruit in the bowl. Help yourself."

Melaia poured water into a stone cup, eyed the dates and dried apricots, and took a round of seeded wheat cake. "Do you want some?" she asked.

"Wine for me." He pointed at a jar and dipper. "Add some to your water if you wish."

Melaia did not want wine, even watered. Now that she was fully awake, she wanted to stay alert to hear the plan of escape. She served wine to Arelin and then sat on a mat on the opposite side of the brazier.

"We've a bit of time together," he said, "but you must be securely back in your quarters before morning."

"You can't help me escape?"

"And throw away our best chance yet?" He sipped his wine.

"Chance of what?"

"Of restoring the stairway and its protective tree."

Melaia leaned forward. "That's my hope as well."

"I know." Arelin cocked one eyebrow. "Rejius plays his game and we play ours, which means we remain alert and change plans as necessary. So I have a strategy. Just be aware that if you went missing, your cell would be searched, and my stairway might be discovered."

Melaia could hardly look away from his eyes, which were distractingly like Trevin's. "Are you a prisoner here too?"

Arelin saluted with his cup. "I'm the product of my choices, some good, some . . . less than satisfactory."

"What is your strategy?" She quickly added, "I might as well warn you, I ask questions, which frustrates some people. Even –" She started to say Trevin, but her throat tightened. "Even my best friends."

Arelin plucked a date from the bowl. "I'm open to questions. I may have a few of my own. You know I'm an angel?"

Melaia nodded. "So was my mother, Dreia. Did you know her?"

"I'm quite familiar with Archae," he said. "I happen to be Exousia, warrior and keeper of history. At the time the Wisdom Tree fell, I lived north of here. During the Angel Wars that followed I fought on the side of the Angelaeon, but I was not in complete favor with them."

"Why?" Melaia munched on her bread.

"Because instead of pressing for complete victory, I supported a truce with the malevolents. You'll ask why, I suppose." He half smiled, like Trevin.

Melaia nodded, wishing that Trevin sat on the other side of the brazier and that the brazier was in Redcliff or Eldarra or anywhere but here.

"I watched too many friends die in the war," said Arelin. "Friends on both sides. At least half of this world's angels were slaughtered. If we destroy ourselves, what hope remains for the restoration of the stairway?"

"Was the truce made?"

"It was, but as the skeptics predicted, the opposition did not drop their grievances against the Most High. Instead they regrouped in support of the immortal Firstborn. At least we stopped fighting each other. Those of us who did not support the Firstborn pursued our futures in the world of humans. I ended up in the mountains of Montressi, defending that small kingdom from invaders, mostly wolves."

Arelin rose on his crutches, strode to the shelf, and removed an egg-shaped stone. "Prince Cadian of Montressi gave this to me." He rubbed the polished, gray mottled stone. "Side by side Cadian and I battled bandits and united the mountain people. His family became my family. His younger sister, Ambria, was like a sister to me. Then one autumn the Dregmoorians invaded Montressi and slaughtered Cadian and his entire family. All but Ambria." He handed the stone to Melaia.

"And you." She stroked the smooth surface.

"And me," said Arelin. "Ambria had married Kedemeth of Eldarra and lived in Flauren at the time. I was visiting the scriptory in Aubendahl when I heard news of the attack. I led Eldarrans into Montressi and retook the region, which has been an Eldarran province ever since."

Melaia handed the stone back. "Did you move to Flauren?"

"I stayed in Montressi as governor." Arelin set the stone back on the shelf. "When the plague swept through Eldarra, Ambria and Kedemeth sent their three children to me in the mountains to spare them from the disease. One day a wandering bard journeyed through Montressi, and I invited him to my manor. Unfortunately along with his entertainment, he brought the plague. All three children took ill and died."

"That's terribly sad," said Melaia.

Arelin leaned against the shelf and stared out the window into the night. "Ambria and Kedemeth were gracious. They forgave me long before I forgave myself."

"Is that when you came to the Dregmoors?"

"Soon after. You know about Windwings?" He slipped the white plume off the shelf and handed it to Melaia.

The feather was as long as her arm. "Did this come from a Windwing?" she asked.

Arelin nodded.

"Trevin told me the Dregmoorians tried to breed their horses with Windwings."

"That's why I led warriors into the Dregmoors. To free the Windwings. We succeeded for the most part, but only after fierce fighting. I was injured by a woman warrior, who battled as fiercely as I've ever seen. She fought me to the edge of a cliff, and I jumped, thinking I could make it to the ledge below, but I miscalculated and paid the price." He patted his leg. "She jumped after me and made it, and I laid down my sword. I assumed she couldn't kill me."

"Because only an angel can kill an angel?" Melaia ran her finger along the edge of the feather.

"Right," said Arelin. "But oh, how I wanted her to finish me off – first because I was in agony, second because dead, I'd be done with my grinding guilt over the deaths of Ambria's children. If I had known the warrior was able to kill me, I might have begged her to. As it was, she took me as a prisoner."

"But if she wasn't an angel –"

"She was immortal, the daughter of the Firstborn. I had heard her story, of course."

Melaia handed the feather back. "The legend of the Wisdom Tree. I've told it dozens of times."

"Perhaps you understand, then, why my heart went out to Stalia. She imprisoned me here in the cliffs, but I pitied her, for she was lonely. She often visited my cell to talk, hungry for advice and encouragement. Eventually we fell in love."

Melaia wrapped her arms around her knees. "What then?"

"Stalia decided to free me so we could marry. I posed as a malevolent." He pushed up his sleeves to show the feather etchings covering both arms. "Though Lord Rejius was not overjoyed with his daughter's choice of husbands, he tolerated 'the cripple,' as he called me."

"Was Varic your son?"

"He was Stalia's son. Her husband – Varic's father – died in the war. I tried to influence Varic for the good, but Rejius filled his head with fear and violence and used the boy for his own ends."

"What about Trevin?"

"He is our son, Stalia's and mine. I should have sent him to safety when he was an infant. If we had known –" Arelin returned to the brazier and stirred the coals.

Melaia stared at the flame. How many times had she and Trevin sat entwined in each other's arms, watching embers of a fire glow to a red gold before they put another log on?

Arelin cleared his throat. "I had no premonition that my position here was crumbling. Our world crashed the day Stalia found her uncle, Benasin, in a cell and discovered that Rejius abused him daily. Late that night we drugged the guards, freed Benasin, and sent him out of the country. Rejius was livid when he found out."

"What did he do?"

"I think he would have killed Stalia if she hadn't been immortal. Instead he ordered her to kill me and Trevin. Fortunately I had a handful of trustworthy friends. I sent one to Ambria with a message advising her to watch for my son's arrival and requesting that she raise him as her own. That was my atonement, giving Ambria a child to replace the three whose deaths haunted me."

Melaia warmed her hands over the brazier. "Why didn't you and Stalia and leave too?"

"Because Rejius enjoys nothing better than to hunt quarry."

"The way he hunts Benasin for sport?"

Arelin clenched his jaw. "Can you imagine our life on the run, never safe, never truly free? We stayed, but we had to convince Lord Rejius that Stalia had followed his orders. Trevin had a malformed finger, which Stalia cut off as proof."

"That's awful."

"Better a finger than a life. Stalia presented it to Rejius, along with the ashes of a pig, to show that she had obeyed his command to kill the child and burn his body. Meanwhile I sent Trevin from the Dregmoors with a nurse."

Melaia looked away from Arelin's pained face. "What about you? She was supposed to kill you, too."

"We stole a corpse, dressed it in my clothes, and staged a burning. I've quartered myself here in the cliffs ever since."

"You never have been discovered?"

"I keep my distance from malevolents and the Firstborn so they won't sense me, and I've tunneled a system of crawlways and linked rooms. I learn all I can about the workings of Rejius's mind and his kingdom."

"Does Stalia know?"

"A well-used tunnel connects her quarters and mine." Arelin winked. "Why do you think she moved you?"

Melaia couldn't picture Arelin in a continuing relationship with the Firstborn's daughter. She knew of Stalia as Lady Jayde, the imposter who had almost tricked her way into ruling Camrithia. "Most High, have mercy," she murmured, narrowing her eyes. "Stalia tried to marry my father, and all the while she was your wife!"

"That entire episode was a complication we hadn't anticipated," said Arelin. "Lord Rejius came up with the idea of establishing a beachhead in Camrithia by marrying Stalia to King Laetham. Stalia couldn't very well refuse on the grounds that she was already married. As far as Rejius knows, I'm long dead. I do have supporters who are aware of our relationship, but Stalia and I are very careful about who we trust."

He leaned forward, his eyes full of expectation. "I've always believed that if I could bide my time, I would one day be able to undermine the structure that undergirds the Firstborn's tyranny. Now that Dreia's child is here, the time is right for us to make our move."

"*Our* move?" Melaia frowned. "I'm not interested in Lord Rejius's political maneuverings. I just want to escape my cell, unite the harps, and find Trevin."

"I'd like to find him, too," said Arelin. "I lost track of him when he was a child and found him again only when a reliable source located him at Caldarius. With you." He half smiled. "I now make it my habit to learn about my son. I scry him on occasion, but I haven't seen him in a while."

Melaia gripped the edge of the table. "Did you see the attack on the Eldarran caravan? I don't know exactly where it happened –"

"In the mountain pass." Arelin rubbed the corners of his mouth.

"What happened to Trevin?"

"He was badly injured and spent some time recovering under Ambria's care in Flauren."

"So he's alive!" Melaia could hardly sit still. "Where is he?"

Arelin hauled himself up on his crutches. "My scrying is tenuous these days, but we can try to see him."

Melaia followed Arelin to the window. The ledge, an arm's length deep, held a jumble of items, including a clear, wide-mouthed jar of water. She watched closely as Arelin swirled citrus scented oil into it.

After squinting at the swirling oil water for an uncomfortable length of time, he scowled. "I fear my scry-bird has deserted me, but I've been told Trevin fought at Redcliff when the gates were breached."

"Redcliff was attacked?"

"For a time the city was under siege, but I hear the attackers were routed."

Melaia peered into the night as if she could see Redcliff, half a kingdom away.

Arelin swirled the oil water and shook his head. "Maybe tomorrow."

A fresh breeze ruffled a bit of embroidered fabric that lay among the jumble of items on the window ledge. Melaia frowned at the familiar embroidery and pulled the cloth out of the pile. It was Peron's cloth doll.

Melaia gaped at Arelin. "You!" She shook the doll at him. "Peron homes to you. You use *Peron* to scry."

He leaned wearily on his crutches. "It's not –"

"It *is.* It's her doll. I ought to know." Melaia stormed to the stairs. "I thought I could trust you, but now I see the truth. You'll use me for your purposes, just as you use Peron!"

"Wait." Arelin's voice was too much like Trevin's. "You *can* trust me. Hear the story."

Melaia swiped at her tears. "I don't want your story. I can't bear it."

"At least leave the doll here. You'll be hauled before Rejius if you're found with it."

Melaia hesitated at the top step and then flung the doll at Arelin and half-ran, half-tripped down the stairs into the dark.

CHAPTER 18

Trevin slumped back on the throne as the steward finally shut the doors to the outside world and Lord Beker dismissed the scribe.

"Did you note the length of that line of petitioners?" Trevin asked. "There were enough people to populate the entire city of Redcliff and its environs." He huffed. "I think most of them came merely to gawk at me."

"Can you blame them?" asked Lord Beker. "I'm sure they've heard a wagonload of rumors."

Trevin could only guess what tales the wagging tongues were spreading. The official rumor was that Melaia, in mourning, had appointed him temporary regent under her counsel until she felt able to resume her duties, but other rumors circulated about comains jostling for authority. Who knew what else was whispered in the streets?

"Must I hold audience again tomorrow?" Trevin asked.

"Every day until you leave for the Dregmoors." Lord Beker cleared scrolls from a side table. "Melaia needs you to leave her kingdom as stable as possible. You're a confident, capable man, appointed by the queen. Don't let her people think otherwise."

"Of course, Lord Beker." Trevin squared his shoulders and returned to what he hoped was a kingly demeanor. Heir to two thrones, he might as well accustom himself to royal duties. "It's just that I find it hard to concentrate on anything other than where Melaia might be – and Dwin."

He had sent Dwin as an envoy to the Dregmoors with instructions to insist on seeing Melaia with his own eyes to make sure she was unharmed. There would be no trade until he had proof. What's more, because he had nothing to trade, Dwin's trip was a play for time. While trusted Angelaeon were searching for Jarrod, sylvans were making copies of the original harps in case the search failed. Trevin intended to head for the Dregmoors with the harps, real or the fake, as soon as Dwin returned.

He stepped down from the throne and unfastened the lion brooch at the neck of his cloak. "Jarrod's done for if Dwin finds him first."

"Dwin won't have time to search for Jarrod," said Lord Beker. "He'll be too busy navigating Dregmoorian intrigues."

"Which may include Jarrod by now."

Lord Beker gathered a group of scrolls. "Before King Kedemeth headed north, he left these five for you."

Trevin selected one and coaxed open the seal. "Any news from King Kedemeth?"

"His men secured all roads between here and Eldarra and destroyed a storeroom of gash at Dahl."

"Gash at Dahl. I'm not surprised." Trevin scanned the scroll. "These are rules and regulations of Eldarra."

"Worthy reading for the heir."

A page entered. "Excuse me, Sire."

Trevin stood tall. "Yes? Is there news of Jarrod?"

"I wouldn't know, Sire, but Livia seeks audience with you."

Trevin tossed the scroll onto the table. "Send her in."

The page scuttled out as Livia entered with a large bundle the size of a harp.

"Did you find Jarrod?" asked Trevin. "Or is this –"

"It's one of the harps you commissioned." Livia handed it over. "It's made of zilwood, which is often mistaken for kyparis. We can only hope Lord Rejius doesn't know his woods."

Trevin knelt and unwrapped the harp. "The zilwood looks like a good match." He stroked the letters carved into the soundboard.

"The runes were a matter of some debate among the sylvans," said Livia. "They asked me the spelling of 'awaken,' but I was of absolutely no help. I know of only one person who is accurate in the old tongue."

"Jarrod," growled Trevin. "If he hadn't taken the real harps, we could have copied the runes exactly."

"And Melaia might still be with us, and *you* might still be wandering somewhere in Eldarra."

"Don't remind me." Trevin clenched his jaw.

"Jarrod made some foolish choices," said Livia. "So did you. All you can do now is take the next step."

"How do I know it will be the right one?" asked Trevin.

"You don't," said Lord Beker. "All you can do is set your feet in the direction of your goal and move forward."

"In that case my feet are pointed to the Dregmoors." Trevin rewrapped the harp. "What about the second harp?"

"It should arrive tomorrow or the day after," said Livia.

"Maybe Dwin will be back by then," said Trevin. "Maybe he'll bring Melaia with him, and I won't need the harps after all." He tried to give Livia a confident smile, which she returned, but he knew they were not fooling each other. The kyparis harps were with Jarrod, Melaia was in the Dregmoors, and the stars were aligning. She would not return to Redcliff until she completed her task – if she completed it.

Livia bowed out, leaving Trevin clutching the wrapped harp in the center of the throne room. He did have a back-up plan. If Lord Rejius did not accept the fake harps in trade, he would offer the hawkman one other item: Stalia's son. Once before, he had offered his services to Lord Rejius, and he had landed in a drak cage. This time, if it would buy Melaia's life, he would willingly play the hawkman's game to the death.

❖❖❖

Melaia's anger at Arelin fueled her pacing for an entire day. At least she assumed a day had passed. She estimated time by meals, one in the morning, one in the evening, brought by the sullen woman who had accompanied her in the carriage from Navia. But Melaia's anger was spent, and now she was bored. Completely and thoroughly bored.

She scanned the back wall. No lighted crack. When she held the oil lamp to the wall, the light revealed only the mottled shades of roughcut stone. No matter. She turned away. Arelin had used Peron. She would not go to him.

Instead she drew her mother's book from her pouch. She had read through it three times, searching its blank pages in vain for some sign of the harps, but maybe this time it would yield a clue. For a moment she simply held the book to her heart to feel its comforting hum. Then she turned to the back and stared at the blank pages, waiting for lines to form a picture that contained some clue about where Jarrod had hidden the harps.

The only picture that appeared was on the last page, and it revealed the same silhouetted figures the page always showed, which meant the third harp had not been moved. The other pages were dark. The harps were still wrapped.

Melaia closed the book. Why had she thought only she could unite the harps? She recalled the night the Erielyon had brought a message to the temple: *Now is payment due in full.* She had been told she was the payment, Breath of Angel, Blood of Man.

According to the story the price Benasin had to pay for taking the fruit of the Tree was the first creature that greeted him when he arrived home. Which was his niece Stalia. Rejius, her father, had refused to allow such a payment. Was that so wrong? After all, Dreia was also at fault, for she was guardian of the Tree. If she had not given Benasin the fruit, the Tree would still exist. So the debt was hers as well. Jarrod's point was logical. As son of Benasin and Dreia, why couldn't he pay their debt?

"Because Benasin is already paying," murmured Melaia. No matter how many times Benasin suffered and died, his spirit returned to his body. Every day he paid his debt as an immortal in a painful, mortal world. That left Dreia owing something of her own, something that did not also belong to Benasin.

"I am Dreia's payment, angel and mortal," Melaia murmured. That's why Jarrod could not and would not succeed.

As she slipped the book into her pouch, she chided herself for being such a dolt. Trevin or Dwin would have gone directly to Arelin for help, and here she was, only a climb away. Who but the Asp could discover where Jarrod had taken the harps?

Melaia ran her hand over the wall until she found the crack. Then she tugged the sliding stone along its groove and groped her way up the dark stairway.

"Arelin?" she whispered. A dim glow came from the brazier, leaving the rest of the room in shadows, but she sensed his rich, dark purple presence.

"Arelin?"

A rustling sound came from the depths of the room. Then she heard a murmur of voices, one a woman's.

"Give me a moment," said Arelin. "I'll fetch a light."

Melaia fought the impulse to crawl back down the stairs.

A light flared from the brazier and then settled into a brass lantern, which Arelin set on the table. Once again Melaia was caught by Trevin's likeness in his face. She looked around, but no one else was in the room.

"You couldn't sleep?" Arelin sat in his chair and leaned his crutches against the wall.

"I didn't know the time. I have no window."

He cocked his head. "Is this a friendly visit, or did you come to scorch me for cruelties I did not commit?"

Melaia's face grew hot with embarrassment. "I have some questions, but I can come back in the morning."

"You should be in your cell in the morning." Arelin yawned and folded his hands in his lap. "What did you want to ask?"

"Rejius keeps one of the kyparis harps in a room with statues. Do you know where?"

"I do," said Arelin.

"Do you know how I can get it?"

"The way will reveal itself when the time comes, which will be soon, I think. I've heard that the other two kyparis harps arrived, but I've not yet discovered where they are."

"I need them. All three. Will you help me find them?"

"In good time."

Melaia fingered her waist pouch. Did she dare trust him? Did she dare *not?*

"Anything else?" asked Arelin.

She took a deep breath. "I apologize."

"I've never turned anyone into a drak, Melaia. It's my business to help, not to harm. The truth is, I was not in a position to save your young friend, but I was able to give her a calming potion before the transformation."

Melaia's eyes filled with tears, and she looked away.

"I knew she needed to be treated gently," said Arelin. "So in a sense I stole her. Stalia brought her to me, along with the doll. Your friend then homed to me, and I cared for her, but I'll not lie to you. I haven't seen her for a while."

"I have. Lord Rejius has her. I'm sure of it."

Arelin rubbed his forehead. "I hoped she had flown far enough to break the tie. Some draks do."

"How far?"

"Across the sea."

Melaia doubted that Peron would ever fly that far. "If you hold Peron's doll, what draws her to Lord Rejius?"

"Her clothing?" Arelin's face softened. "Don't worry too much about Peron. I've trained her to spy on you and Trevin, so she's valuable. Lord Rejius won't treat her too harshly."

"He spies on Trevin?"

"With or without Peron, yes. You can be sure Lord Rejius knows exactly where Trevin is."

Melaia returned to her cell and slept fitfully, dreaming of harps and draks, Trevin and the hawkman, Dreia's book and the overlord's tower. Every dream ended in fire. She was glad to awaken to the turn of the key in the lock.

First the guard entered, followed by the taciturn woman, who served the morning meal. As the woman slipped out the door, another guard with intricate arm etchings ushered in a young man, who bowed, eying her through his black curls.

"Dwin!" Melaia clasped her hands to keep from hugging him, which would no doubt embarrass him and spoil his decorum. "Are you a prisoner here too?"

Dwin grinned. "I'm an envoy sent to verify that you're alive and well, my lady."

The etched guard poked Dwin in the back. "Take your look."

"Raise the light," Dwin barked over his shoulder.

As the guard lifted his lantern, light pooled toward the corners of the dirt-streaked cell.

Melaia wrinkled her nose. Darkness had done the room a favor.

Dwin scanned the cell. "Not exactly royal quarters." He glanced at the crack that led to Arelin's chambers. "You're well?" His eyebrows asked the rest of the question.

"Yes." Melaia nodded. "I'm well."

He snooped around her food like a dog looking for scraps. "You're not injured?"

"No, but I'm terribly bored. What's the news from Redcliff?"

"Trevin is prepared to trade two harps for you, but he wants to make sure Lord Reijus isn't lying about your well-being."

Melaia bit her lip in an effort to refrain from pelting Dwin with questions. Obviously they had found the harps. Perhaps Jarrod too. "You can't simply hand the harps to Lord Rejius," she said.

"Oh?" Dwin snatched the water jar in the corner, sniffed, and nodded, satisfied. "Watch what they bring you." He pointed to the jar. "It might not always be the real thing."

Dwin sauntered to the door. "I wish I could stay for more of your hospitality, my lady, but I'm off to Redcliff with my report. You'll hear from us." He nodded to the guards, and they left.

Melaia listened as their footsteps faded into silence. The sight of Dwin and his mention of Trevin had heartened her, but now that Dwin was gone, she felt lonelier than ever. She sank to the floor by the food tray. When she reached for her cup she saw, behind the water jar, a small, rolled scrap of papyrus. Holding it to the light, she unrolled it. Two harps had been inked in the center, placed together to make a heart. Trevin had signed his name underneath.

Chapter 19

Trevin knelt at the altar. He had always flung his prayers high and wide in the midst of riding the plains or battling a foe. Especially battling a foe. But he never had burned incense or bowed before an altar. Nor would he have done so now if Hanni hadn't insisted that he spend time in prayer before journeying into the Dregmoors.

He had protested, claiming ritual held little meaning to him, but Hanni claimed that ritual did not give the heart meaning. Instead the heart gave ritual meaning. Still he had resisted until she handed him the incense and pointed him to the spot where Melaia always knelt. That was what drew him.

On his knees in her place, Trevin felt Melaia's serenity. He bowed his head and basked in the peace of the moment. When he looked up again, the smoke of the spice-scented incense was thinning here, thickening there, forming the image of a tree. Its trunk grew, looming higher and higher. Then a distant, indistinct figure appeared within the tree, walking toward him. He knew her stride, felt her energy, sensed her silver pulse.

"Melaia!" Trevin reached for her, and the vision faded. For a moment he waited, barely breathing, his arms extended, her name on his lips. When the figure did not return, he sat back on his heels, his heart pounding.

"Foolish imagination," he said. Dwin had returned earlier that afternoon and had reported that Melaia was well, kept in a cell near Arelin. Such news brought limited comfort, for Trevin knew by experience that the hawkman was unpredictable and wily, and the Dregmoorian caves held danger at every turn.

Once more he knelt, but peace refused to return, so he rose and strode from the temple into the dusk. His next prayers would again be flung from the back of a horse.

The following morning at dawn, a small drak left the parapet of Melaia's tower garden and flew east, trailing two mounted and cloaked travelers, who rode out of Redcliff side by side. One was Benasin, the Second-born immortal. The other was the Prince of Eldarra, seed of wind, heir of fire, born to free.

"You can still turn back," said Benasin. "I'm at the root of this. You're neither the cause nor the solution, and you may come to grief before we're done."

"I know." Trevin kept his eyes on the eastern horizon. "My choices are entirely my own."

Benasin gazed ahead as if he could already see the Dregmoorian cliffs. "She's worth it. In your place I'd take the risk too." He broke into a gallop, and Trevin followed.

For three days they rode hard, changing horses at towns along the route. Two groups of warriors had gone before them to clear Dregmoorian troops from their way. The Camrithians under Main Catellus fanned out to the south, those with Main Undrian pushed north. At times the noises of battle sounded uncomfortably near, but Trevin and Benasin held to their path.

On the fourth day they rode through the eastern woods with its blighted trees bare and skeletal as if the season were midwinter instead of early summer. Beyond the woods lay the Davernon River. When they reached the riverbank they dismounted, and Trevin led the horses to the shallows to drink.

Benasin looked upriver and down. "I could have sworn this was where we were to meet the ferryman."

"I say we're too far north." Trevin studied the shadowy, cave-pocked cliffs across the river. The face of the bluff seemed to change shape, moment by moment, as the sun lowered. "We might find the ferry before nightfall if we head out now."

Benasin filled his water flask. "The river turns to whitewater farther south, and I'm not of a mind to trust the ferryman's skills in the dark."

"But I –"

"I know. You can see after nightfall, but I'm not so gifted. Nor, I wager, is the ferryman."

"Tomorrow then." Trevin walked out his stiffness. "Once we cross the river, where shall we go?"

"I expect a welcoming party will escort us to Lord Rejius. No doubt my brother knows precisely where we are."

"No doubt." Trevin scanned the trees and located the small drak who had been their constant companion. She fluttered from branch to branch, restless, which seemed strange. Normally when they stopped for the night, she plumped into a ball on a limb overhead.

Benasin set flatbread and dried meat on a large rock and uncorked a flask of watered wine.

Trevin rummaged through his travel bag for a packet of raisins to add to the meal. As he plucked it out he caught the edge of a net of finely woven silver that lay at the bottom of the bag. He had impulsively grabbed Varic's net from his trunk when he was packing. Used together, sword and cloak could be formidable in a fight. Sword and net might be just as effective.

As he stuffed the net back into the bag he realized that he felt no pain at the base of his missing finger. Usually the ache returned as he neared the Dregmoors, but it hadn't bothered him when he rescued the children, and it wasn't painful now. In fact his hand had not hurt since his confrontation with Stalia, his mother, the source of his terror dreams. The dreams and the pain had vanished at the same time.

After supper Trevin took the first watch. While Benasin snored he leaned against a tree and stared across the sloshing river. On the far shore some of the caves glowed with an inner light as if they were the open eyes of an animal in the dark. Other caves were dark pits in the cliff face. From one of the darker caves a figure in flowing white emerged and crossed the rocks at a daunting height.

Trevin walked to the river's edge for a better view. It was his mother. Stalia. Known as the ibex. Was she watching for him? Did she live in one of those caves? Her last words to him at Qanreef had been,

Come with me. Bring the harps. Bring Melaia. He had yelled back a defiant *NO,* but – blast it all – he had come.

The ibex glanced upriver before slipping into a dark cave. Trevin looked north as well. Over the water a mist crept toward him, steadily progressing south like a vanguard sweeping across a field. As he watched he realized it *was* a vanguard of sorts. A vanguard of spirits. On they came – men, women, children, dwarfs, sylvans.

As the spirits neared Trevin, they saluted with three fingers. He recognized one man as a Navian who had followed him into battle. Another was a Camrithian who had died on the bridge to Redcliff. Four were from King Laetham's guard, killed on the stairs to the king's quarters. Trevin held three fingers over his heart, but his stomach twisted. If the dead were massing and marching, had Jarrod already restored the Tree and stairway? Had he released these spirits? Had Melaia?

Seaspinner wove toward him through the mist. "Earthbearer blocked the flow of spirits into his realm, as he warned Rejius he would," she said. "The stars are aligning. The fate of the dead will soon be decided." She waved the spirits forward.

Trevin palmed the hilt of his sword as he watched them throng downriver. So the harps had not yet been united. He was right to be here, back at the place of his birth. *Born to free.* The freedom of the spirits, the Angelaeon, the entire world could depend on his choices in the next few days.

❖❖❖

From Arelin's window Melaia looked down on the mist of spirits that shrouded the whitewater below. A gentle breeze drifted in, carrying a soft, splashing whisper. "The stars are aligning. The fate of the dead will soon be decided."

Melaia turned to Arelin. "Did you hear that?"

"I did." Arelin smoothed a wax tablet with the blunt end of a stylus to erase the map of tunnels and caves he had drawn for Melaia.

She clenched her fists so tightly her fingernails bit her palms. "If the stars are aligning, I need the harps. Where are they? Where is Trevin? Where is the strategy you keep hinting at?"

"Our strategy is here." Arelin tapped his temple. "And here." He patted his heart. "We move as Lord Rejius does, and I hear that he is about to take a turn at his game. Stay alert – and get a good night of sleep."

"How can I do both?"

Arelin laughed. "I'll stay alert, and you get a good night of sleep."

Melaia trudged down the stairs to her cell. After her first meeting with Arelin, she had prayed for patience, but she didn't like the practice she was getting.

A thud woke Trevin during Benasin's watch in the wee hours of the morning. He sat up and saw Benasin lying on the bank of the river, an arrow in his chest.

Trevin snatched his sword and leaped to his feet, sensing the impure, olive colored presence of a malevolent. Gash warriors emerged from the woods on every side, their arrows trained on him. Some brute jerked him backward and clamped an arm around his neck. Another snatched his sword and dagger. Then a feather-etched malevolent strutted out, took Benasin's weapons, and tugged out the arrow.

The Dregmoorians grabbed the journey packs and the covered harps and hauled Trevin and Benasin upriver, where a raft waited. Two warriors escorted Trevin on board and tied him to a central post, while the others threw down the packs, along with Benasin's body.

As the ferryman poled the raft across the river, Trevin eyed Benasin, trying to determine if he was alive. He couldn't tell. The raft dipped and swayed, and he leaned his head against the pole, watching the woods of Camrithia fall away. *Welcome to the Dregmoors,* he thought.

Melaia estimated that it was late afternoon when guards ushered her to a lower level of caves and into what appeared to be an anteroom. Torchlight danced off polished, black marble walls. At her approach portal guards swept open two tall, gilt doors, and the guards nudged her into a cavernous chamber studded with gems. The floor was etched with a giant circle sectioned into six wedges, each marked with a symbol. The guards walked Melaia to the center of the circle and left her in front of the hawkman, who sat on his gilded throne.

Lord Rejius leaned forward, his gold-eyed gaze sweeping over her. "You like my throne room?"

Melaia gritted her teeth and bowed, forcing herself to be civil, for she had no notion of which way the tide ran for her mission. "It is truly a marvel," she said.

"You will address me as 'my lord.' Now let's begin again. You like it?"

"A marvel, my lord," said Melaia.

"Surely not as marvelous as these." He motioned to two harps carried in by gash servants, who set them at his feet.

Melaia stared at the harps, clasping her hands in an effort not to tremble. How did Lord Rejius get the harps? Where was Trevin or Dwin or whoever made the trade? Why had she not been freed?

"Come." The hawkman's voice was like ice. "Play one of them."

As Melaia knelt to choose a harp, her stomach knotted. The grain of the wood didn't look right. These harps were too new, and the runes were misspelled. One harp bore *Dedrumaki* instead of *Dedroumakei*, which meant "to awaken," and the other read *Tremlaki* instead of *Tremulakei*, which meant "to shake."

Watch what they bring you. It might not always be the real thing. Someone had gone to great pains to create these fakes, and Dwin had known about it, but what role was she expected to play? Was this Lord Rejius's ruse, his attempt to bait her? Or was it Trevin's doing? Did the hawkman believe the harps were real, or did he know they were fake? Maybe she could test him and find out.

She took a deep breath and picked up the harp that read *Tremlaki*. Surely he would stop her if he considered it real, for its music caused earthquakes.

Lord Rejius smirked at her and said nothing.

Melaia hesitated. The hawkman might be using her to discover whether the harps were real or fake. If so, choosing this harp would prove it was fake, because she would not knowingly play a harp that would bring down the mountain around her. She set it down.

She reached for the other harp, but Lord Rejius kicked it aside, and she recoiled. He picked up the first harp she had chosen and ran his talons down the soundboard, gouging long scratches. Then he shoved it into her hands, demanding, "Play this one."

"I don't dare, my lord," said Melaia.

He narrowed his eyes. "Why?"

"The runes, my lord. This harp will cause an earthquake."

"Play it," he barked.

Melaia felt her face redden. She held the harp close and plucked a melody. The tone sounded mellow and full, but the only thing it would shake was someone's cunning plan.

"Is this the kyparis?" hissed Lord Rejius.

Melaia stopped playing.

With his palm under her chin, he turned her face to his, cocking a single eyebrow. "Is this harp kyparis?"

"You know the answer, my lord."

"So I do." He released her chin. "Kyparis is a hard wood. Zilwood is softer, easier to scratch. And whoever carved these runes must think I'm ignorant." He snatched the harp from her hands and dashed it against the wall. The strings twanged as the frame snapped.

"Do *you* think I'm ignorant?" He grabbed the second harp and smashed it against the steps to his throne. "Do you?" he shouted.

Melaia shrank back. "No, my lord. I've never thought you ignorant."

"So you say." He tugged her to the door. "Come and see how I treat guests who think I'm ignorant."

As they strode through the anteroom, Stalia swished in, her sheer white cloak flowing around her. "Where are you going?" she asked.

"To see my guests." Rejius pushed past her, hustling Melaia along.

"Exactly my interest. I heard you had guests." Stalia followed. "I'm here to learn about them."

"Of course you are," said Rejius. "One of them is your son."

Chapter 20

Sunlight streamed through a gap in the cavern's rock ceiling and crept slowly across row upon row of stone statues far below. High above the cavern floor, Trevin wondered if the beam of sun edging his direction would eventually shine on him and Benasin. Chained to the rock face, his arms ached from their constant outstretched position. His legs and feet were cramped from hours of standing barefoot on the ledge, but because he was stripped to his leggings, when he tried to shift his stance, the rough stones cut into his back.

Although Benasin was dead, his immortal body had been treated the same and hung, rag limp, beside Trevin. "Good thing you're secured, or you'd tumble straight down," Trevin rasped. His throat felt as dry as sunbaked dirt. He shifted and grimaced. "You're not much company." He hoped the immortal's spirit lingered somewhere nearby, but there was no answer, only an intermittent whimper, which he attributed to the birds roosting in the rocks high above the tunnel mouths that pocked the cavern walls.

Trevin tugged at his wrist cuffs again, in case they had loosened. "Remember when we escaped by running through the statues down there? Escape would be welcome right now. Benasin?" There was no answer. "Oh Most High!" he whispered. How long would it take to die?

A movement crossed the floor far below. The figure in black was Lord Rejius. The one in white, Stalia. The one in a plain brown robe . . . "Melaia," he rasped.

Melaia gazed in amazement at the rows of stone figures. Then Lord Rejius pointed up to his guests, and she cried, "Trevin!"

Trevin's answer came out as a cough. He straightened, hissing as the stones cut his back, but worse was the hot shame that flooded him. The courageous hero had turned into a pitiful pawn.

"Is this part of your game?" Stalia's strident voice echoed through the cavern. "You set both my sons against each other, didn't you? You wanted to see who would win. Is this the way you reward the winner?"

"This is the way I reward my deceitful daughter," said Lord Rejius. "Unfortunately your son inherited your deceptive ways. He tried to pawn off two zilwood harps as kyparis."

The hawkman tugged Melaia into a tunnel. Stalia stood for a moment, gazing at Trevin and Benasin. Then she, too, left.

"Life is twisted, Benasin," Trevin croaked. "I wanted Melaia to look up to me, but not this way."

A few moments later Lord Rejius appeared at the mouth of a tunnel on the same level as Trevin, but across the open expanse, a bow shot away. The hawkman drew Melaia to his side as Stalia joined them.

Trevin concentrated on Melaia's pure silver aura and stood as tall as he could, hoping to look indestructible.

"Treachery deserves death, my dear," the hawkman said to Melaia. "As you can see, Benasin has already died. You might prevent the young man's death by telling me where the true harps are."

Trevin gritted his teeth. Melaia was staring at him, and he would have shouted the answer if he had known.

Without taking her eyes from him, Melaia said, "My half-brother, Jarrod, stole the harps. That's all I know. I've no idea where he took them, and that's the truth. The full truth, my lord. Now let Trevin go."

Lord Rejius rested a taloned hand on her shoulder. "Jarrod? I believe he was apprehended this morning trying to steal the third harp. He mentioned nothing about having the other two."

"I told you what you wanted to know," said Melaia. "Release Trevin."

"First I must question Jarrod." Lord Rejius drew Melaia into the tunnel.

As Trevin stared after them, wishing for one more glimpse of Melaia, the sunlight fell directly on him. He squinted at the place where she had stood and saw that Stalia remained there, watching him. He closed his eyes. How sane was a mother who gloated over the torture of her son?

By the time Trevin opened his eyes again, dusk had claimed the cavern. He realized that he had dozed and fallen into a slump that looked much like Benasin's. He straightened, wincing at the pain, and felt something wet poke him in the ribs.

A bony, etched man stood on a ledge not a stone's throw away, holding a dripping wet sponge on the end of a pole. The sponge bobbed toward Trevin's mouth. He caught it in his teeth and sucked the moisture. Water. Fresh water. The man stayed, holding the sponge toward him as long as he took it.

Trevin nodded gratefully to the man as he lowered the pole. "So they want me to live a little longer," he murmured. "Not necessarily good news."

"Surely you wouldn't give up. Not *you*." The ibex strolled toward him, stepping nimbly from ledge to ledge as dusk seeped toward darkness.

"Are you here to taunt me?" Trevin asked. "A useless sport at this point, don't you think?"

Stalia crossed a lip of rock to reach him. "I see you've inherited my biting wit."

"You said I would come, and I've come," said Trevin. "Do what you want with me, but please see that Melaia is released."

Stalia took a key from her waist sash. "I don't know if I can do anything for Melaia." She unlocked his wrist cuffs and said, "Follow me."

Trevin rubbed his wrists as he watched his mother step across the narrow ledge. "Easy for you, ibex," he muttered. "You'll live even if you fall." He took a deep breath and edged across the wall behind her, reminding himself that he had crossed cliff faces before. But not lightheaded. He didn't dare look down.

As Trevin crossed the last gap from the ledge to the mouth of the nearest cave, Stalia grabbed his hand to steady him. She pulled him into the tunnel. "I would allow you to rest," she said, "but there's no time." She snatched a lantern from a wall bracket and dashed through the stone corridor, her sheer white robe billowing behind her.

Trevin stumbled after her as fast as his stiff legs would go, wondering what trickery she had in mind. Then he heard the whimpering sound, louder and nearer, coming from a side tunnel. Slipping into the tunnel he followed the sound to an open door a stone's throw away. He crept to the edge of the door and peeked in. Children lay on pallets behind bars.

Stalia yanked him aside and shoved him against the corridor wall. His eyes watered as the stones slammed his stinging back, but he threw a punch. A weak one. Stalia easily blocked it and grabbed him around the throat. Nose to nose with him, she hissed, "Senseless."

Trevin tried to protest, but he could barely breathe.

"Don't speak." She eased the pressure. "I know you want to save them, as do I, but do you know the way out? How will you escape leading a score of children with gash guards and malevolents on your tail? Their rescue is at hand. Trust me."

Stalia clutched his arm and trotted him out of the corridor.

Trevin rubbed his throat. "Are you . . ." He swallowed. "Are you the ghost lady? Do you rescue the children?"

"Silence." She jerked Trevin down one tunnel after another, pausing once in a while to scan an intersecting corridor. Then she slipped into a storage room and handed Trevin the lantern. Behind a stack of barrels, she slid aside a slab of rock, revealing a tunnel with a lower ceiling. Trevin followed her in, and she slid the door back into place.

Once more Stalia took the lantern. She hooked it onto a bracket and eased through a narrow gap in the rock.

For a moment Trevin considered turning back and searching for an escape route, but his legs felt as if they would buckle at any moment, and his stomach was a hollow, growling pit. He could die of exhaustion somewhere in the maze of tunnels or, with his luck, end up back in Lord Rejius's throne room. He slipped through the gap and entered another storeroom, smaller than the first.

Stalia was already pushing past a thick curtain. Trevin followed her into a spacious chamber furnished with a canopy draped bed, cushioned benches, a half-moon table, and shelves lined with gem-studded boxes, shapely vases, and delicate bottles of colored glass. On the far wall, veil-thin draperies fluttered softly in the night breeze that drifted through an open, latticed window.

"Verria!" Stalia called, tossing her cloak aside. A sapphire brooch pinned her gown at one shoulder. The other shoulder was brown and bare.

Trevin stared at her, trying to force his mind to accept the fact that she was his mother. She was no demure Ambria. How did a son relate to this kind of mother?

A dour looking woman entered and bowed. "My lady?"

Trevin suspected that the woman could see him from the corner of her eye, but she did not look his way or indicate that she was aware of his presence. She saw only what she was told to see, and heard only what she was told to hear. He remembered suggesting that the priestess Melaia do the same at Redcliff. That day seemed long ago.

"Bring a small supper," said Stalia. "Then leave me alone for the night. I wish not to be disturbed."

As Verria bowed and left, Stalia waved Trevin to a padded bench by the window. He gratefully sank to the seat, watching Stalia as a field mouse would eye a falcon. Their last encounter at Qanreef had not been pleasant.

Stalia tied back her black hair and rummaged through the contents of a trunk. "I told you at Qanreef that you and I desire the same thing. You didn't believe me, did you?"

"You expect me to believe a deceiver, a seductress, a murderer?"

She tossed a tunic at him, glaring. "I'm sure you're as pure as springwater. You've certainly never deceived or betrayed or killed have you?"

Trevin tugged the tunic over his head, glad to hide the heat in his face.

"I did only what my father commanded," said Stalia. "Besides I want the harps."

They hushed as Verria brought in a cloth-covered tray and set it on the half-moon table.

"My son will need boots . . . sandals . . . something for his feet." Stalia waved the woman out.

Trevin narrowed his eyes at Stalia. "The harps belong to Melaia. I intend to do everything I can to help her unite them."

"How surly you are." Stalia lifted the cloth from the tray and surveyed the meal. "I can return you to the cavern wall after supper, you know. Pin you there like an insect. But I suppose if I did that, you never would believe we're on the same side." She handed him a bowl of stew.

Trevin's stomach rumbled at the savory aroma. His mother could do whatever she wanted with him as long as he could eat first.

Stalia watched him slurp his stew. "I, too, wish to bring the harps together and restore the stairway to heaven."

"Only Melaia can unite the harps."

"Because she's Dreia's daughter?"

"And King Laetham's." Trevin licked his lips. "Breath of Angel, Blood of Man. That's the prophecy. She was born to the task. Just as I was 'born to free.'"

Stalia's eyebrows rose. "Who told you that?"

"Flametender named me, and Seaspinner told me about my heritage. But I plan to see that Melaia completes her task."

"I shall do everything in my power to ensure that you and Melaia succeed."

Trevin nearly choked on his stew. "*You* want to help? In that case, we've circled back to the subject of trust."

Stalia handed Trevin a round of brown bread. "All right. I deserve your wrath, but you should know I grieved for you."

Trevin ripped the bread in two and dunked half of it in his stew. "Maimed me, yes. Abandoned me. Haunted me. But grieved? I hardly think so."

She huffed. "I'm well aware that I cannot demand your respect, much less your love, but I ask that you hear me out. After that you can hate me if you wish."

"All right," he mumbled with his mouth full.

She folded her arms and leaned against a carved post that supported the canopy over her bed. "Take your time eating," she said. "The story is a long one. I'm starting with my youth."

"Stretch it out then," said Trevin. "I'll have a second bowl of stew."

Stalia's face softened into a near smile. "When I was a girl, my father, Dandreij – or Rejius as he is now called – saw me, his only daughter, as a trophy, a prize, a possession, while my uncle Benasin treated me as a person. He was as kind as my father was violent and unpredictable."

Stalia poured two goblets of spice-scented wine. "The day Benasin's old hunting dog died, I wanted to be the first to tell him, so I watched for him and ran to meet him in the field. I knew he would be sad. I did not expect him to be inconsolable."

She sipped her drink and set the other on a table beside Trevin. "Imagine how terribly guilty I felt when Benasin told my mother about his vow to take Dreia the first creature that greeted him on his return home. If only I had waited, perhaps a sheep would have greeted him. Or a pig. Or a bird."

Stalia sat on the edge of her bed and stared into her wine. "Benasin told me not to worry. He said he would beg mercy of Dreia when he returned the seeds of the fruit. But I offered to go with him. I *wanted* to go. The anticipation of a journey thrilled me, as did the prospect of seeing a guardian angel." She looked up sheepishly. "I must admit I was also enticed by the thought of making the trip behind my father's back."

Trevin mopped his bowl with his bread. "So did you see Dreia?"

"We didn't make it to the Tree. Rejius and his men rode in to 'rescue' me. I never had seen him as upset as he was that day. He refused to hear my explanation. Instead he beat Benasin senseless and scavenged his pack, crowing when he found the seeds. He swallowed one, ordered me to eat the other, and crammed the third down Benasin's throat along with so much water I thought Benasin had drowned." She fingered the stem of her goblet. "I'm sure you've heard how Rejius and his hoard destroyed the Wisdom Tree."

"Several times." Trevin took a sip of his wine. Peppery. He licked his lips. "When did you realize you were immortal?"

"Rejius married me off to the son of a tribal leader. My husband aged and died, my children grew old, and I remained in my prime. When Rejius realized that I would never grow older, he pawned me off, time and time again, in marriage alliances with tribal princes – for the sole purpose of adding their lands to his expanding possessions."

"Why didn't you run away?"

"I was frightened. Who can an immortal depend on but another immortal? Rejius provided my only longstanding security – but only if I remained obedient and loyal."

Trevin leaned against the wall and stretched his legs. "So how many half-brothers and sisters do I have from ages long past?"

"Not as many as you might think." Stalia set her goblet aside. "Rejius didn't want to contend with heirs, so he felt free to test his alchemy and shape-changing arts on my children. I shunned the men he married me to, although I did bear a child to a prince who helped Rejius breed Windwings."

Trevin folded his arms. "Varic?"

"A creative little boy corrupted by Rejius." Stalia pulled an embroidered cushion into her lap and fingered the poppy design. "I thought I could shield Varic, because Rejius was preoccupied with fighting the Angelaeon over the Windwings. Varic's father was one of the first casualties of that war. I fought as well."

She cocked her head. "That's when I met Arelin. You look a lot like him."

"So I've been told." Trevin pictured the broad-shouldered man reflected in his sword and was sorry that Rejius had confiscated the blade.

"Arelin was badly wounded," said Stalia. "I easily cornered him and could have killed him if I had wanted. Instead I decided he would be *my* trophy. For the first time in my life I chose my husband."

"Arelin was willing?" asked Trevin.

"Is that so hard to believe?"

"What did Rejius have to say about it?"

"Arelin posed as a malevolent, and Rejius thought a crippled angel was a great joke, an interesting twist in his game. He toyed with Arelin, but Arelin is no fool. He held his own and always kept Rejius guessing."

"Your father's tolerance obviously didn't last," said Trevin.

Stalia sighed. "Arelin and I released Benasin from a cell where Rejius was having him flogged. Somehow Rejius discovered that we had set Benasin free. He decided to use the occasion to rid himself of the threat Arelin and his son posed."

"Meaning me," said Trevin, "but how could a young child possibly be a threat?"

"You were not *any* young child. You're the son of an immortal and an angel." Stalia's hand trembled as she rubbed her forehead. "My father demanded that I kill both you and Arelin. Of course I couldn't. Neither could I leave you to Rejius. That's when I took your finger. It was crippled anyway. I presented it to Rejius as proof of your death."

Trevin studied his right hand. He had always imagined his missing finger as whole as anyone else's. Now he tried to envision his small finger bent and stunted.

"We sent you with a nurse to Arelin's friends in Eldarra. As for Arelin's 'death' we dressed a corpse in his clothes and staged a burning. We had already taken pains to create a secret dwelling within the cliffs, a place of escape in case of danger. That's where Arelin hides, and I retreat to him when I can."

"And betray him when you can?" Trevin ran his hand through his hair. "You were set to marry King Laetham if I recall."

"On Rejius's orders." Stalia lobbed the cushion to the head of the bed and rose. "Do you think I could simply say, *Excuse me, Father, but I'm already married to the angel you thought I killed years ago?*"

She paced the room barefoot. "I've only myself to blame. When Rejius returned after failing to kill King Laetham and win his throne, I was in a foul mood. I remarked that an underling could have done a better job of procuring the kingdom of Camrithia. Rejius replied, 'So be it' and sent *two* underlings."

"You and Varic," said Trevin. "But neither of you won the throne."

"Because of you." Stalia laughed. "*That* made a stunning countermove to Rejius's game – and a blow to mine. My own son faces me down and swears I'll never get my hands on the harps I so badly want."

Trevin studied his mother as she studied him. It was easy to believe her, but should he? Everything depended on caution – his life, Melaia's life, the restoration of the stairway, everything. "Why should I believe you?" he asked. "You played the part of Lady Jayde to perfection. Do you play a different part now, advancing the game in Lord Rejius's favor as he instructs you?"

"No." The word shot out like an arrow. "I'm on your side."

Trevin rose, his fists clenched. "Prove it."

"I freed you from the cavern wall, didn't I?"

"That doesn't prove you're on my side."

Stalia threw up her hands. "I was a child when the Tree fell, Trevin. A child. I had no idea what the destruction of the Wisdom Tree meant to the world. It was Arelin who told me. He says the stairway can be restored. It's the only way out for us."

Benasin's spirit stepped through the heavy curtain on the far side of the room. "She's trustworthy, Trevin."

"I intend to prove exactly that," said Stalia, unshaken at the sight of Benasin in his spirit form.

Trevin dropped to the bench, staring at Benasin. "You left your body hanging in the cavern?"

"I released the cuffs," said Benasin. "My body now lies on the floor among the statues. While Rejius watches my corpse, expecting me to enter my body again, perhaps I can move about undetected."

"Do you know anything about Melaia?" asked Trevin.

"She's safe in her cell," said Benasin.

"Cell," Trevin muttered. He hated picturing her in a cave-cell. "What about Jarrod?"

"Not as safe," said Benasin. "But that's hearsay. I've not seen him."

"If you had a part in releasing me, you have my thanks," said Trevin.

"The thanks belong wholly to your mother. It was her idea and her risk. I can vouch for her."

Stalia slumped to the bench beside Trevin. "I'm weary of being an immortal in a mortal world," she said. "I want to end it, to cross the stairway. That's the complete truth."

Trevin clenched his jaw. Stalia. Lady Jayde. The ibex. The ghost lady. Daughter of the immortal Firstborn. His mother. He took a deep breath. That's what he wanted. His real mother.

He opened his right hand to her. One thumb. Three fingers. No pain.

Stalia cupped her hands under his and bowed her head to his palm.

Her tears were warm.

Chapter 21

Melaia lay on her mat, haunted by the sight of Trevin and Benasin chained to the cavern wall. At last she gave up trying to sleep and paced her cell instead. Her heart wavered like the flame of her oil lamp. She was desperate to run to Arelin for help, but no light crept in from the hidden stairway, and she cringed at the thought of interrupting him in bed again.

When she could no longer bear the anxiety, she slid the stone aside and tiptoed up the stairs. At the top, a faint light flickered off the wall.

"Arelin?" she murmured.

He looked up from a lamplit desk, where he was writing on a scroll.

"Trevin was discovered entering the Dregmoors," said Melaia.

"Benasin, too, I heard."

She approached the desk. "Lord Rejius chained them to a wall high in a cavern. Can you help me release them?"

"It's too late." Arelin set aside his stylus.

Melaia felt the blood drain from her face. She could hardly breathe. She grabbed the edge of the desk to keep from collapsing.

"Most High, have mercy, I'm incorrigibly obtuse." Arelin hoisted himself up on his crutches and paced to her side. "I said it's too late, because Benasin's spirit was already free, and Trevin has been released."

"Oh!" Melaia steadied herself. "He's released." She hugged Arelin around the neck. "Thank you. Thank you."

"It was not my doing," said Arelin, "although I'd gladly take the credit in return for this kind of thanks."

Melaia reddened. "You didn't free him?"

"Stalia did. I think he's safe in her quarters."

Melaia bit her lip. *Safe* was not how she would describe Stalia, in spite of Arelin's story. "Can't Trevin stay with you?" she asked. "Can I see him?"

"Not without risk to the plan." Arelin stepped to the window and gazed into the night. "As long as you two stay apart, Lord Rejius will be torn in two different directions, which will serve us nicely."

As Melaia leaned against the window ledge, both relieved and disappointed, a black bird flew past only an arm's length away. Arelin shrank back from the window, but Melaia reached out, calling, "Peron!" She turned to Arelin. "Where is her doll? If I hold it, maybe she'll come."

"Do you truly want her to come? You know who sees through her eyes."

"You sound like Trevin."

"Do I?" Arelin half-smiled. "He must have a good deal of common sense."

Melaia found Peron's doll on the shelf. "Do you think Rejius saw me? Or you?"

"That I don't know, but the dark of night is in our favor."

Melaia stroked the doll's wool-fiber hair. "If you caught Peron, could you change her back to herself?"

"Not I. Benasin might. Or someone loyal to him."

"Loyal to Benasin? Here in the Dregmoors?"

"Few are pleased with the way Lord Rejius reigns, but most have neither the courage nor the means to stand against him."

"Did Benasin re-enter his body?"

Arelin shook his head. "Lord Rejius has it guarded. Until we can take it to a safe place, there's no reason for him to take on flesh again. If we can't free his body, he may have to wait until you restore the Tree."

"Do you think I still have a chance?"

"Many are working to give you that chance, but the choice will ultimately be yours."

"Help me get the harps, then. Help me take them back to Camrithia."

"That pathway may not be open." Arelin headed deeper into the shadows of his room. "Come. There's someone you should see."

Melaia followed as he slipped past a drape behind his bed and ducked through a narrow doorway into a completely dark tunnel. She groped along, listening to the Asp outpace her somewhere ahead.

"Is there no light?" she called as loudly as she dared.

Arelin's crutch steps halted. "I forget. I can see in the dark."

"Like Trevin," said Melaia.

"Is that so?" asked Arelin with a smile in his voice. "Fetch the lantern in my quarters. I'll wait for you."

Melaia groped her way back, grabbed the lantern, lit it by the lamp flame, and soon joined Arelin.

Their trek was not long, but the last few corners turned sharply, passing crevices tinged with the odor of prison cells. Arelin selected one, and they entered at a rear corner of the room.

Benasin's spirit stood in the center of the cell, glaring down at the prisoner, whose feet and hands were clamped in stocks.

Melaia's heart sank. The man's bare back bore the bruises of a beating and the lacerations of a flogging. His hair, long and hay-colored, hung wildly, half in and half out of the thong that bound it at his neck. Jarrod's spirit edged his body, and her anger at him melted.

Benasin huffed. "Who is worse – the one who flaunts evil, or the one who hides it under the guise of good?"

"I meant no evil," murmured Jarrod.

"Melaia was sold to Rejius." Benasin waved his hand toward her. "Trevin and I went through agony trying to procure her release. We failed."

Jarrod tried to raise his head. "Melaia?"

She stepped to Benasin's side. Jarrod's eyes were slits in his swollen, bruised face. "Most High have mercy," she murmured. "You've paid dearly. You're dying."

"I know, death-prophet." Jarrod's smile twisted with pain. "I tried for the harp." He snatched a sharp breath. "They changed the trap."

"He took precautions against a net like the one that caught Trevin," said Benasin. "Instead it was a lance to the thigh."

"And they still beat him?" asked Melaia.

Benasin's angry brow softened. "They wanted to know where he hid the other two harps."

Melaia's stomach knotted with guilt for naming Jarrod to Lord Rejius.

"I didn't tell," Jarod rasped.

Arelin stepped from the shadows. "Rejius will be back."

"Let him come," said Jarrod. "He won't find me alive."

"But the harps," said Melaia. "Where are they?"

"Jarrod told me," said Benasin.

"Serai?" moaned Jarrod as his spirit fought to stay within him.

Melaia knelt and brushed strands of his long hair back from his face. "She flew from the tower to find help."

"And arrived safely in the Durenwoods," said Benasin.

"Tell her . . ." Jarrod struggled to breathe. " . . . I'll meet her in Avellan."

Melaia blinked back tears. "I'll tell her."

"Restore the Tree." Jarrod bowed his head.

Melaia felt as if her insides were shriveling as his spirit eased away from his body and swirled cold around her. "My brother," she whispered. His spirit thinned and seeped away through a crack in the stone floor.

She hardly felt Arelin draw her to her feet, barely heard him say, "We should not linger." She numbly followed him from the cell, leaving Benasin's spirit bowed over Jarrod's body.

Arelin pressed her to hurry. Every step returned her to the present, to the seriousness of her situation. There was no question now. Jarrod would not unite the harps.

Before they reached Arelin's quarters, Benasin caught up with them. "The two harps are at Philea Falls," he said, a determined look in his eyes. "In the cave behind the waterfall."

"I know the place," said Arelin. "Stone Grove."

"Maybe you were right, Benasin," said Melaia. "You said I might need to restore the Tree where it was destroyed."

"I once told Jarrod the same," said Benasin. "I'm sure that's why he brought the harps here."

"All I need is the third harp," said Melaia as they slipped into Arelin's chamber. She couldn't stop trembling. She rubbed her arms. Jarrod had been foolish, but he had been brave, too. She couldn't afford to be any less brave than he. "We should steal the third harp today, before they change the trap again. I'll take it straight to Stone Grove."

"The third harp has been moved," said Arelin. "Those who are eyes and ears for me are searching for it now."

The sullen woman did not leave after bringing Melaia's morning meal. Instead she stood by until Melaia finished and then escorted her to a room that contained a pool of warm spring water. There she helped Melaia bathe and then dressed her in a gown of soft-flowing, purple fabric.

Although Melaia was grateful to be clean, she was too tense to enjoy the experience. "Why am I bathing and dressing?" she muttered. She expected no answer, for the woman never spoke, presumably because she understood only the Dregmoorian tongue.

"Lord Rejius is taking you to an assembly," the woman said softly.

Melaia tried to make eye contact, but the woman remained intent on draping the shift properly around a gem-studded sash. "What kind of assembly?" she asked.

"A trial," said the woman.

Melaia's stomach rolled. "Whose trial?"

The woman clamped her lips shut as a guard appeared and motioned Melaia to the door.

Once again Melaia was escorted to the black marble anteroom, where Lord Rejius waited in a cloak of iridescent black feathers that glinted blue and violet in the lamplight. His round, gold eyes studied her as she entered. Then he nodded his approval and led the way through an arched door into a corridor. Four bodyguards whose arms bore etched feathers accompanied them down the hall to a series of stone stairways that took them deeper into the earth.

With each flight of stairs they descended, Melaia grew more apprehensive. Jarrod had died, so the trial was surely not his, but it might be hers. She wiped sweat from her forehead as Lord Rejius paused at the entrance of a cavern so dark that Melaia could not see the other side. The only light came from a flickering lantern held by a man who stood at the mouth of a wide tunnel. He beckoned them forward.

As they approached the tunnel, a clatter of hoofs echoed from within. Two massive, black, winged horses emerged, one harnessed in front of the other. Melaia recoiled. The Firstborn *had* bred Windwings. These two pulled a gilded, jeweled chariot.

Lord Rejius linked his arm in Melaia's, walked her to the chariot, and hoisted her in. Then he climbed in beside her, and guards stationed themselves behind – two guards, she thought, but she didn't look. She couldn't take her eyes off the horses' beautiful, frightful wings.

The Windwings eased into a walk, drawing the chariot across the cavern floor. Melaia braced her feet and gripped the rig's round, gilded railing as the horses picked up their pace and entered the darkness of a wide corridor. She could see nothing ahead until the horses broke into a gallop. Then two dim lights appeared in the distance, one on each side, illuminating the stone floor. As they neared the lights, the chariot gained speed, and Melaia saw that the beams marked the end of the tunnel, the place where the floor disappeared.

Before Melaia could cry out, the horses galloped off the ledge and into total darkness, and her stomach lurched into her throat. They were airborne. Her knees felt weak, but she dug her nails into the chariot rail and forced herself to remain standing.

The trip was not short, although Melaia had no way of measuring the passage of time in total darkness. There was absolutely nothing to see, but she sensed the expanse of the cavern by listening to the echo of falling water, the sharp pip and flutter of bats, and the steady pulse of the horses' wings, which occasionally paused as they angled left or soared right. She preferred those more distant sounds to the nearer noises of guards shifting behind her, Lord Rejius's raspy breath, and the nervous tap of his talons on the railing.

Her thoughts wandered to Trevin – to the time he gave her a dried apricot and asked for her forgiveness, to the evening they first held hands in Qanreef, to their first kiss, to the sight of him hanging on the wall. Trevin was presumably safe now. Unless this trial was for him. Her palms grew clammy, and she tightened her grip on the rail.

At last two lights appeared ahead at the mouth of a tunnel. The horses folded their wings, glided between the lights, and galloped through the stone corridor, slowing until they came to another large chamber, where bare-chested, spear wielding guards waited to receive them.

Lord Rejius grunted as he disembarked, and Melaia eased out behind him, her legs wobbly. They followed the spear guards down a lantern-lit hallway, through an arched door, and into a chamber twice as large as Lord Rejius's throne room. More bare-chested guards stood among pink, green, and blue columns that encircled the chamber. Some columns were fully formed. Others hung down from the ceiling or jutted up from the floor. Melaia had seen the same type of formations, though not as grand, in the caverns of Aubendahl when she was escaping the talonmasters. With Jarrod. Her throat thickened.

Lord Rejius's bodyguards stationed themselves at the entrance to the cavern, and one of the pale guards stepped forward. He made no sign of deference to Lord Rejius or Melaia, but led them across the mosaic floor and left them standing on the image of a gryphon at the midpoint of the tiled pattern, which formed a giant multicolored star. Each point of the star extended about five paces from the center.

Melaia's pulse quickened. She had seen this place before, but from a different viewpoint. At the far side of the chamber, an arched doorway framed a small font that contained a bowl lamp with a flaming wick. Though she couldn't see past the font, she knew what lay beyond: an iron latticework gate that blocked a steep stairway leading to the library of Redcliff.

She clasped her hands in front of her, stifling the impulse to run to the hidden stairway and yell for help. Surrounded by guards with spears, watched by Lord Rejius and his bodyguards, she would have no escape. More important her purpose now lay in the Dregmoors with Trevin and the harps, Benasin and Arelin. No matter what happened in this trial, she had to return to her task.

"They keep me waiting," growled Lord Rejius.

"Who, my lord?" asked Melaia.

"Earthbearer and his cronies. Forcing me to wait is a strategy of the simple-minded. Perhaps they forget I'm immortal. Time means nothing to me."

Melaia shifted uneasily. A trial before Earthbearer? Was she guilty of some offense against the Archon?

She tried to calm herself by studying the mosaic floor. Each arm of the star contained a different design. Directly in front of her the point held a pattern of brown mountains and stones. To the right the tiles appeared as sea blue waves. Inlaid tongues of fire filled the point to the left. Behind them to the left, swirls of gray and white formed the design, while leaf shapes in every hue of green decorated the right rear section.

A deep melodic chant now rose from the guards and brought Melaia to attention. As their thrum echoed through the cavern, four mist-like figures entered. The Archae. Melaia knelt in reverence.

Windweaver swept in first, his long, white hair flowing and his cloak billowing as if he faced a breeze. Flametender strutted in behind him, dark of skin, her copper hair frizzing wildly about her face. Seaspinner, with the pale blue skin and short white hair of a water spirit, fairly danced across the stones. After her a black-haired, bare-chested, rock-brown man strode in, his coal black eyes surveying the scene. Earthbearer.

As the procession entered the star at the point in front of Melaia, she remained on her knees, her pulse pounding in her ears. Had the stars of the beltway passed alignment? Was she on trial for failing to restore the Wisdom Tree and its stairway to heaven?

The chant swelled when Earthbearer halted in the section patterned with mountain formations. Flametender took her place within the fire-designed tiles, while Seaspinner swept to the wave pattern. Windweaver breezed past to the section adorned with swirls, and the chant faded into silence.

"Rise, daughter of Dreia." Earthbearer's deep, stone-hard voice echoed through the chamber. "You are here to take your mother's place. Enter your domain."

Melaia blinked at the Archon, trying to understand. Was she not on trial? She looked around. When the other three nodded, she rose and stepped into the only vacant section of the star, the one patterned with leaves.

Lord Rejius remained in the center, flexing his talons, his jaw clenched.

"Rejius, formerly Dandreij, Firstborn immortal and guest of my realm," boomed Earthbearer, "you stand at the center of our council in the place of the Gryphon, whose realm of man and animal you have long abused."

Rejius held his chin high. "Is it your place to accuse me of abusing a realm you don't preside over?"

Earthbearer appeared unmoved. "I accuse you, Rejius Firstborn, not only of abusing the Gryphon's realm but also of encroaching on *my* realm. You brought the treacheries of the upground into my peaceful domain and used the bounties of Deep Earth to further your villainies."

"You welcomed me here," said Rejius.

"So I did, for the spirits of the dead had nowhere else to go as a consequence of your unbridled arrogance. You destroyed the stairway to heaven, their bridge to Avellan, assuming for yourself the responsibility for their afterlives. You could have discharged that responsibility faithfully, but you did not."

"Do you discount the protection I provide for the spirits?" Rejius slowly turned, addressing the Archae, his eyes as wide as an innocent. "Do you discredit the years I spend creating potions that renew the dead and extend the lives of the living?"

"For whose benefit?" asked Flametender. "Who is the beneficiary of their drugged servitude? Who reaps the rewards of compliant spirits so controlled?"

"I say you trifled with the alchemies of Deep Earth," said Seaspinner. "You took its gems and potions for your own use."

Rejius thrust a taloned finger toward Earthbearer. "He gave me that authority. He allowed me to rule the Shallows. He deceived me with his words of welcome. What more can you expect from the lie-monger?"

Earthbearer's chest swelled. "I am not in the habit of lying." He pointed to Flametender. "I sculpt molten rock that holds the heart of fire." He nodded at Windweaver. "I lift mountains and extend plains to sculpt the wind." He gestured toward Seaspinner. "I spread the stone that beds brooks, the mud that lines ponds, the scree that edges rivers and seas." He inclined his head to Melaia. "I plow my fingers through the soil that nurtures tree and flower."

Earthbearer narrowed his eyes at Rejius. "The lie is that the earth is the source and end of life. That lie is born not of me but of your kind, Rejius, you who consume and abuse the gifts of the earth."

"*That* is a lie," said Rejius.

"*That* is the truth," said Earthbearer. "I serve truth to those who refuse to believe, and so the lie is spun."

"You tie your reasoning in knots to exonerate yourself," said Rejius. "Let us come to terms and be done with it. Here is my offer: I shall limit myself to the Shallows and block access to the Deeps. I shall ensure that no one bothers you from this day forth."

"Bother me?" Earthbearer's voice shook the cavern. "What about the spirits that daily swarm into the Under-Realm? They arrive faster than you can deal with them. They fill your halls and walls and overrun mine."

Rejius extended his hands, palms up, as if he were blameless. He scanned the circle of Archae. Melaia suspected there was more to this discussion than she would ever know, but when Rejius turned his pitiful gaze on her, she knew she was not on his side.

"How can I satisfy Earthbearer the oath-breaker?" asked Rejius.

"I am not the one on trial for breaking oath," said Earthbearer. "You ask how I can be satisfied? My answer: We shall vote. Do we limit the Firstborn immortal to the Shallows, or do we banish him upground?" He snapped his fingers, and a steward entered, bearing a tray that held ten gems – five rubies, five sapphires – each the size of a large grape.

"Only a stone-hard heart would banish me," whined Rejius. "You think I'm welcome upground? I sacrificed myself to my experiments, and now I'm a miscreation, an unnatural beast, a hell-hawk. I'll be mocked and isolated."

"You sacrificed yourself?" asked Windweaver. "Now who knots reason?"

Rejius fumed as the steward carried the tray to each Archon in turn, starting with Earthbearer.

Melaia noticed that each Archon took one ruby and one sapphire. When the steward offered the tray to her, she took one of each as well.

Servants placed two pottery urns halfway between Earthbearer and Rejius.

"For the sake of Dreia's daughter, we should explain," said Seaspinner.

"We vote with these gems," said Flametender. "The ruby indicates a vote to allow the Firstborn to continue in the Under-Realm."

"Shallows only," said Earthbearer.

"The sapphire is a vote to banish him upground," said Seaspinner.

"The urn on your left, Melaia, will receive the votes," said Windweaver. "The urn on the right will receive the unused stones."

Earthbearer motioned for Melaia to follow him as the Archae slowly circled the star. "We walk three turns around and then place our stones in the urns," he said.

The Archae hid the stones in their cupped hands as they walked, so Melaia did the same, fingering the gems as if they were worry stones. Why try the Firstborn now? Why didn't the Archae simply wait to see if she succeeded in uniting the harps? Better yet, why didn't they force Rejius to release the third harp?

As Melaia circled the second time, she realized why – because angels did not interfere, they merely influenced. This trial served as their move in Rejius's game, their attempt to force his hand and provide her with an opportunity to unite the harps. But which way did they want her to vote? If she succeeded in uniting the harps, it wouldn't matter, but what if she failed? The grief of failure would be burden enough without the added guilt of having unleashed Rejius's tyranny upground.

During the third circuit around the star, as Rejius seethed at its center, the Archae lowered their hands to their sides in such a way that the gems remained hidden, one enclosed in each fist. Melaia noted which stone she palmed in each hand.

As Earthbearer finished the circle, he thrust one fist into the right hand urn. A single gem clattered in. He released the other gem into the urn on the left and returned to his place on the star.

Melaia followed, dropped the ruby into the voting urn, and discarded the sapphire in the other.

One by one the stones rattled into the urns. When all the Archae had returned to their stations, Earthbearer carried the voting urn to Rejius and emptied it at his feet. Four sapphires rolled out. One ruby.

Earthbearer left the gems on the floor before the hawkman and strode back to his place. "Only one voted to allow the Firstborn to remain in the Under-Realm," he proclaimed. "The decision is made. Rejius Firstborn, you are hereby banished from the Under-Realm for the remainder of your immortal days. You will leave within seven sunsets."

At the snap of Earthbearer's fingers, five pale guards stepped toward Rejius. He did not wait for them to reach him. He stormed toward the door, jerking Melaia to his side as he went.

"They will rue this trial," he muttered.

Melaia dared not complain about the tightness of his grip as they strode through the corridor toward the waiting chariot. But she wondered if the Archae had given serious thought to her safety.

Chapter 22

From Stalia's open window Trevin gazed east across desolate mountain ridges riddled with mines. As Queen Stalia's son he was heir to the Dregmoorian throne, the future ruler of this land, but in reality Stalia was immortal, so an heir was unnecessary. Besides, Lord Rejius was truly the power behind the throne. If the hawkman ever saw the necessity of having an heir, he would make the choice.

Voices murmured behind Trevin, and he sensed a deep, blue-purple presence. He turned to see Stalia embrace a balding man with a close-trimmed brown beard and mustache. When she backed away, Trevin saw the crutches.

"Arelin!" he murmured. "Father?"

Arelin strode easily across the room on his crutches, grinning as he studied Trevin's face. "I've waited a long time to hear that word." He swept his right crutch to his left hand and wrapped Trevin in a firm hug.

"Ambria gave me your sword," said Trevin.

"Did she reveal its secret?"

"He saw the truth of *me* in it," said Stalia.

"Ah, yes." Arelin gave her an amused smile.

"Rejius has the sword now," said Trevin.

"I wager he has no notion of its powers," said Arelin. "I'll get it back."

"The Asp has his ways." Stalia's voice sounded as alluring as Lady Jayde's. She nodded toward Trevin. "Upground our son is a prince. He has accepted his heritage."

"You follow a path I forsook," said Arelin. "Not the proudest moment of my life. But you –" His smile warmed Trevin. "I trust you will fulfill your destiny. We've much to share. Shall we start with an errand?"

Stalia frowned. "Is it wise to remove Trevin from my quarters?"

"Is it wise for him to be sequestered here?" Arelin nodded at Trevin. "I'll let you decide. I'm going to Stone Grove to ascertain the truth of a rumor that may be of interest to you. I've heard that two kyparis harps lie concealed near Philea Falls."

Trevin grabbed the boots laid out for him. "Lead the way," he said, tugging them on.

Moments later Trevin was following the Asp through pitch-black tunnels without lamp or lantern. He smiled. His night-sight came from his father, whose pace on crutches amazed him, as did the Asp's familiarity with the twists and turns of the underground maze. Trevin trotted to keep up.

The rushing echo of the cascading water grew louder as they entered the last corridor, approaching the falls from behind. Arelin held up his hand, and they paused, surveying their surroundings. A bowshot away, a veil of water spilled over the mouth of the tunnel, which smelled of damp earth and a whiff of rot.

Arelin crossed the dirt floor to a large, flat stone that lay atop a mound of earth. "I wager something's buried under there."

"The harps?" Trevin tugged away the stone. With sharp rocks he and Arelin dug through the soil.

A putrid odor set Trevin back on his haunches. "Smells like a dead animal."

Arelin rubbed his nose. "Not likely." He tugged at a russet fleck, which lengthened into a corner of cloth. "Were the harps wrapped in a cloak perhaps?" He delicately followed the hem of the fabric until he reached a dirt-encrusted emerald brooch the size of a walnut.

Trevin envisioned the sneer that matched the brooch and heard the slur aimed at him across the tavern in Dahl. "It's Hesel," he said. "I can't say I'm sorry."

"You know him?"

"A gash runner. Dealt in kidnaped children."

"I knew of him," said Arelin. "He was a friend of Varic's." He heaped the dirt back over the corpse. "With that jewel on him, it's obvious that robbery wasn't the motive. You think Jarrod killed him?"

"That's my guess." Trevin tugged the flat stone back over the grave. "I was told that Hesel provided Jarrod's way into the Dregmoors. Maybe they argued about the pay or the plan. Or maybe Jarrod didn't trust Hesel to keep quiet."

Arelin rose on his crutches and ambled back along the corridor, eying the rock. "Here it is." He edged through a narrow opening.

Trevin followed Arelin through the slit into a small room that had been recently occupied. A lamp and wooden cup sat on a stone ledge. On the opposite wall a rolled mat lay on top of two large cushions. A journey pack was on the ground nearby.

"No harps." Trevin picked up the cup, the simple kind used in the temple, and a small scroll fell to the floor. He squatted, unrolled it, and frowned. "This is a map to the the third harp, including a warning about the net trap. It was scrawled in haste."

Arelin peered over his shoulder. "What makes you think so?"

"Dwin writes this way only when he's in a hurry."

Arelin scratched his chin. "I saw Dwin recently when he came to check on Melaia. We met only briefly, but he said he was looking for Jarrod."

"He obviously found him, but I'm surprised Dwin helped Jarrod. He has good reason to shun him. For that matter, so do I." Trevin crushed the scroll in his hand and scanned the room again. "Could Jarrod have moved the harps?"

Arelin circled the cave, tapping his crutch against the rocks. None sounded hollow. "According to Benasin they're here."

"How did Benasin know? Did he speak to Jarrod?"

"He did. He was present at Jarrod's death." Arelin tapped the cushions with a crutch. "See what's in these."

Trevin gaped at him. "Jarrod died?"

"He was caught trying to steal the third harp. The trap had been changed to a lance. That was bad enough, but Rejius beat Jarrod to within a breath of his life in order to find out where the other two harps are."

"Did Jarrod tell?"

"He claimed not, and he died of his injuries before Rejius could question him further. But I want to make sure Jarrod told us the truth." Again Arelin tapped the cushion.

Trevin crouched and felt for an opening. "Sewn shut," he said.

Arelin handed him a knife and then rummaged through Jarrod's journey pack.

Trevin slit the seam of the cushion and reached in. He touched the soundboard, ran his fingers across the carved runes, and felt the strings. "This is it." He tapped the second cushion. "Shall we take them back with us?"

"They're probably safest here, due to the Lady of the Falls. Most folk are too frightened of her to come this way." Arelin took a yellowed scroll from Jarrod's pack and untied its red, tassled cord.

"Would the Lady of the Falls be Seaspinner?"

"The same," Arelin murmured, scanning the scroll. He stiffened and frowned. "God bless us. How did Jarrod intend to use this information?"

"What is it?" asked Trevin.

Arelin exhaled slowly. "It's something Stalia should see." He tucked it into his waist sash and headed out of the room. "We need to bring the third harp here."

Trevin followed. "How do we get the third harp?"

"That remains to be seen." Arelin picked up his pace as they entered the downhill tunnel. "The harp was moved, and my informants have yet to locate it."

"How many informants do you have?"

"I have a small, trusted network."

"Which once included Dwin."

"Still does, when he's here."

Trevin pondered the message Dwin had scrawled on the map. No doubt he had renewed at least some of his contacts on his last trip.

Enough to learn that the trap at the third harp had been changed? Trevin couldn't prove it, and he didn't intend to try, but he suspected Dwin had avenged Nuri by killing Hesel and sending Jarrod straight into Lord Rejius's trap.

❖❖❖

Lord Rejius shoved Melaia to a bench at the side of his throne room. "Your vote to oust me will be of no avail to you, my dear."

Melaia blinked at him wearily as she rubbed her arm where he had gripped her. "Mine was the vote to let you stay, my lord."

"Is that so?" The hawkman's gold eyes studied her. "Perhaps I misjudged you. If you are willing to play by my rules, you might go far." He strode to his throne and then whirled to face Melaia. "I'm truly a likeable man. You see that, don't you? You see why I should be allowed to stay here."

"Indeed, my lord." The hair on Melaia's neck prickled as he strolled toward her.

"It's for the good of mankind that I pursue my alchemies," he said. "Yet Earthbearer has no appreciation for my toil. He cannot admit that with his molten earth, I work a great good. My alchemies will bring an end to suffering. I'm to usher in an age of immortality for all people, but do the Archae see that?"

"It seems they don't, my lord, for the vote went against you. What will you do now?"

"That, my dear, I did not know until now." He took her hand and walked her toward the door. "I'll clean house before I leave, starting with three harps, which I'll bury in three different graves deep underground. One harp is already at its gravesite. You gave me the opportunity to discover the other two."

"So you found them."

"Not yet, but soon. One more meeting with Jarrod should yield what I wish to know."

Melaia's throat tightened. *Play your part,* she told herself. She cleared her throat. "After the harps are buried, what then, my lord?"

He paused at the door and breathed a mock sigh. "I'm afraid I'll be forced to go upground. Fortunately I have a companion who will go with me." He stroked her cheek with the back of a talon. "The Firstborn immortal and Dreia's daughter. A perfect coup. I should have thought of it sooner. People will not call me monster if you are at my side. Some already honor me as hawk-god, but now everyone will bow before me, for you, my queen, will worship me, and they will follow your example."

Melaia swallowed a bitter taste and tried to look pleasant. "If you desire me as your queen, then you must make a pledge to me, which I will receive if custom is followed."

"What custom, my dear?"

"You seal your pledge by giving me a token. Something of value."

He locked his gaze on her as he slipped a topaz ring from a talon.

Melaia shook her head and hoped she wasn't pushing her luck too far. "To seal the pledge," she said, "the gift must be something of value to *me.*"

Lord Rejius smirked. "What might that be?"

"A drak. The little one. Peron."

"A drak?" He laughed and motioned to a guard. "Bring the little drak." He drew Melaia toward him.

Her mind spun. If he meant to kiss her, she dared not resist. Peron, Trevin, the spirits of the dead, the whole of the Angelaeon – everyone depended on her.

She lowered her gaze and leaned into his embrace. The harp pendants beneath her gown pressed against her chest as the hawkman clutched her and kissed her neck.

Melaia climbed the stone stairs to Arelin's quarters as quickly as the weight of Peron's cage allowed her to go. She had slept most of the day with the cage in her lap. After supper was cleared away, she had eased the sliding rock aside. She could hardly keep her voice low as she ascended. "Arelin! Arelin!"

She heard his crutches crossing the floor. "I have Peron!" At the top of the stairs she proudly set down the cage.

"Shades!" Arelin tossed his cloak over it. "The hawkman sees through her eyes!"

Melaia reddened. It had not occurred to her that the hawkman might use Peron's new vantage point, but of course he would. "Perhaps he wasn't watching."

"We'll know soon enough. How did you manage to get her?"

"Rejius plans to make me his queen upground. I asked for Peron as a pledge of his intentions."

Arelin snorted. "A pledge of his intentions." He bent over his desk, dipped a stylus in ink, scratched a few words on a scrap of papyrus, and blew it dry. Then he tied a weight to it, slid aside a stone in the wall, and dropped the scrap in.

"What's that?" asked Melaia.

"It's a message from the Asp to Benasin, asking if he can change a drak into a little girl – at his earliest convenience." He sat down in his chair, eying the cloaked cage. "Tell me more about your conversation with Lord Rejius."

Melaia sat on the floor beside Peron's cage and told about her time with the hawkman, starting with his trial, ending with his intention to bury the harps deep underground. "The third harp is already at its grave," she said.

"Where is this grave?" asked Arelin.

Melaia cringed. "I didn't ask."

"Ask what?" Benasin's spirit entered, carrying a pack.

"Where the third harp is," said Melaia. "Lord Rejius intends to bury it."

"Old news," said Benasin.

Arelin cocked an eyebrow. "Oh?"

"At least a few hours old." Benasin chuckled. "I've located the third harp." He squatted by the cage. "Is this Peron? How did you catch her?"

Melaia repeated the tale while Benasin laid out the contents of the bag. One large flask, one small. Several pouches, the type Hanni used for storing small quantities of crushed herbs. Two sharp knives, one that tapered to a needle-sharp point. Staring at the implements, Melaia trailed her tale to a close.

"Trevin once asked me if I could change Peron back to herself," said Benasin. "I told him I never had tried to undo the transformation. Since that time I've given it much thought. I'm almost certain I can make the change." He looked Melaia in the eye. "Almost. Are you sure you want me to try?"

Melaia bit her lip and nodded. If Peron didn't survive the process, at least her spirit would be set free.

Benasin turned to his implements. "I suggest that you not watch."

"You were once a priestess, weren't you?" asked Arelin. "Go sit by the window and say your prayers." He gently drew Peron from the covered cage, his hands over her eyes.

Melaia stepped to the window, picked up Peron's doll, and knelt, listening to the quiet murmurs that passed between Benasin and Arelin. She was certain they would give Peron something to block the pain and keep her calm. Even so, she couldn't stop trembling. She leaned her head against the cool stone and prayed, and prayed, and dozed.

A soul-ripping scream brought Melaia to her feet, clutching Peron's doll to her chest.

Arelin rose to his crutches, mopping sweat from his brow. "She's back."

Melaia darted past him. "Peron?" She scooped the thin, blotched body into her arms and stroked the matted, black-streaked curls.

"Mellie?" Peron rasped.

"That scream will bring guards," said Arelin. "You'd best return to your cell."

"But Peron –"

"We'll take care of her." Benasin wrapped Peron in his cloak and took her from Melaia.

"Hurry now." Arelin waved Melaia toward the stairs.

She paused at the landing. "I don't know how to thank you enough."

From below came the grating sound of a cell door opening. Melaia dashed downstairs and yanked on the stone slab, but before she could close it completely, two guards were on her. One dragged her up Arelin's stairs, and the other followed with a lantern.

When they reached the top, Arelin's chamber was dark. As the light from the guard's lantern chased the shadows, Melaia held her breath, expecting it to reveal Arelin, Benasin and Peron, but they were gone.

Then from the shadows, swift as the strike of an asp, a crutch crashed down on the head of Melaia's guard. As he fell she wrenched away.

The second guard clamped his arm around her waist and held her as a shield while he yelled the alarm. He continued to yell as he backed down the stairs with Melaia and dragged her into the corridor. By the time they were halfway down the hall, guards were swarming into her cell like vultures after carrion.

Chapter 23

Trevin adjusted his sword belt as he stood in the sitting room of Stalia's quarters. Arelin had enlisted an underling to fetch his sword and journey pack from a weapon storeroom. Just in time. The alarm had shot like thunderlight through caves and caverns, along with word that a system of secret tunnels had been discovered. Word had come, too, that Melaia had been locked in an isolated cell under constant watch.

He thrust the familiar blade into its scabbard and approached Stalia's door, eager to show her the sword. Her guard nodded and stepped aside, and Trevin entered, ready to deliver the news of the day, but he paused when he saw Verria spooning broth into a little girl who sat on the bed, propped up by cushions.

Stalia was stuffing clothes, blankets, and packets of who-knew-what into two journey bags as she spouted instructions. "Verria, you'll take Peron into Camrithia. Make your way to a temple, either at Navia or Redcliff."

Trevin stared at the pale girl whose hands were brown and leathered from serving as drak feet. "Peron?" He expected her to shrink back. Instead she smiled shyly, and he realized that she knew him. She had tailed him around the kingdom, followed him to Eldarra, watched him court Melaia. He was not in the habit of blushing, but he felt heat rush to his face. Who knew what she had seen?

Arelin and Benasin slipped in from the side room. "My aides are sealing the tunnels," said Arelin. "Two remain open, but only because we blocked off corridors that feed into them."

"Did you leave open the route we mapped?" asked Stalia. When Arelin nodded, she turned to Verria. "You and Peron will use the escape tunnel." She closed and tied the journey bag. "Leave before dawn."

Verria's stony composure eased into a concerned frown. "What about you and Arelin?"

"We'll not leave." Stalia looked at Arelin, her gaze locking onto his. "This is where our future will be decided. Here is where we win or lose."

"If you're to win, you'd best strike first," said Benasin.

Arelin straightened on his crutches and studied Trevin. "I see you have your sword. Do you have a knife or dagger as well?"

"Both." Trevin patted his side, where his dagger was sheathed. He had also tied Varic's silver net around his waist. *If only Varic could see me now*, he thought.

Arelin beckoned to Trevin. "Come with me. You and I have a task to do." He headed through the storeroom.

Trevin dashed after his father. Finally they would rescue Melaia. He caught up with Arelin at the entrance to the tunnel.

As Arelin led the way he said, "We're going to nab the third harp. It's in the lower Shallows. Or the Upper Deeps, according to which way you look at it. A grave has been dug for it."

"What about Melaia?" asked Trevin. "Shouldn't we free her first?"

"She is not about to be buried. The harp is."

Trevin swallowed his disappointment and thought instead of how grateful and impressed Melaia would be when they *did* rescue her – and handed her the third harp. "Should we have brought a shovel?" he asked. "In case the harp is already buried?"

"I doubt it's in the ground yet," said Arelin. "Rejius will insist on watching the burial with his own eyes to ensure that it's done to his liking. I've had the hawkman watched, and so far he's not made a move in that direction."

They crept through the back corridors and entered the main caves through a room that contained empty cages and the sharp odor of drak droppings. Trevin fought the impulse to retch as he remembered being caged there. He kept his eyes on the Asp, following as he threaded his way between the cages and out the door into a straight, dark, downward sloping corridor.

Quickly and quietly they slipped through the tunnels, ducking into side halls or alcoves at the approach of servants or guards. They had crept into one of the side corridors to wait for two serving girls to pass with their lantern, when Trevin sensed someone in the hallway with them.

He flattened himself against the wall and reached for Arelin's sleeve, then recoiled and stared at his hands. His palms were warming as they had before he released the comains from their shields. What's more the silver sash was growing hot around his waist. But why? Then he noticed the wall paintings of robed men and women and sensed their thoughts floating around him, though their words were unclear.

Arelin mouthed, "What's wrong?"

Trevin untied the mesh sash and spread it over the nearest figure, a young man. As he pressed the net to the wall, his hands burned.

"Are you daft?" Arelin whispered at Trevin's shoulder. "These are spirits of the dead."

"I know," said Trevin, "but I can release them."

"We've no time."

The net bulked and billowed, and Trevin removed it. A mistlike man knelt at his feet.

"Great shades!" said Arelin. "What now?"

Trevin moved to the next figure. A spirit-woman emerged and knelt with the man.

As Trevin moved to the third figure, Arelin snatched away the net. "You can't release all of them," he whispered. "There's no time." He turned back to the two spirits.

Trevin blinked heavily. He felt as if he were waking from a deep sleep or a drunken stupor. The two spirits rose and conversed briefly with Arelin before dashing away.

Arelin handed Trevin the sash. "Put this back around your waist and keep it there. At least for now."

Trevin stared after the spirits as he retied the mesh. "Where did they go?"

"I sent them to find Benasin," said Arelin. "He is also in spirit form, so he will know what to do with them. I hope." He drew Trevin back into the main tunnel, and they followed it until they reached a dead end at an intersecting corridor. Arelin peered both ways before creeping around the corner to the left.

Trevin followed. At the end of the tunnel, a patch of dim light spilled into the hall from a crudely hewn doorway half his height.

Loosening his dagger Arelin moved to one side of the door and motioned for Trevin to stand on the other side. Trevin slipped out his dagger and took his place. Then Arelin scratched on the wall with a crutch. All was silent. Arelin scratched again. A grunt and murmur came from within. Arelin tapped, and a shadow fell across the patch of light.

Trevin stood motionless, dagger ready, glancing back and forth between the shadow and his father. When a gash guard emerged from the door, knife in hand, Arelin's crutch felled him.

Trevin ducked into the room, taking another gash guard by surprise. Before the man could strike, Trevin's dagger found its mark.

"The harp," said Arelin, staring into a hole in the ground.

Trevin crouched and peered down at the half buried harp. The hole appeared to be only a bit deeper than he was tall. He lowered himself in and eased down. With the toe of his boot he loosened the dirt around the base of the harp. Then he wiggled it out and handed it up to Arelin.

With a hand from his father, Trevin hauled himself out of the hole. They looped a guard's sword belt through the harp frame and slipped the belt over Trevin's shoulders. As Trevin adjusted the weight of the harp on his back, he sensed the approach of a decayed, gray presence.

Arelin nodded. "A malevolent." He positioned himself in the center of the cave. "Captain of the guard."

Trevin pressed himself to the wall at the side of the entrance, motioning for Arelin to do the same on the opposite side.

Arelin shook his head and held his blade ready. Between his teeth he said, "You'll get the harp out."

Trevin clenched his jaw as the malevolent, fully etched in black feathers, raged into the room, his dagger aimed at Arelin.

Before Trevin could leap on the man from behind, Arelin barked, "Get out."

The captain, obviously thinking the command was for him, growled and struck.

Arelin blocked the man with his crutches and struck back, yelling, "Get out! Only I can take a malevolent."

Trevin ducked through the doorway and ran, hating it. Hating it. Hating it. He felt as if he were betraying his father. Why did he always abandon people? The old guilt returned, weighing him down as if he bore boulders on his back, but he kept running. He darted through the room of cages and did not pause until he entered the relative safety of the back tunnel. Then he bent forward, his hands to his knees, and caught his breath.

A cold hand grabbed his shoulder, and he whipped around, drawing his dagger.

Benasin's spirit stood there, a finger to his lips. "No noise," he hissed. "Come."

"Arelin." Trevin panted. "He's fighting a malevolent."

"But you have the harp," said Benasin. "That's what matters – that, and a short side mission."

Trevin shifted the harp but kept his dagger in hand as he retraced his steps, following Benasin through the drak room and out the door. The path they took sloped upward and ended at a cave that sent a shudder up Trevin's spine. He had spent days chained at the bench next to the wall, his only company the stone statues positioned around the room: a soldier, an old shepherd, a seated woman and girl, and Dreia.

"I met two spirits," said Benasin. "They said you released them."

Trevin nodded. He understood what Benasin wanted, for his hands were warming again. He sheathed his dagger, slipped off the harp, and set it on the bench. Untying the mesh at his waist, he walked among the statues, the friends Benasin had loved. Rejius had trapped their spirits in stone, but Trevin sensed a surge in the energy of their thoughts. Who should he release first? The moment he formed the question, the answer was clear. He had to release the one who had died as a result of his treachery, the one who looked like Melaia.

Trevin draped the silver net over Dreia's statue, placed his hands on her shoulders, and bowed his head. Heat billowed from the mesh, and sweat dripped from his forehead. Then the stone beneath the silver net softened and shifted.

"Trevin," a voice said. "I am free."

He backed away, and Dreia removed the mesh herself. Eyes like Melaia's studied him, and he bowed to his knees. "I –"

"No more apologies." Dreia laughed. "You apologized so profusely when you were here in chains that I began to feel guilty myself. I forgave you each time, but you couldn't hear me." She drew the mesh to her chest. "I'll release the rest. No doubt you have other duties." She nodded at the harp. "Am I right?"

Trevin rubbed his hot palms on his tunic. "You don't need my hands?"

"I'm an Archon, Trevin," she said. "I can call upon my powers now." She turned her generous smile to Benasin, who handed the harp to Trevin.

"I'll escort you back to the inner tunnels," said Benasin. He wove among the statues, touching each on his way out of the room. "I'll be back," he said. "I will see all of you freed."

Trevin followed Benasin to the room of cages and into the back tunnel, where Benasin left him. Weary, Trevin leaned against the wall. Where should he take the harp? Stone Grove was the obvious choice, although he didn't know the way. What's more he had no idea whether the tunnel to Stone Grove remained open. But it was worth a search.

He tramped along looking for a passage that sloped up, but every ascending tunnel he ventured into ended abruptly, blocked and sealed. In the end he headed back to Stalia's quarters, hoping at every turn to see Arelin approaching.

After meandering through the deserted back tunnels and finding more roadblocks, Trevin at last arrived at Stalia's storeroom. He pushed past the heavy curtain and entered her bedchamber. The sky outside her window was dark, and the chamber was silent, but she was not in bed.

Exhausted he clutched the bedpost to steady himself. Maybe Stalia had gone after Arelin. Surely she had helped him reach safety. Trevin slipped the harp off his back, his knees buckled, and he crumpled to the bed.

When Trevin awoke, dawn was filtering through the latticed window and a breeze was rippling the sheer drapes. There was still no sign of Stalia, but a murmur of voices drifted in from her sitting room. Trevin rose, smoothed his hair, adjusted his tunic, and slipped the strap of the harp over his shoulder. Then he strode through the doorway.

Stalia glanced at Trevin from the table where she sat eating breakfast. Across from her Lord Rejius looked up and smiled.

Chapter 24

Trevin froze. Whose side was Stalia on? Or was she playing both sides?

She glanced at the door behind him, and a look of concern flitted across her face, an unspoken question about Arelin.

Trevin tried to mask all emotion as he weighed his options.

Stalia's face grew stony. "Come break your fast with us." She beckoned to a servant, who set a third cup on the table along with a bowl of dried fruit.

Trevin retreated. "It seems I've interrupted a private meeting. I'll wait for you elsewhere."

"Stay!" Lord Rejius pointed a talon at Trevin. "You are a thorn in my side." He stabbed a piece of bread and dipped it in honey. "It didn't take me long to discern who took you from the wall." The large bite dripped all the way to his mouth.

Chewing loudly he rose and strutted around Trevin, looking him up and down. "Was it your plan to ingratiate yourself with my daughter by bringing her the harp?" He licked his honey-smeared talon. "Or was it her idea?"

"My idea," said Stalia.

"A poor one," said Lord Rejius, "but easily remedied since, I assume, this misbegotten did not waste his time filling the hole. You may both join me for the burial." His gold eyes bored in on Trevin. "Keep the harp on your back. There's room enough for two in the grave."

"There will be no burial." Stalia continued to eat as if they were engaged in common, everyday conversation.

"Ah, but there will, and someday you'll be grateful," said Lord Rejius. "I'll soon be installed as the supreme ruler upground. I shall be a god and you, my Stalia, shall be a goddess, but our future is assured only if we are rid of all three harps. We must be rid of this thief as well."

"You speak as though I'm opposed to destroying the harps," said Stalia. "I'm simply against your plan."

He grunted. "You have a better one?"

"I do." Stalia poured spiced cider into the cups. "Sit, both of you. At least hear my suggestion."

"Goddess indeed." Lord Rejius returned to his seat. "Just remember who is god."

Trevin pulled a stool to the table, eased the harp off his back, and set it on the floor between him and Stalia. "I'm here to serve the goddess," he said.

Stalia inclined her head to Lord Rejius. "You see? He serves me."

Lord Rejius snorted. "Are you crazed? You trust him?"

"He has no choice if he wishes to live," Stalia said flatly. "Besides, he agreed to be initiated. By the time he is etched, it will be obvious where his allegiance lies."

"When will that be?" asked the hawkman.

Stalia waved away the question. "You ask for minor details when we have more important topics to discuss." She slid the honey toward Trevin. "Fetching the harp was a test of my son's loyalty and your security."

Lord Rejius grunted as he stuffed his mouth with a chunk of fish.

"Not that your security is especially lax," said Stalia. "I'm sure he overcame many challenges to accomplish the task." She gave Trevin a joyless smile. "Excellent, my son. You have succeeded admirably."

Trevin acknowledged her praise with a nod and dipped a piece of bread into the honey. There was no excellence in abandoning his crippled father to the mercy of a fully armed malevolent. A good son would have not have run. A good son would have defended his father.

Rejius popped a prune in his mouth. "Your son is a proven betrayer, you know. Unworthy of your trust."

"Leave him to me," said Stalia. "I'm perfectly capable of taking care of betrayers."

Lord Rejius pushed back from the table. "Tell me. Why should I not bury the harps? I've chosen three different grave sites, three different locations far removed from each other and as deep in our realm as I can go without Earthbearer's permission."

Stalia leaned toward her father. "These are not ordinary harps. The kyparis wood lives. What if these harps take root and grow? Then you're not burying them, you're planting them."

Trevin decided his best bet was to play out the game, at least until he saw where the loyalties lay. "Besides that," he said, "I just proved that a buried harp can be found and dug up."

"I have a foolproof plan," said Stalia. "The Angelaeon wish to see a stairway rise to heaven, do they not? Instead let them see smoke rise from a pyre." Her eyes brightened. "Burn the harps, all three, and you'll be rid of them. What's more, you'll have plenty of kyparis ashes to add to your gash."

Rejius cocked his head. "I suppose you have already chosen a site for this pyre of yours?"

"High in the cliffs. The rising smoke will be visible from a great distance," said Stalia. "Stone Grove is the perfect spot."

"Isn't that where the Wisdom Tree originally stood?" asked Trevin. He had visited the grove with Windweaver when they walked the wind together.

"Where the Tree once grew, its last remnants shall be destroyed. It's genius, isn't it?" hissed Stalia.

"Brilliant," said Trevin. But did Stalia plan to bring Melaia to Stone Grove to unite the harps before they burned? Or would she burn the harps before they were united so she could be a goddess? Her face held no clue. Who was she duping – her father or her son? One of them at this moment was a fool.

Lord Rejius's smile turned into a wicked grin. "A pyre high in the cliffs. A splendid display of my power. A perfect proclamation of my reign. I must bring my beloved to witness it."

"Your beloved?" Stalia snorted. "Since when have you had a beloved?"

"Since Dreia's daughter entered my domain," said Lord Rejius.

Trevin forced himself not to reach for his sword. Skewering the hawkman might be satisfying, but the man would only come back to life. He took a fig from the fruit bowl. *Play the game,* he told himself. *Play it and hope the last move is yours.*

"Build the pyre, then," said Lord Rejius. "Build it today. We've no time to waste. We'll burn the harps after the evening star rises. My beloved must witness the death of her mother's dream. Tonight Dreia's daughter shall be liberated from duty to the past. I will free her to look upon a glorious future with me. The debt shall be paid today. To me. *I* will take Dreia's *Breath.*"

Trevin squeezed the fig so hard it oozed from his fist.

Melaia sat in her cell, clasping the two harp pendants in one hand and her mother's book in the other. Her cold supper lay uneaten, because her stomach churned with apprehension. As much as Peron's recovery encouraged her, the discovery of Arelin's chambers grieved her. She was afraid she had ruined everything, and her mind insisted on conjuring distressing images. Arelin in chains. Benasin trapped. Peron caged again. Trevin beaten like Jarrod. The harps buried. She laid a hand on her mother's book, but its peaceful thrum no longer stilled her soul.

At the sound of a key turning in the lock of her cell door, Melaia hurriedly tucked the book into her waist pouch and slipped the harp pendants beneath her tunic. When two gash guards entered and prodded her into the hallway, she braced herself to again face Lord Rejius in his throne room.

But the guards led her up the slanting corridor instead of down, and she was startled when they ushered her into a brightly lit anteroom, where a wide window stood open to the rising evening star. On the far side of the room a door opened, and Lord Rejius emerged in his feathered cloak, smiling smugly. The two gash guards who flanked her stood at attention.

"My dear," the hawkman crooned, strutting to her as Stalia appeared behind him, wearing an elegant, sheer white cloak over a sky blue gown.

Then Melaia sensed a familiar golden presence. She hardly noticed when Lord Rejius bent to kiss her, for at that moment Trevin strode into the room, securing his sword belt. His eyes caught hers for only a moment, but they held no warmth of recognition, and as he looked away, she went cold, head to toe. With his severe, detached glare, and his face set like stone, he looked like a gash man.

Then Stalia picked up a harp, and Melaia stiffened. She knew it was the third harp not only by the care with which Stalia held it, but also by the runes that graced its soundboard: *Illumakei*, meaning *one shall light the way*. But she suspected Lord Rejius had invited her here to attend its burial. How could it light the way from a grave?

"We have a grand evening ahead of us, my dear," said Lord Rejius. "Tonight you shall be released from your bonds to the Wisdom Tree and its stairway." With a flourish of his hand, he cried, "To Stone Grove," and swaggered out the door, flanked by his bodyguards.

Trevin grabbed Melaia's arm and shoved her through the door. She gasped as the point of his dagger prodded her back. "A feint, my lady," he murmured.

She gritted her teeth. If this was a feint, it felt a bit too real. Besides, Trevin's footsteps were not the only ones she heard behind her as they marched down the corridor. She picked up her pace, but the dagger stayed. Which way had the game tipped?

The afterglow of sunset was fading as the hawkman's procession left the caves by an opening high in the cliffs overlooking the Davernon. As they ascended a narrow trail crossing the cliff face, the whispered rush of whitewater met them, and when Melaia looked down, she saw spirits gathering on the river. Her stomach gnawed at her. The spirits were depending on her to restore the stairway, a feat that now looked highly unlikely. What would become of them if she failed?

The cliff trail ended at a cirque, a wide field shaped like a colossal amphitheatre. Bluffs bounded three sides, and standing stones were scattered throughout. As the procession entered, Benasin, in the flesh again, looked up from where he sat on a boulder.

Lord Rejius hissed. "The debt will be paid to me," he called to Benasin. "Tonight." He skirted the cirque, keeping his distance from the Second-born

"Surely you didn't think I would miss it," said Benasin.

"Stay if you wish, but do not interfere." With a flick of a talon Lord Rejius directed a feather-etched malevolent to keep an eye and a sword trained on Benasin.

Melaia glanced around the field, searching for the two other harps. When she didn't see them, she looked instead for the most promising place to make an escape. One possible route was the trail they had just climbed, which lay on the west, the only open side of the cirque. The trail afforded a bird's eye view of the Davernon and the woods and fields of Camrithia beyond, but it was narrow, and a single misstep would result in a terrifying fall to the whitewater below. Even so it might be the only choice because of the rocky bluffs surrounding the rest of the field. At the foot of the north bluff stood a grove of leafless trees. The south ridge was a sheer cliff lined with torches wedged into its stone face. A waterfall cascaded down the rocks of the eastern ridge.

But perhaps there was another option. Two of the Archae were in attendance. Seaspinner stood in the spray of the falls, and Windweaver walked the south bluff. Since angels did not intervene in human choice, they were most likely here to observe. Still, their presence raised Melaia's hopes. Perhaps they would point a way out if the need arose.

Then she noticed the hill of dry brush atop layers of logs. A pyre. It stood among the standing stones in the center of the field and was clearly the intended hub of activity. But what – or who – was destined for the blaze?

Stalia leaned the third harp against the south bluff and barked orders to her gash guards, who ducked behind the waterfall.

Lord Rejius turned to Melaia. "You'll not mind a bit of precaution, will you, my dear?" He waved two gash guards to her side. "Bind her to a tree," he ordered, "but make sure she has a clear view of the proceedings."

She felt Trevin's dagger leave her spine. "Can I not watch beside you, my lord?" she asked. "I'm well guarded."

Lord Rejius simply turned away, rubbing his palms together and muttering, "It shall be done. It shall be done."

When the guards grabbed Melaia's arms, she pulled back. "I can walk on my own," she said and marched between them to the stand of leafless trees on the north side of the cirque. She hoped Trevin would follow, but she didn't hear or sense him, nor did she feel his dagger. Then the guards backed her against a tree trunk, and she saw him standing beside Lord Rejius as if he were the hawkman's guard. But with two dagger-wielding gash warriors behind him, he was obviously under guard himself.

As the gash men firmly bound Melaia to the tree, she pressed her fingers to the bark, feeling for its pulse. But it had no pulse. Nor did she hear its voice. "Stone Grove," she murmured. The standing stones were lone tree trunks. Even the trees with branches, including the one she was bound to, were petrified. She had a sickening vision of all the world's trees turning to stone.

Stalia's guards waded out from behind the waterfall, carrying the two cushions Jarrod had stolen. Melaia craned her neck to watch. At Stalia's direction the guards ripped open the cushions. As they pulled out the harps, Dreia's book pulsed hot in Melaia's waist pouch. All three harps were in the grove now, out in the open, two with Stalia and the third across the field, leaning against the south ridge.

Melaia looked up through the bare branches overhead. The stars of the beltway were aligned in a perfectly straight path. They would hold their position for only so long. "The time is now," she said. The harps were together. Why was the Tree not rising? Did they need to be closer to one another? Did they need her touch? She strained against the ropes. They held tight, but she continued to tug as she planned the path she would run in order to dodge the guards. She had to unite the harps tonight.

Stalia called to Rejius, "Dreia's daughter should pile the harps on the pyre and light it herself. Let her know the futility of her efforts and the transcendence of your power."

Melaia flexed her fingers and called, "Allow me to demonstrate my loyalty to you, my lord. Let me reject my past by carrying the harps to the pyre."

Lord Rejius grinned at her, raised his arms, and shot a flash of thunderlight across the grove. The pile of brush exploded in flames.

"Wait, my lord!" Melaia yelled, tugging at her bonds. "You gave me your pledge. It's time for me to give you mine. If the harps are to burn, allow me to throw them into the flames."

Lord Rejius strode to the south ridge, grabbed the harp that lay there, and bowed to Melaia. "This is for you, my dear." He hurled the harp onto the pyre.

"Fool!" shouted Stalia.

Benasin lunged toward Rejius, but a malevolent's sword blocked him.

Flametender appeared, circling the harp as the flames devoured it. Seaspinner watched from the waterfall. Windweaver paced the ridge.

Melaia huffed. Angels didn't interfere with human choices, but confound it, couldn't they make an exception? As the harp turned to ashes, she slumped against her ropes.

Lord Rejius turned to Benasin. "Tell me, my brother, how will you pay your debt now?"

Melaia blinked to clear her eyes. Was it a trick of the firelight, or was Lord Rejius younger than he was a few moments earlier?

Benasin, too, looked more youthful, more like Jarrod. "Haven't we both paid?" he called. "You and I have died a score of agonizing deaths. If you burn these harps, we will only face death again and again. Is that what you want? Already you're more animal than human. You'll never walk among people without being called a monster."

"A god!" Rejius shouted at the onlookers. "You shall call me god!"

"God of a blighted earth," yelled Benasin.

Rejius wagged a taloned finger at him. "That, my brother, is your fault."

"It's both your faults," cried Stalia, now a young woman.

"Ingrate!" Lord Rejius snatched a second harp and hurled it into the blaze.

As flames engulfed it, Melaia leaned her head back against the tree and groaned. How had all their efforts come to this? How had it all gone so wrong?

Warm fingers touched her wrists, and a cold blade sliced at the ropes. She thought it was Trevin until she spotted him lurking among the onlookers. He appeared as shocked as she felt. Everyone's attention, including that of her guards, was completely given to the bonfire and the three immortals, who were regaining their youth and circling each other like dogs before a fight. Although Rejius's feathers and talons remained, his jawline was more pronounced, and he swaggered like a young man. Benasin was younger as well, handsome and stalwart, but it was the change in Stalia that transfixed Melaia.

"She's younger than I," said Melaia.

"Both a blessing and a curse," said a familiar voice as the bonds fell away from her hands.

"Arelin?" whispered Melaia. She rubbed her wrists.

"I normally don't interfere –"

"Please! Interfere!"

The ropes on her ankles loosened, and Arelin slipped the hilt of a dagger into her hand. "Look to the cliff trail," he murmured. Then he was gone.

Melaia looked west. The spirits of the dead were surging over the top of the cliff like a rising fog. She wanted to shout at them, *Too late.*

But then she realized they might provide cover for her escape. Her guards were edging toward the fight in the center of the grove as if they expected the hawkman to call for their help.

No longer watched, Melaia slipped into the cold, whispering flow of spirits and headed for the cliff trail. She had failed. How could she ever face angels again? She wanted to run into the darkest cave and hide forever. Would Trevin understand? Maybe Arelin would send him after her and they could flee together.

As Melaia reached the top of the trail, a child's shout split the air. She turned to face the cirque and saw that the shout had come from Stalia, who was now a young girl with long dark hair.

Stalia shook a yellowed scroll at Rejius, one bound with a tassled red cord. "I know the truth," she cried with a child's rage. "My birth is recorded here. Benasin is my father, and *that* is the root of your hatred. My mother loved Benasin, not you, and I was born of that love."

"Take her weapons," Lord Rejius ordered his guards. As they relieved Stalia of her knife and dagger, the hawkman hurled the last harp into the fire.

Melaia clenched her teeth. She would not run away. She would not hide. She would die fighting.

Lord Rejius crowed. "There is no Tree! No stairway!" He pointed his sword at Stalia. "You are no longer needed."

Melaia shot toward the hawkman, screaming like a madwoman, brandishing Arelin's dagger. As Lord Rejius turned toward her, she struck up against his sword. The blade flew from his hands, but he grabbed her wrist and she lost her grip on the dagger. As it fell the hawkman flung her at the stone wall of the south bluff.

Melaia stumbled before she hit the wall full force. Even so the fall knocked the breath from her. As she gasped for air she saw two of Rejius's bodyguards drive Trevin back. At the same time, Benasin struck his guard and lunged at Rejius, who wrestled him to the ground. Angels, both Angelaeon and malevolent, emerged from the perimeter of the grove and slowly circled the field, their auras swirling in a myriad of colors.

Stalia, a somber little girl, darted to Melaia and tried to pull her to her feet, but Melaia shook her head and hugged her pouch with Dreia's hot, thrumming book inside. It was the only remaining fragment of the Tree. The heartwood.

I am the heart
that makes three one.
I am freedom,
the curse undone.

But the harps were gone, and the heart was broken. Melaia leaned her head back against the stone. Her eyesight blurred as she stared at the line of stars.

Stalia crouched beside her, holding Arelin's dagger. "I can help you escape."

"And Trevin?" As Melaia scanned the grove, trying to locate him, the fight exploded.

Stalia whirled toward the battle and stood before Melaia in a protective stance, her dagger in hand. Throughout the grove angels and malevolents clashed, while the spirits of the dead crowded in like thick fog. Malevolents, who could see the dead, tried unsuccessfully to strike them down. Gash guards, who could only feel their presence, swatted as if they were flailing at swarms of horseflies.

Only Seaspinner, Windweaver, and Flametender stood still. Melaia noticed that they were watching her with the same expectant confidence they had shown when she entered the fifth arm of the star on the mosaic floor. Earthbearer had said, *You will take your mother's place.*

Melaia wiped her eyes. *You will take your mother's place.* She rose to her feet, clutching Dreia's book. *I am the heart that makes three one.* She understood. The three harps were united in the ashes of their death, but the Tree would not rise until its heart was restored. The book, bound in heartwood, was the heart of the Tree. As Breath of Angel, Blood of Man, she held the heart. She would take her mother's place.

She looked around the grove for Trevin and saw him as he lunged at a gash warrior. "Remember me," she whispered. Then she darted around Stalia, ran to the blazing pyre, and dived in.

Chapter 25

Trevin had been biding his time, aware of the presence of both Angelaeon and malevolents ringing the field. He wanted to free Melaia, but the odds were not good for him, on his own, to confront the gash warriors in attendance, much less Lord Rejius's bodyguard of malevolents, not to mention the hawkman himself. So he watched for an opening, a moment when he could make a move.

He was stunned when Lord Rejius threw the first harp onto the pyre. Then as each harp hit the flames, the three immortals grew younger, which amazed him even more. When his guards backed away staring at the transformation, he eased into the distracted, gawking assembly of gash men.

He glanced around the grove, looking for a way to reach Melaia unnoticed. Clearly she could no longer unite the harps, so the challenge now was to help her escape. Then he spotted Arelin with her and every muscle surged with energy. His father was alive. Arelin would secure Melaia's safety. Now he had to get out of the grove himself.

Trevin was edging toward the cliff trail when he saw Melaia rush at Lord Rejius. He sprinted after her, but then she struck the hawkman, who threw her at the bluff. As he swerved to follow her, he met the swords of two gash warriors. He parried, dodged, and struck back, but he could not reach Melaia before the entire field erupted in battle.

"Melaia!" he called, ducking, blocking, swinging. "Melaia!" But he knew she couldn't hear him over the roar of the fighting and the flames, and try as he might, he could not get near her. As soon as he struck down one warrior, another would lunge at him.

Trevin had just felled one of his attackers when he saw Melaia run for the pyre. He leaped over the man's body and ran after her, but Flametender, standing in the blaze, held up a hand to halt him. As he jerked to a stop, his palms burned with the memory of his naming. *Born to free.* Like a double-edged sword, the truth sliced into him. Freedom had a price. To free Melaia, to free the world, he had to let her go.

Helpless he watched her dive into the flames. With a flash of blinding light the stairway streaked into the heavens. A succession of cracks echoed through the grove as trees broke through their stony bark.

Trevin was conscious of a gash warrior rushing him, sword raised, but he couldn't move, and he didn't care. This is where he wanted to die. But the spirits of all the gash men were escaping their bodies, and before the warrior reached Trevin, the man's sword clanged to the ground, his body crumpled, and his spirit snaked toward the Tree.

When Melaia dived into the flames, she hoped to land in the center, the heart of the harp ashes, but she never knew whether she made it or not, for white hot flames shot up around her, joined the burn of her soul, and exploded in a mighty roar that surged toward the heavens in a column of light. For a moment she felt she *was* the light rushing upward, the stairway to heaven. All her senses sprang to life with the intense swirling colors, the sharp fragrance of kyparis, and the rich melody of harps.

Then her spirit settled within the boundaries of her body. Although she felt light enough to float upward forever, she did not rise but stood, stable and solid at the foot of the stairway, while spirits crowded past as they climbed. Young and old, rich and poor, man, woman, child, and angels ascended the lightbridge.

Only one lingered. As Jarrod knelt before Melaia, her anger, pity, resentment, and sorrow washed away in a wave of love. "Jarrod," she said, "I've already forgiven you."

"I know, and I'm forever grateful." His eyes searched hers. "What about Serai? Has she ascended the stairway?"

Melaia shook her head. Would Serai ascend too? Although she was uncertain she said, "She'll come. Sooner or later she'll come."

Jarrod stood to his feet and gazed up the stairway, his lips pressed in a tight line. Then with a nod to Melaia, he ascended.

Windweaver's voice thundered, "The debt is paid."

"Settled," said Seaspinner.

"In full," said Flametender.

As spirits continued to ascend, a protective mist began to rise like a wall around Melaia and the stairway. At first it was as transparent as a veil, but as it thickened, she realized that it was the Tree, the stairway's protection. Soon it would solidify into wood and block her view of the grove – and Trevin.

Trevin's arms hung listless at his side as he watched the trunk of the Tree take shape. He was aware that Arelin had chased Rejius into the caverns behind the waterfall and that Benasin and Stalia had disappeared. The clash of battle and the crackle of the pyre had subsided, leaving the air thrumming with the beat of Camrithian victory drums. Through it all Trevin had stood unmoving and numb, staring at the Tree, trying to glimpse Melaia within it.

At last he turned away, trudged to the cliff, and gazed at the glow of Camrithian campfires across the Davernon. He knew he should rejoice at the victory, but he felt empty. Completely and utterly empty. He told himself he should have known it would end this way. He had been warned a dozen times. He had seen the vision in the temple. He should have expected it. But he hadn't wanted it, and he didn't want it now.

He looked up at the beltway of stars, connected now by a streak of light. His vision blurred. He never knew emptiness could hurt so much.

Through the rising veil and the mass of spirits, Melaia saw Trevin turn away from the Tree. Then one of the approaching spirits caught her eye. When had he died? How? She should have been at his side.

"Father!" she cried.

King Laetham smiled, walking with ease. "My daughter." He bowed his head. "My queen."

Melaia started to point out that she never would be queen – not now that she was guardian of the Tree – but when he raised his head, he gazed past her, and she felt a presence behind her.

"Laetham," said Dreia, touching his cheek.

Melaia stepped aside, gaping at her parents. Dreia's nose and brow favored Jarrod. Otherwise Melaia felt as if she were watching her reflection.

King Laetham kissed Dreia's hand. Then he, too, ascended.

Melaia was conscious that Trevin still stood in the cirque beyond the Tree, but she dared not look away from her mother, for she expected Dreia to follow King Laetham at any moment. Melaia wanted to stand in her mother's presence as long as she could.

"Well done, my daughter." Dreia smiled proudly and surveyed the interior of the Tree.

Melaia glanced around too. The trunk was hardening now, taking on the appearance of the inner walls of Wodehall. Only the west side of the Tree continued to shimmer like a veil of light. Beyond, at the edge of the cliff, stood Trevin. Alone.

Melaia's throat tightened. "Why do I still see him through the Tree?"

"You have a strong connection with him," said Dreia. "You may join him if you wish."

"But I thought –"

"My dear Breath of Angel, you restored my guardianship of the Tree, so you may ascend to Avellan or return to your world, as you choose. But you must make your choice before the Tree closes. After that you may enter only as a spirit."

Melaia clasped Dreia's hand, and an old ache, long locked within her, sprang open, yearning for the mother she had never had.

Dreia cupped Melaia's face in her soft hands, which held the scent of woodlands and herb gardens and flowering meadows. "Your world is renewed, my daughter." She nodded toward Trevin. "He will find someone to share it with. Do you want to be the one?"

Melaia leaned into her mother's embrace, absorbing her scent, her warmth, her fullness, her love.

Trevin stared at the moonlit whitewater far below and rubbed his right hand. The pain from his missing finger had been replaced by a sharper pain, a heart-deep pain, one he would carry forever. For a moment he thought he might shorten 'forever' by throwing himself into the raging river, but Seaspinner was walking the rapids. She had warned him that Melaia's destiny was not his. He squeezed his eyes closed. He could live without her, but he didn't want to.

Then a hand touched his back, and he sensed a silver presence. He turned, barely breathing, afraid his agonized mind was playing cruel tricks on him. But she smiled. Her touch felt solid and real.

"Melaia?" He drew her into his arms, felt the harp pendants she wore pressing against his chest, felt her heartbeat quicken. He closed his eyes and held on.

How long they clung to each other, Trevin didn't know, but when he became aware of his surroundings again, the soft light of dawn was filtering into the grove.

Melaia traced his brow, his jawline, his mouth. "So many are gone now," she said. "My father, Jarrod, the angels – they climbed the stairway."

Trevin wiped a tear from her cheek. "But so many are still here." He nodded toward Camrithia. "Dwin is waiting for us with Nuri, Hanni, and Iona."

"Nuri?"

"She's awake now and mending with the sylvans, who are safe in the Durenwoods. The comains await our return too – Pym and Main

Undrian and Catellus. Besides, look at the green across the treetops. I think the trees are in leaf."

"And is that a new star?" Melaia pointed to a brilliant speck in the dawn sky. "It's a bright one. Maybe it's a good omen."

Trevin squinted at the gold gleam. It was too large for a star. What's more, it was growing – not larger, but closer. He laughed. "It *is* an omen, and a good one."

A golden, white winged horse soared toward them.

Melaia's eyes widened, and her grip on his arm tightened. "A Windwing?"

"Not just any Windwing," said Trevin. "That's Cherrim, Queen of Windwings. Shall we fly home, my lady?"

Melaia gasped. "I'm a poor rider on land. How can I hope to stay on the back of a Windwing?"

He nuzzled her hair. "I'll hold you."

She smiled at him, her cheeks flushed. "In that case, let's fly."

CHAPTER 26

Melaia's open carriage, wreathed in greenery, rolled past the newly repaired gates of Redcliff and began a regal descent across the bridge toward the festival grounds in the valley below. A contingent of guards marched ahead, the comains of Camrithia flanked the carriage in single file, and Serai rode behind on a white horse.

The waiting crowd cheered, waving newly budded branches and jostling for a good view as they lined the road from the end of the bridge to the festival field. The battle-scarred ground had been concealed by a scattered carpet of flowers in every color. Perfume from the fragrant blossoms drifted on the breeze and sweetened the air.

Melaia waved as she scanned the crowd, hoping to see Angelaeon, although she doubted that any would attend. The stairway and its protective Tree had risen only a fortnight ago. During those two weeks all Angelaeon except the sylvans had returned to the heavens for new assignments. Only Arelin and Serai had stayed behind for today's betrothal and the upcoming wedding.

Melaia glanced back at Serai, glorious with her long copper hair curling loosely over her broad shoulders. She had claimed that she needed to sort out her feelings toward Jarrod before she saw him again. Melaia understood the hurt feelings, but her heart ached for Jarrod. Would he wait for Serai? Or would he be assigned to some distant world?

The cart hit a bump, and Melaia reached up to steady her new gold crown. She ran her fingers across the engraved lions, the emblem of Camrithia, entwined – at her insistence – with fruiting apricot branches, a symbol of the mercy she hoped would mark her reign. After two hundred years of rivalry and vengeance, the world was ready for peace. She hoped.

The strains of a jaunty melody floated above the din of the crowd, and Melaia leaned forward to see beyond her driver. A section of the festival field was roped off to form a flower-strewn green. Onlookers thronged around the outside, while Caepio pranced in the center of the green with his lute. His musicians paraded behind him, playing reed pipes and tabors.

Melaia spied Iona in the stands to the east of the green. Dwin and Nuri, already betrothed, sat arm in arm beside her. Seated in front of them was Hanni, with Peron on one side and the novice Claudia on the other.

In the stands on the west side, little Stalia sat beside her father, a young Benasin. Melaia's heart went out to Stalia, a woman in a child's body, forced to grow up once again. Her relationships with Arelin and Trevin were so awkward that she had hesitated to attend the ceremony. Even now she planned to leave immediately afterward to return to the Dregmoors, accompanied by Benasin, who had been appointed governor there.

A dais at the south end of the green held the guests of honor with Trevin seated in the center. King Kedemeth, to his right, surveyed the grounds with an ease and authority that Melaia hoped to have one day. Beside the king sat Queen Ambria, dressed in the royal blue of Eldarra. Melaia noticed her glancing at Arelin, who sat on Trevin's left. Queen Ambria had been trying to persuade Arelin to stay at Flauren, at least for a while.

The guards leading Melaia's procession parted and stationed themselves along the rope encircling the green. Then the carriage halted, the comains retreated, and Lord Beker extended his withered fist to Melaia, steadying her as she descended. Serai stepped to her side, and as they strode onto the field, all the seated attendees rose.

Trevin descended from the dais. From his commanding stride to the confident set of his shoulders, from his rich blue tunic and shining sword to the band of gold that crossed his forehead, he looked every bit a prince. Melaia would have run to greet him if they were still priestess and kingsman, but Queen Ambria had coached them both on the protocol required for this occasion, and running was not on the approved list.

As Trevin took his place at the foot of the dais, his eyes met hers. From that moment on, Melaia's gaze did not leave his, nor did his waver from her. Not when the crowd cheered her approach. Not when she placed her hands on his palms. Not when Arelin and King Kedemeth announced the banns. Not until Trevin looked down to prick her right forefinger.

In that moment a movement in the crowd beyond Trevin's shoulder drew Melaia's attention. She looked up, and as the needle-knife bit, she found herself staring into the golden eyes of a dark-haired, sharp-nosed man. Then the crowd shifted, and he was gone. A chill rippled through her. Arelin had chased Lord Rejius into the tunnels of the Dregmoors, but had lost him there. Even now the caves and caverns were being searched and barred to entry. Surely the hawkman was not here. Not now.

Gently holding her blood-tipped finger Trevin looked up and then frowned. "What's wrong?"

She returned what she hoped was a reassuring smile. "Nothing." She turned to Serai, who handed her a needle-knife.

Melaia pricked Trevin's right forefinger, and they pressed their wounds together, mingling their blood. Again their eyes met, and then their lips, and both wished the crowd would vanish.

Serai cleared her throat. "I believe Caepio has a gift for you."

The bard was supervising two servants, who lugged his trunk onto the green and set it at Melaia's feet.

Trevin laughed. "Is this the Pageant Players' trunk? The one we hauled into Qanreef when we entered in disguise with Pym and Livia and –" He looked at Melaia.

"And Jarrod." She knelt before the trunk.

Trevin crouched beside her. "I'm sorry," he whispered.

"I do wish Jarrod were here. And Livia." She ran her hand across the lid of the trunk. "But this memory is a good one."

As Trevin raised the lid Melaia braced for another round of bittersweet memories, but the trunk contained only the sweet, none of the bitter. On a padded scarlet cushion lay two masks, the lioness and the eagle.

Trevin lifted the lioness. "May I?" He held it over her face while Serai tied it in place. Then Melaia held the eagle to Trevin's face, and Caepio secured it. As the servants carried away the trunk, Caepio swept up his lute and launched into a melody that transported Melaia back to the square in Qanreef. She had been a simple chantress then, and Trevin had been an escaped prisoner, both of them hiding from Lord Rejius.

"The Tantelais." Trevin extended his right hand, palm out. "Remember?"

She pressed her right palm to his. "How could I forget our first dance?"

They bowed their heads toward one another, walked in a circle, moved apart, turned, came together again, fingertips touching, palms together. Melaia felt the same warm blush she had experienced the first time they had danced. She entwined her fingers with Trevin's and leaned into him, and they danced as one, claiming the entire green as their ballroom. Unlike the abbreviated version of the song that Caepio had played in Qanreef, this rendition was delightfully long. Long enough for Melaia to lose herself in the melody and the movement and the magic of her partner.

"They're here!" Trevin murmured into her ear.

Melaia shook off her reverie and blinked at his half-smile before she felt a buoyant light encircling them. "Angelaeon!" she said, sensing sea blue, leaf green, fiery red, storm gray, rich brown.

"Archae, I think." Trevin slowed as Caepio headed the Tantelais toward its final notes.

Then Melaia saw them – Windweaver, Seaspinner, Flametender, Earthbearer, and Dreia – forming a circle around her and Trevin. The last time she had been surrounded by all the Archae but Dreia, she had stood in the center of the mosaic star on the floor of the underground meeting hall, across from the barred stairway that led to the library through the statue of the Gryphon – the same Gryphon depicted in tile at the center of the star mosaic.

Melaia gasped and drew Trevin close. "We're the Gryphon!"

Trevin laughed. "The what?"

"The eagle and the lion. *Unity will not return until the Gryphon dances.* We are the Gryphon!"

Trevin grinned. "I don't know about the Gryphon, but I like the *we* and the dancing part."

The crowd appeared to be unaware of the presence of the Archae. As the people applauded, Trevin and Melaia removed their masks and slowly turned in a circle, waving to the crowd. The Archae bowed, and Melaia knew that the next time the Archae met in their great underground hall, she and Trevin would represent the animal and human world. They would stand in the center of the mosaic star. Together.

Once again Caepio's music swirled into the night. Melaia and Trevin faced each other unmasked. Beneath the stars, fingers entwined, they danced. The chantress and the thief. The priestess and the swordsman. The silver and the gold. The king and the queen.

ACKNOWLEDGMENTS

Many thanks:

To my friends, mentors, and fellow grads from Vermont College of Fine Arts. You are a delightful foundation of confidence, creativity, and comraderie. Cheers!
To my husband, Ralph, for your trust, creative skill, and willingness to help wherever it's needed.
To my agent, Cheryl Pientka, for your constant support and wise words of encouragement.
To the readers who wanted to know how this part of the Circle's story ends.

ABOUT THE AUTHOR

KARYN HENLEY grew up on myths, fairy tales, and spiritual stories and began writing because she loved to read. She is now an award-winning author with more than one hundred titles to her credit, including books for children, parents, and teachers, as well as CDs and DVDs of original music. She received an MFA in writing for children and young adults from the Vermont College of Fine Arts and has traveled worldwide as an educational speaker and children's entertainer. She lives in Nashville, Tennessee, with her husband, a jazz drummer. Visit her at www.AngelaeonCircle.com.

Enjoy all the books in the **ANGELAEON CIRCLE**:

www.ingramcontent.com/pod-product-compliance
Lightning Source LLC
Chambersburg PA
CBHW050507190726
48284CB00003B/715